DEATH AT POMPEIA'S WEDDING

A Libertus Mystery, set in Roman Britain

Libertus is at a society wedding on behalf of his patron when the father of the bride is poisoned while testing the wedding wine. Pompeia, the bride, declares that she has caused the death, but Libertus is retained by the bridegroom to prove her innocence. His investigations uncover hidden tensions, and when another guest is discovered murdered at his home, events take a different and more sinister turn...

DEATH AT POMPEIA'S WEDDING

A Libertus Mystery of Roman Britain

Rosemary Rowe

Severn House Large Print
London & New York

This first large print edition published 2010
in Great Britain and the USA by
SEVERN HOUSE PUBLISHERS LTD of
9-15 High Street, Sutton, Surrey, SM1 1DF.
First world regular print edition published 2008 by
Severn House Publishers Ltd., London and New York.

British Library Cataloguing in Publication Data

Rowe, Rosemary, 1942-
   Death at Pompeia's wedding. -- (A Libertus mystery of Roman
   Britain)
   1. Libertus (Fictitious character : Rowe)--Fiction.
   2. Romans--Great Britain--Fiction. 3. Slaves--Fiction.
   4. Great Britain--History--Roman period, 55 B.C.-449
   A.D.--Fiction. 5. Detective and mystery stories. 6. Large
   type books.
   I. Title II. Series
   823.9'2-dc22

   ISBN-13: 978-0-7278-7841-0

Printed and bound in Great Britain by
MPG Books Ltd, Bodmin, Cornwall.

For Jakob

Author's Foreword

The story is set in AD 189. At that time most of Britain had been, for almost two hundred years, the most northerly outpost of the hugely successful Roman Empire: subject to Roman law, criss-crossed by Roman roads and still occupied by Roman garrison legions in the major towns. The province was normally governed by a provincial governor, answerable directly to the Emperor in Rome, but the previous incumbent, Helvius Pertinax, (the supposed friend and patron of the fictional Marcus Septimus mentioned in the book) had recently been promoted, first to the African provinces and more latterly to the exceedingly important consular post of Prefect of Rome – making him effectively the second most powerful person in the Empire.

There is scholarly doubt as to who was acting as Governor of Britannia at this time, one theory being that several candidates were appointed and then un-appointed by the Emperor – the increasingly unbalanced Commodus, whose erratic and scandalous behaviour was a byword by this time. He had renamed all the months, for instance, with names derived from his own titles (which he had in any case given to himself); declared that unlike his predecessors (who had been deified at death) he was the living incarnation of the god Hercules; and announced that Rome itself was to be officially retitled 'Commodiania'. He was unpopular and feared, but still clung tenaciously to power and (perhaps justifiably) feared plots against his life. He therefore had a network of secret spies throughout the Empire.

This is the background of civil discontent against which the action of the book takes place. Glevum, modern Gloucester, was an important town: its status as a 'colonia' for retired legionaries gave it special privilege – all free men born within its walls were citizens by right – and a high degree of responsibility for its own affairs (local tiles of the period describe it as a 'republic'). The members of the town council were therefore men of considerable power. They were also, by definition, wealthy men: candidates for office were obliged by law to own a property of a certain value within the city walls, and any councillor or magistrate was expected to contribute to the town, by personally financing elaborate games, fountains, statues, arches, drains and public works. Though they might expect to gain a little too, in service or in kind, from the contractors whom they appointed to the work. The sudden rise of a comparative unknown – like Antoninus in the story – seeking to be made a councillor, would therefore be a matter of concern, not least in case the newcomer might be the Emperor's spy.

Councillors were often local magistrates as well, like the ageing Honorius in the tale. Roman law was universal at this time, but it did make clear distinction between the punishment which might be meted out to citizens, and that which might be given to other freemen for the same offence. (Slaves, of course, were in a different class again.) Many of the more savage punishments had by this time been repealed, and others (such as the 'sack' for parricide) had fallen out of use, though there is evidence that some jurists wanted them renewed – rather as the hanging lobby does today. The right of the paterfamilias to wield life and death over his children was by this time largely gone, except in the case of a father who – as in this story – catches his married daughter with a man who is not her husband, if not 'in flagrante' then at least in part undressed. In this case the father was entitled to execute the man – to protect his family honour – provided that he killed his daughter too, otherwise he might be charged with homicide.

Power, of course, was vested almost entirely in men. Although individual women might wield considerable influence and even manage large estates, females were excluded from civic office, and indeed a woman (of any age) remained a child in law, under the tutelage first of her father, and then of any husband she might have. Marriage officially required her consent (indeed she was entitled to leave a marriage if it displeased her and take her dowry with her), but in practice many girls became pawns in a kind of property game, since there were very few other careers available for an educated and wealthy woman – though some low-ranking citizens (like Maesta in this story) might continue to help their husbands in some form of trade.

The wedding ceremony might take several forms. The most prestigious was the oldest form, the 'confarratio' which required a solemn religious ceremony and the sharing of a special wheat wafer (hence the name) in the presence of a group of Roman witnesses. This kind of marriage was indissoluble and by the time of the narrative was becoming very rare – for one thing it required the presence of two senior priests of Rome (the Flamen Dailis and the Pontifex Maximus) so it was not available in the provinces, and for another it removed the bride from her father's 'manus' to her husband's power and her former family had no further claim on her (or on her dowry or her children) even if he died. Another form, the 'usus' marriage, which simply required uninterrupted co-habitation for a year, was widespread among the poor; there are instances of women annually spending a night with their sister or mother so that the marriage was not finaliz-ed, and thereby keeping a degree of indepen-dence in their own affairs.

Pompeia's marriage, the basis of this book, is an example of a further kind – and by the time of the story a pattern for such a mar-riage had emerged. The bridegroom – wear-ing a wreath of flowers on his head, and accompanied by his male friends and rela-tives – led a procession to the home of his prospective bride. There, in front of the assembled guests who were the witnesses, a sort of contract was exchanged (originally a fictitious bill of sale between the father and the groom!). A short religious ceremony and sacrifice took place at the family altar, where the bride, dressed in a saffron veil with matching shoes, crowned with flowers and with her hair plaited in a symbolic way, took the bridegroom's hand and uttered the marriage promise: 'Where you are Gauis, I am Gaia.' There was usually a feast, and then the bridegroom dragged his wife away – it was polite to show reluctance – to her new home, whose portals had been decked with

11

greenery, and in order to avoid a stumble (which would have been a dreadful omen for their life) he picked her up and carried her inside. As the story suggests, the bridegroom usually scattered walnuts to the onlookers en route – a symbol of fertility and longevity.

All this pertains to Roman citizens, but many of the inhabitants of Britannia were not citizens at all and might come from a variety of tribes. Celtic traditions, languages and settlements remained, especially in the remoter country areas, but after two centuries most people had adopted Roman habits. Latin was the language of the educated, and Roman citizenship – with its legal, commercial and social status – the ambition of all.

However most common people lacked that distinction. Some were freemen or 'freedmen', scratching a precious living from trade or farm; thousands more were slaves, mere chattels of their masters with no more rights or status than any other domestic animal. Some slaves led pitiable lives, but others were highly regarded by their owners and might be treated well – like Pulchra in this story. Indeed a slave in a kindly household, certain of food and clothing in a comfortable home, might have a more enviable lot than many a poor freeman struggling to eke out an existence in a squalid hut.

The Romano–British background to this

book has been derived from a wide variety of (sometimes contradictory) written and pictorial sources. However, although I have done my best to create an accurate picture, this remains a work of fiction and there is no claim to total academic authenticity. Commodus and Pertinax are historically attested, as is the existence and basic geography of Glevum (modern Gloucester).

Relata refero. Ne Iupiter quidem omnibus placet. I only tell you what I heard. Jove himself can't please everybody.

One

The wedding of Pompeia Didia was an elaborate affair – not at all the sort of thing I usually attend. Anyone who was anyone in the colonia was likely to be there, and Glevum was founded for wealthy veterans, and was thus one of the richest towns in all Britannia. Not generally an event for humble slaves-turned-pavement-makers then, but His Excellence, my patron, had requested me to go – actually as his personal representative – and when Marcus Aurelius Septimus offers one an honour of that kind, it is not something that a man can readily decline – not if he hopes to live a long and happy life.

Of course, I was not expecting any such request so I was surprised early one morning to get a messenger at my home summoning me to come at once to Marcus's country house which was only a mile or two from where my roundhouse was. I put on my toga, collected my young slave Minimus – himself on loan from my patron for a while – and set off at once. I was duly ushered into the *triclinium*, where I found him reclining on a

14

dining couch, languidly nibbling a bowl of sugared figs – most unusual at this time of day.

'Ah, Libertus, my old friend!' He waved a hand at me so I could kiss his ring.

I performed the usual obeisance rather cautiously. When Marcus greets me as 'old friend' like that, it is usually because there is some favour that he wants to ask. 'You wanted to see me, Excellence?' I said.

'I did.' He waved the hand again, this time to indicate a stool where I could sit and keep my head politely below his. When I had perched on it, he smiled approvingly. 'I'm sorry to have to greet you in the dining room like this. The household is in sorry disarray, I fear. As you know, in just a day or two we are setting off for Rome, and the slaves are busy packing everything we need. I am leaving it to Julia to supervise the task, she has strong ideas about the quantity to take. This seems to be the only room where there is any peace.'

I nodded. I had seen the evidence of this as I came into the house. Much of the normal household furniture had been stored away, and there was already a pile of wooden boxes stacked beside the gate, obviously awaiting the arrival of the luggage-cart. 'She will need a good deal for the child, I expect,' I said, thinking of the quantity of crates – then rather wished I hadn't. Marcus was unfashionably devoted to his wife and son, and this might seem a little critical.

I need not have worried. He gave another smile. 'My old friend Pertinax, who used to be the governor of this very province, is Prefect of Rome now, of course, and he has invited us to visit him, so we shall be seen at the Imperial Court. I believe that Julia would take every robe she owns, and she would take a similar quantity for Marcellinus if he were not likely to grow out of it all.' He leaned forward and selected another sugared fig. 'And your own wife and son? They are well, I trust?'

'Very well, I thank you, Excellence,' I answered, still more cautious now. Marcus was well aware of my household circumstances. Indeed, he had given me a plot of land to build a roundhouse on, when I was reunited with my wife after years of painful separation when we had both been captured and sold separately as slaves. And he had done the same thing for my adoptive son, who until recently had been my faithful slave. But Marcus did not usually trouble to ask after them like this. Whatever this favour was, I thought, it must be onerous. I sighed. He had used me in tricky situations once or twice before, but I had hoped to escape these duties while he was away. I glanced doubtfully at him.

However, he seemed to be waiting for me

to tell him more. 'Junio is enjoying his new role as freeman and citizen,' I said. 'All of which he owes to your advice. And, of course, he is now a husband on his own account. I must thank you once again for your handsome wedding gift.'

'Ah!' His expression altered, and he ceased to meet my eyes. 'Weddings! That reminds me. That is why I called you here. You know the citizen Honorius, I believe? Honorius Didius Fustis, the town councillor?'

I nodded. Honorius was not merely an important figure in the town, he was one of the most wealthy citizens in the area. 'I recently installed a pavement in his town house,' I replied.

Marcus grunted. 'I have visited the place. Rather a vulgar ostentation of wealth and privilege, I thought.' There was some truth in that. It had been built with the obvious intention to impress, on an enormous site which Honorius had obtained by buying up a number of little businesses and having them pulled down. Town houses on that scale were not common here, though any public officer of any rank is obliged to maintain an establishment within a certain radius of the basilica. Marcus himself kept up only an apartment in the town, which – although it was luxurious enough inside – was nonetheless over a public wine shop and had attic flats above.

I looked at him, surprised. Marcus did not usually stoop to jealousy. Perhaps there was a certain animosity between the pair of them. Honorius set great store by his wealth and rank, and claimed to come from a patrician family, but my patron easily outstripped him on all counts. Marcus is the wealthiest man in all Britannia and – especially now that Pertinax was appointed to the Prefecture of Rome – one of the most influential in the Western Empire. Honorius may pride himself on his patrician blood, but Marcus is said to be related to the Emperor himself.

But Honorius had paid me fairly handsomely. I did not wish to criticise the man. 'Well, I did the pavement, if you noticed that. I dealt with the steward, I did not meet the man himself.'

Marcus paused in the act of nibbling his fig. 'Well, now you will have an opportunity.' He gestured towards a piece of scrolled vellum on the floor beside the couch, which I had not noticed up till now. 'His daughter's getting married. He has invited me – but the ceremony will take place after I have gone. But I should make a gesture – he is rewriting his will, and I am to be appointed residuary legatee.'

I nodded. It is not an uncommon thing to do, in fact, to nominate an influential man as heir of last resort. It is a kind of compliment of course – and it does prevent the estate

18

from being forfeit to the Imperial Purse, as it would be otherwise, if any primary legatees should die or be untraceable, and thus cause a 'querella' about the provisions of the will. Marcus had been named in this way many times, and more than once had benefited from the inheritance. I saw where this was leading, or I thought I did. 'You wish me to deliver a gift on your account?'

Marcus bit thoughtfully into his fig before he said, 'A little more than that. I have written suggesting that you should take my place, and go as my personal representative. Oh, don't look so reluctant, it won't be difficult. No temple rituals, or fictional sales before the court – it isn't to be an old-fashioned *manus* wedding of that kind. Just a modern wedding in the family home – a simple civil contract exchanged between the bride and groom in front of the proper number of Roman witnesses, and then a small offering to the household gods, follow-ed by a cheerful party afterwards.' He grin-ned. 'You'll like that, Libertus. You'll have a good feast there. Tell me all about it, when I get home again. No need even to take a din-ing knife with you – the family is so wealthy they provide one for their guests, even on a large occasion such as this. Oh, and speaking of the guests, you can keep a watch on one of them for me: one in particular, I'm certain he'll be there.'

19

So this was the reason for the summons. I said nothing, and after a moment he went on again.

'Antoninus Seulonius, he's a merchant in the town, and he's clearly aiming to be elected as *decurion* next year. Wants me to propose him as a candidate. But I'm not sure that he's honest. He's risen very quickly – and I'm not sure how. He's not well-connected so he may be using bribes – or have some secret influence over somebody in power. He'll be at the wedding, but he won't be on his guard. Keep an eye on him. See who he consorts with, and write and let me know.'

So that was it. I felt my spirits sink. I was to attend the wedding of a girl I'd never met, in a class of society where I did not belong, simply to spy for Marcus on a fellow guest. It was not an appealing prospect. 'I don't imagine that the father of the bride – anxious about his standing in the town – will be altogether delighted at this substitution, Excellence. I might be a citizen, but I am a tradesman all the same – and an ex-slave at that. Everyone in Glevum will be aware of it. Hardly the social equivalent of a great man like yourself.'

He looked more flattered than disturbed by this. 'You were born a Celtic nobleman and I have told him that. In any case, it has all been arranged. I have instructed him to send you an invitation scroll, and you should be receiving it within a day or two. A pity I could not have asked him to invite your wife and son – they might have enjoyed a Roman wedding, I suppose – but since you are specifically representing me and none of you are known to the household socially, I could hardly impose on him for that.'

He helped himself to the last remaining fig, saying as he did so, 'Well, we seem to have eaten the very last of those. I don't suppose we shall buy figs again until I'm back from Rome. Of course, if you would care to take a little wine, I can try to find a servant – I'm sure one could be spared. Meanwhile take this silver platter with you, it's rather coarse and heavy, but you can take it as my gift to Pompeia and her husband on their wedding day.'

I recognized the signs that I was now dismissed, so I excused myself and went back to Minimus, who was still waiting for me in the anteroom. He grinned at me enquiringly, but I was in no mood to talk. I gave him the silver salver and we walked back to the roundhouse as quickly as we could.

My wife was remarkably sanguine when she heard the news – though, of course, I hadn't told her about the spying task. 'I will get your toga to the fuller's straight away. You can't go to a place like that with damp bedraggled hems. A really wealthy town

21

councillor, you say? What an opportunity for you, to mix with folk like that! Why, one day you might be elected to the *curia* yourself.' She fussed around the fire, stirring something delicious-smelling in a pot.

I refused to share her optimistic view. 'I don't know what Honorius will make of this at all – knowing the kind of man he is,' I said. 'He is notorious for his old-fashioned attitudes, you know, especially where law and order is concerned. He has made speeches on the steps of the basilica for years, urging that the state should reintroduce the sack for parricides.'

She gaped at me. 'Not really? Not the dreaded sack?'

'The whole thing,' I said, remorselessly. 'Thrashing the father-killer to within an inch of death, and then sewing him, bleeding, into a leather bag together with a bunch of frantic animals – a live dog, monkey, snake and rooster, I believe it is – and then throwing the whole lot into the sea to drown. The condemned man has a variety of painful ways to die. Honorius says the very threat of it helps to prevent the crime.'

She was so startled she almost let the dinner burn. 'Well, people say these things in public life, I suppose.'

'He carries the same principles into his household too. You've heard the rumours about his eldest daughter, I am sure. How, when he went to visit her and her new husband, a month or two ago, he found a strange man hiding in her room and killed the pair of them. He claimed the ancestral right of a paterfamilias to avenge his family's honour in that way – and the local courts declared that he was justified.'

There was a silence, then she said suddenly, 'Where was this then?'

'Aqua Sulis – so the gossips say.'

'That's miles and miles away, so it's more than likely an exaggerated account. These stories have a habit of growing in the telling, as you know.'

'But the fact that it was told at all gives you a vivid indication of the man,' I said. 'He is an old-fashioned paterfamilias who runs his household like a military camp, and insists on doing things the strict, old-fashioned way. Can you imagine him being pleased to have me as a guest?'

'Why are they having a private marriage, then? I must say I'm surprised. From what you say, I would have expected him to want the old traditions. The whole thing – from temple rites and sacrifices to symbolic cakes. Though, I suppose that *conferratio* is only for aristocracy of the highest ranks – doesn't it require the High Priest of Jupiter in Rome to officiate in person, and that sort of thing?'

I grinned. 'But that is exactly why he would have wanted it. And his mother too.

She's worse than he is, so I heard them say when I was laying that pavement in the house. She would have loved all that. But of course it couldn't really be made to happen here, and anyway it's almost unheard of nowadays. Honorius did not even have one for himself, when he remarried a year or two ago – nor did that other daughter that I told you of. Anyway, under the old system the father lost his power – and Honorius would not want to lose the right to have her dowry back if by any chance the marriage failed. He is too fond of money for anything like that.'

'So you see,' Gwellia said, triumphantly, 'he isn't such a stickler for convention as you say. And if Marcus has told him to invite you, he can hardly refuse – in fact he'll have to make a special fuss of you. So eat your dinner while it's hot and let me have those clothes. And you can go to the barber's shop tomorrow for an hour, and have your chin scraped and your nose hairs plucked. At least we can have you looking halfway decent for the day.'

'I still don't want to go at all,' I said. 'But I suppose I'd better do it, if the invitation comes.'

And so I did. But if I had been a rune-reader and known what lay in store, I might even have disobeyed my patron and declined to go.

Two

So there I was on the appointed day, arriving at the house. Minimus, who had accompanied me, had already gone round to the back to join the other slaves in the servants' quarters there, and I was left to walk up to the front entrance on my own, clutching the piece of silver plate and trying to look as if I often did this sort of thing. In fact it was the first proper Roman wedding feast I'd ever been to in my life, and I was not quite sure what was expected of a guest. I said as much to the tall, stooping, lugubrious-looking slave who was acting as doorkeeper for the afternoon.

He appraised me silently from top to toe. I clearly didn't match his picture of an honoured guest. The toga I was wearing was my best one – true – and it marked me as a proper citizen, but it lacked the telltale purple stripe which would have indicated high-born rank, or even the dazzling whiteness and high quality of cloth which might be expected of the other invitees. But I had produced the special invitation scroll, and

25

there was no doubting the quality of that silver plate I held. His discomfiture was so visible it almost made me smile.

He must have decided that it was safe to let me in. His face relaxed and he was almost friendly as he said, 'I shouldn't worry about the customs, citizen. There isn't much to do except stand and watch, then eat. And it's likely to be a good feast too, judging by the other wedding that took place in this house.'

'Then I hope for your sake that the guests are not too hungry – or for that matter the gods.' Leftovers from important feasts were always offered to the household deities, in addition to the normal evening sacrifice, but anything remaining on the altar the next day was generally shared between the household slaves. I grinned at him. 'Though I hear the last marriage did not work out very well – let us hope this new one is far happier.'

He gave me a wary smile. Most guests, I realized, would not stop to stand and gossip with the doorman in this way. He leaned forward, confidentially. 'I hope so too, for Pompeia's sake – even though her bridegroom is almost twice her age. She didn't even choose him, her father did all that. Mind, she's so plain, poor thing, no doubt she is glad of anyone at all – and her father's so restrictive she hardly leaves the house! I tell you, citizen, if I were Pompeia, I'd marry the one-eyed beast of Hell himself if it would earn my freedom from Honorius! Though, of course, I'm just a slave, and I'm talking out of turn.' He had bent so close towards me I thought for a moment he would clap me on the arm.

I took advantage of his friendliness to say, 'Then there's something else that you can tell me, friend. A guest called Antoninus is expected, I believe. Can you tell me if he's already here?'

This simple enquiry had an unexpected effect. He took a step backwards, and abruptly changed his tone. 'Almost all the other guests are here already, citizen. Only two more are expected – I see their litter now. So, if you'll excuse me, I can't stand here chattering. I should call an attendant and have them show you in.'

I looked over my shoulder in the direction of the street. Sure enough a double litter had drawn up just outside and a sour-faced merchant and his wife were being assisted to clamber out of it. I knew them slightly. They were very rich and dealt in the expensive wines which Marcus sometimes bought, and they were already looking disapproving at the sight of me. They turned their backs and made a show of paying off the litter. I was equally anxious not to talk to them – or to be ushered in with them. If they learned that I had been asking after Antoninus, they would make a point of telling him, and put him on his guard.

I turned back to the doorman urgently. 'You're right,' I said. 'I'd better go inside.' I slid him a half-sestersius as I spoke. Marcus had advised me that I should tip the staff, though of course he had made no provision for my doing so, and my humble offering was out of my own purse. Too humble, it appeared. The doorkeeper looked unimpressed.

However, he did his duty – all cool politeness now. 'Give me that cloak you're carrying, citizen. And I'll take your offering for the bride as well. The bridegroom and his procession will be here very soon.'

I gave him the cloak, which had been folded on my arm, but did not relinquish the solid silver plate. If anyone was going to hand over such a splendid gift, I would have the pleasure of doing it myself.

The doorman shrugged and put the cloak into an ante-room – a sort of little cubbyhole where waiting slaves could sit. There were several cloaks already, draped across a stool, but I would have no trouble locating mine again. It was the shabby one.

'I'm sorry citizen. There are no house-slaves about. I'll have to summon one.' He struck a little hanging gong beside him as he spoke. 'The pages are all busy, by the looks of it. Wait for a moment till these other guests are here, and I'll find an attendant for all three of you.'

I shook my head. 'I know my way about. I've walked unescorted in this house before.'

That impressed him, I could see. Not many people are accorded such an intimate privilege. I did not tell him of the circumstance – that I'd been laying the mosaic in this very entrance way.

I gave him a bright smile. 'I'll go straight along this passage to the atrium. There are certain to be several servants waiting there, in that big vestibule beside the door, in case they're needed to attend to guests. One of them can show me in.' I saw his startled look. 'I know it isn't usual,' I added wickedly, 'but I'm certain that even your master would approve. I'm representing Marcus Septimus, after all, and I'm sure he would be given the freedom of the house. Besides, you don't want to upset that wealthy wine merchant and his wife – they won't want to be seen walking in with me. You must have noticed the look they gave me when they saw me here.'

He glanced at me uncertainly. 'Well, citizen, if you are sure. There's certain to be someone outside the atrium, as you say. They will take care of you.' He turned his back and went to greet the newcomers.

So I didn't even have an escort as I walked into the house. I strolled along the passage, clutching my present like a talisman, and wishing – not for the first time – that I had my son Junio with me. He had been married only recently, himself. That had been a simple wedding, with just the family there. I wondered what he would think about all this.

'All this' was evident on every side of me. The door to the nearby *triclinium* was ajar, and I could see a low central table lit with scented oil lamps and festooned with flowers, though the perfume was more than half-obscured by delicious aromas from the kitchens, which must be somewhere through the door down the little passage leading to my left. From immediately ahead of me, behind the screen door to the atrium, a hum of muted conversation reached my ears – no laughter or raised voices, merely that formal murmuring that Romans think polite on ceremonial occasions before the feasting starts. But though I looked up and down the vestibule, and even down the corridor that led off to the rear, there was no sign of an attendant anywhere.

I peered around the screen door, which was ajar. It was much as I expected. I could see the splendid togas of the most important guests – a score of them at least – ranged not only around the corners of the room, but through the back into the courtyard garden which Honorius had carefully installed, at great expense, in imitation of a country house.

Against the far wall, I could see the preliminaries for a feast set out: tables crammed with dates and fruit and little sweetened cakes, and jugs and craters full of wine, but nobody was eating or drinking them as yet. Beside it, the household altar had been adorned with boughs of scented blossom round the base, while on the shelf above were the childhood toys which the bride would have ritually given to the gods the day before, together with her girlhood clothing. A fire was burning on the Vestal hearth, and at last I saw the slaves – moving through the crowd of younger men and handing out festive wreaths and sprigs of marjoram. Which of the guests was Antoninus I did not yet know.

By leaning further forward could I glimpse the womenfolk. There were fewer of them, but they were just as fine – decked out in tunics and stolas of the finest cloth, their arms, necks, ears and ankles hung with jewellery. They were clustered round a temporary dais set against the wall on which three women were enthroned on stools. This was the bridal party, that was clear. I craned a little more to get a better look – Gwellia would want to hear the details of all this.

Seated nearest to the entrance was the eldest of the group, a tall thin woman of advancing years. Her hair was dyed elaborately black and her skin was unnaturally white with powdered chalk, although – together with the wine lees tinting on her cheeks – this only emphasized her wrinkles and the gauntness of her face. This was the redoubtable grandmother, I guessed, as she surveyed the room with a disdainful air and brushed imagined creases from her golden robe.

Beyond her, on the farther stool, sat a plump and pretty girl – she might have been twenty-one or so at most. She was dressed from head to toe in pink, and her complexion and neatly braided golden hair needed no assistance from the cosmetic box.

And sitting between them, what was obviously the bride.

Poor girl. She was as plain as the door-keeper had said – round-faced as a pudding and graceless as a pig – but all the same my heart went out to her. Though she sat there conspicuous in her saffron-coloured veil, I have never seen a girl look more forlorn.

Her bridal costume somehow only made it worse. The plain white tunic, tied beneath the breasts with that suggestive knot which only the bridegroom is entitled to untie, gave her the appearance of a carpet tied with string. The traditional yellow mantle – to match the leather shoes – accentuated the sallow colour of her cheeks. Her mousy hair hung lankly beneath the flimsy veil, though it had obviously been carefully arranged. Gwellia had explained to me last night how it was done – she having done it for a Roman mistress once. It was groomed and parted with a special spear-shaped comb, and carefully formed into the traditional six plaits, representing the six great tribes of Rome. I could just make out the droopy ends of them. The bridal wreath of marjoram and myrtle which held the veil in place, far from being a floral crown of joy, only made her look more pathetic and absurd.

I was just making a mental note of all of this, so that I could tell Gwellia when I got home again, when a voice spoke at my elbow, 'Can I help you, citizen?'

I whirled round to see a little fair-haired slave, no more than eight or nine, wearing the light-blue tunic of the house, and carrying a large basket of walnuts in his hand.

'I could not find an attendant to announce me,' I explained, embarrassed at being found skulking in the hall, spying on the wedding guests like this.

I meant only to offer an excuse, but he took it as a serious rebuke. 'I'm sorry, citizen. I should have been on duty at the door to help escort the visitors, but I was called away. My master sent me to fetch these from the store.' He shook the basket at me, rattling the nuts. 'I didn't expect that it would take me very long, but the kitchen slaves were very busy with the feast, and I could not find where they had stored the nuts. No one expected that we'd be needing them – usually the bridegroom brings some for himself, to throw to the crowd as he takes his bride back home – but the ones that he had ordered turned out to be bad. We had a message from him, just a little while ago, when he was ready to set off from home. Fortunately my master remembered we had these, so I was sent at once to look for ours. It would be an awful omen, wouldn't it, to give away bad walnuts on your wedding day?'

He was prattling out of nervousness, I saw and I tried to reassure him with a smile. 'Never mind, you're here now. You can show me in.'

He nodded earnestly. 'I'm very sorry citizen, to have left you standing here – I came as soon as possible when I heard the gong. I didn't even stop to put the basket down – but ... Oh, dear Mars! – there goes the gong again. There must be other visitors waiting at the door.'

I nodded. 'Two important ones,' I said. 'I saw them in the street. They've taken a few minutes to come up to the door. I think they were waiting for me to be safely out of sight. So, if you'll announce me, I'll go and join the crowd.' I gave him a conspiratorial wink.

'And if I were you, I'd put those walnuts down. You look like a street vendor with that basket on your arm.'

He gave me a grateful look and put the basket down beside a handsome wooden table with a shoe-shaped lamp on it. 'You won't tell my master that I was delayed?'

'Nor that you stood here chattering when you did arrive!' I said. In fact, his artless prattle was delaying me – though a sign, at least, that I hadn't frightened him. Perhaps I could ask him to point Antoninus out. I raised an eyebrow in mock severity. 'So, now perhaps, you'd kindly show me in.'

He had the grace to look a bit abashed. 'Who shall I tell them, citizen?' he asked. He pushed wide the door that I'd been peering round and took a step into the room, just as the gong rang out again – more insistently than ever. He looked back at me, uncertain what to do.

I was on the point of giving him my name, when I was rooted to the spot by an amazing sight. Minimus had appeared in the court-yard from somewhere at the rear, and was jostling his way through the distinguished guests. He was acting in a most un-slave-like manner, too – almost in danger of elbowing one fat young councillor aside.

He saw me standing at the inner door and his face cleared at once. He wriggled out into the atrium and hurried up to me, oblivious to the fact that half the wealthy citizens of Glevum were staring after him.

'Master,' he blurted, not even waiting for me to give him leave to speak. 'I think you'd better come. His Excellence would have sent for you, if he had been here himself, instead of being on his way to Rome – even if you hadn't been invited as a guest. I told the chief steward so and managed to persuade him that I should come and look for you. He's in no state to do anything himself. And someone must take over. There's been an accident.'

Three

There was a dreadful hush in which I became uncomfortably aware that the eyes of the whole room were fixed on me. For a fraction of a moment no one moved at all. Then suddenly the gong boomed out again, and – as if it were a signal – an outraged murmur of whispering began.

Then one voice rang out above the rest – a creaking high voice, like a wheel in want of oil – 'What is the meaning of this disgrace, young man?'

It was the grandmother. She rose to her

feet and marched down from the dais, more like an ex-soldier than a woman in a gown. 'And what do you mean, there's been an accident? Don't you realize that even to mention such a word is a terrible ill omen on a day like this?' She seemed oblivious that her own voice rang out across the room so that – if there was an omen – she was redoubling it. She stood, arms folded, as if confronting us. 'If there has been some kind of unfortunate event, it should be dealt with quietly in the servants' room upstairs – not trumpeted in public to disturb the guests.'

She gestured towards the company as she spoke, and at once the men at least began to turn away and talk in loud voices about other things, pretending – like the well-bred Roman citizens they were – not to have noticed anything amiss, though they had all been staring, goggle-eyed, till then.

She noticed and lowered her voice into a hiss. 'You have embarrassed us, young man. When we've taken such trouble to consult the auguries – and at such expense. It's unforgivable. So kindly take your impudent young slave, and leave the house. Who are you anyway?'

I had not realized till that moment that she was addressing me. Perhaps I should have guessed – she was not the sort of person who would waste her personal attention on a slave like Minimus – but it is a long time since anybody called me a 'young man', and longer still since anyone had rebuked me like a child. I am over fifty and, though this woman was my senior by ten years or so, we two were much the oldest people in the company. Her stinging onslaught took me so much by surprise that for a moment I could not find my tongue.

Minimus answered for me, apologetically, 'This is the citizen Libe—'

She turned and rapped him smartly on the ear with the ivory handle of her folding vellum fan. 'Silence, oaf! I was not asking you. If he's too ill-bred to answer for himself, I will consult my page.' She turned to the youngster. 'Slave! Who is this ... citizen?' The sneering pause before the final word made it quite clear what her opinion was of my bedraggled toga and its presence in her house.

The page looked sheepish. 'Madam, excuse me, but I do not know. He was just about to tell me when his servant came.' He flinched as if he expected an angry blow for this, and when none came he burbled on again. 'I have not seen his invitation scroll because in fact I did not escort him in. I found him waiting outside the atrium.'

She turned to me now, jabbing the fan handle almost in my face. 'So, he was walking unaccompanied around my house, was he? And where did he get that silver platter from?'

'Madam, it was a present from His Exc—' I said, just as Minimus began to tug my sleeve.

'Master, it really is important that you come. There's no time to be lost.'

This time the rap was very sharp indeed, and left a weal across my servant's face. 'Is there no limit to your insolence? I shall send for the household guard and have you flogged. And as for you...' She glared at me. 'I shall summon the doorman and see you are removed. I don't know what my son Honorius will say when he learns of this intrusion on a day like this.' She turned back to the page. 'Where is your master, anyway? I thought he went out with the steward to select the banquet wines.'

The boy looked sheepish. 'Forgive me, lady, but again I do not know. I haven't seen him since he sent me off to find the walnuts, a little time ago—'

Minimus astounded me by breaking in again. 'Your pardon, madam, but I know where he is.' She turned to him, eyes flashing, but he persevered. 'Let me give my message and you will understand. If Honorius is your son, then what I have to say concerns you very much. He was the victim of this accident. Two of his slaves have taken him and laid him on his bed.'

The skin beneath the careful face paint paled visibly. 'Great Mars! What accident was this? No, don't answer now. Wait a minute!' She turned to the invited guests, who had given up pretending and were listening openly. 'Citizens and ladies,' she said with dignity, 'will you pardon me. A slight hitch has arisen, which I must attend to straight away. Please continue to talk among yourselves – and, slaves, you may begin to serve the sweetmeats now. Please forgive me, I shall not be long.' As she spoke she shepherded us out into the hall, where she addressed us in an urgent undertone.

'Now, then, what accident was this? And on his daughter's wedding day, as well! What a dreadful portent! The guests will be distressed, and the bridegroom might cancel if he hears of it and we would lose a strong alliance with a wealthy family.'

I gulped. I know that Roman society considers it good form to keep one's private emotion under strict control, but her apparent lack of feeling quite astonished me. If I had heard such news about my adopted son, I would have insisted on being taken to his side at once, at the risk of offending Jupiter himself. She seemed less concerned about the welfare of her son than about the effect upon her guests.

She was still frowning thoughtfully, and when Minimus made a sign as if he wished to speak, she silenced him with an imperious hand. 'Do not interrupt me when I'm trying to think. I am deciding what it is best to do. My son is receiving good attention, I suppose?'

Minimus had learnt his lesson with the fan. He contented himself this time with a nod.

The woman inclined her own head, as if satisfied. 'Then perhaps it need not come to cancellation after all. If we need a medicus, we will send for one. But we must act speedily. The bridegroom will be here, and somehow Honorius must be present then. We need his hand to sign the contract – though the dowry is arranged. What exactly happened? Is he seriously hurt?' She turned to my servant. 'Speak up, stupid boy!'

Minimus looked demurely at his sandal straps. 'The steward told me to say "accident", as being more polite, though perhaps that does not quite describe it properly,' he said. 'It appears that your son was sampling the wine—'

'You are not going to tell me that he sampled too much and contrived to have a fall?' She shook her head. 'My son Honorius would not do a thing like that. And he always takes wine watered, as I taught him to – even when he is simply tasting it.'

Minimus replied simply, 'Madam, I'm afraid that it is rather worse than that. Perhaps there was something the matter with the wine. Or possibly the water that he put into it. At all events he was taken very sick and almost collapsed on to the floor.'

'Well, it can't have been the water – that comes from our own well, and the whole household has been drinking from it half the day. But I don't understand how it can have been the wine. That was delivered only this morning from the wine merchant. Oh! And here's the very man that it was purchased from.'

The sour-faced merchant and his wife had just appeared from the front door, looking even more sour than they'd looked earlier, and accompanied by the lugubrious door-keeper himself.

'A thousand pardons, Helena Domna,' the attendant said, 'but here is Lucianus Vinerius and his wife. I fear they have been kept waiting at the door for far too long...'

Helena Domna – since that seemed to be her name – was scowling so much that he stopped and stared at her in some dismay. Then obviously sensing that something was amiss, he attempted to excuse what he had done. 'I have been gonging for several minutes for a slave, but nobody has answered, so in the end I brought them in myself.' There was still no answer and he hurried on. 'But I must hasten back, if you'll excuse me, citizens. There are shouts and cheers already in the street – I think the bridegroom's procession must be almost here.' And he bowed himself backwards down the passageway.

Helena Domna watched him out of sight, and only then did she address the rest of us, though there was a sarcastic note in the cracked voice as she said, 'Lucianus Vinerius – and Maesta too, of course. I am sincerely happy to find you here at last. I only wish the circumstances were happier, that's all. It seems that my son Honorius has been taken ill, after tasting one of the new wines he bought from you. I'm sure you'd wish to be the first to know – and perhaps you have some suggestion as to what we should do now? We may require a medicus to find an antidote, no doubt you would be anxious to assist us with the cost?' There was no question about it, she was half-threatening them.

Vinerius looked wary. 'Taken ill?' he said.

Minimus stepped forward. 'Very ill indeed, from what I understand. One minute he was talking to the steward in the court, and the next he had turned pale and collapsed on to a stool. Someone came up to the slaves' room with the news, and we all went running down. By the time I got there his speech was very slurred and he was seeing imaginary things.'

The wine merchant exchanged glances with his wife, a look which said as clearly as if he'd uttered it aloud, That sounds like simple drunkenness. Then Vinerius spoke. 'What sort of things? Pink hippogriffs, I suppose?'

Minimus raised his eyes and looked at him steadily. 'He seemed to be seeing people who were dead, or so the steward said. Somebody called Miles – I think I heard that name. But that was not the worst. A moment later he said his legs were numb. His face turned crimson and he was retching hard. The steward fetched a feather to start him vomiting, but Honorius was almost fainting on his feet, and stumbling so much it took three servants to escort him to his room. They are still at his bedside looking after him.'

Helena Domna drew in a swift, shocked breath but it was Vinerius who spoke. 'Nonsense, boy. It would take a whole amphora to make a man so sick – and it would have to be taken undiluted too. Honorius would never drink to such excess – certainly not on an important occasion like today. It's the kind of bad behaviour he would not tolerate!'

Helena Domna shook her head. 'Then perhaps this boy was right. There must have been a problem with the wine. Thank Jupiter we hadn't yet served it to the guests – or we should have been accused of attempted poisoning. Don't shake your head Vinerius – it could only be your merchandise that brought all this about, Honorius was perfectly all right when he left the atrium. I spoke to him myself, just after we had the message about the walnuts, earlier.'

'And when he sent me to fetch them, he was his normal self,' the little page piped up. I had almost forgotten that he was standing there. 'Whatever happened, it was very fast.' Vinerius gave him a baleful glare and cleared his throat. It was clear that he was seriously worried now. 'Helena Domna, I am desolated by this news. But I assure you it was nothing to do with my goods at all. It would take an amazingly strong drink to cause intoxication of that kind so soon – some rough and undiluted home-made brew perhaps – and there was certainly nothing like that in the batch I sent today. They were splendid, most expensive wines – the finest that I have – part of a shipment that arrived from Rome a day or two ago. I personally sampled each variety and invited Honorius and his wife to my humble table so that he could do the same. That was the basis on which he made his choice.'

Helena Domna's thin nose had turned as scarlet as her face was pale. 'And is it not possible that one amphora failed, and there was contamination of the wine inside?'

She had a point. Vinerius countered it. 'That has been known to happen – even with fine wines. Doubtless that's why he was testing each of them – but there couldn't be anything that would have this effect. The wine might taste a little peculiar, that's all. And of course – if that proves to be the case and he sends it back to me, I will replace it instantly and refund the cost. But I'm sure the goods I sent to him were sound.'

Helena Domna gave him a mirthless smile. 'Then you will do me the favour of testing them yourself, since you are so confident of their quality. Even if Honorius is too ill to appear we shall have to offer something to our invitees, especially if they are denied a wedding and a feast. I should hate to cause illness among our other guests. But you are confident...?' There was a painful moment. I saw him hesitate.

'Wait a minute,' I said suddenly. 'This may not be simply a problem with the batch. You spoke of attempted poisoning a little while ago. Vomiting and weakness and numbness of the legs? You don't suppose it might be ... aconite?' It was such a bizarre suggestion that I almost hesitated to express it, and they were all staring at me as though I were deranged.

'Poison?' Helena Domna was incredulous. 'In wine intended for a wedding feast? That is nonsensical. Who could possibly want to do a thing like that? And why? One couldn't know who'd drink it – it might make everybody ill. And, more particularly, how could it occur? The wine was only delivered this morning at the house.'

'Someone might have tampered with an amphora since, I suppose.' Vinerius was positively anxious to approve my reasoning. 'Some sort of enemy of the family, perhaps? There must be lots of strangers in the house today.'

His stout wife nodded. 'And the citizen is right. Those could be symptoms of wolfsbane poisoning. If so, poor Honorius needs treatment urgently. Salt water to make him vomit and purge the poison out, and mallow and crowsfoot as an antidote. I make a few decoctions, I could go and fetch them now ... there wouldn't be a charge.' She caught her husband's eye. 'Or Honorius can add it to the wine bill later on...'

But the warning head shake had not been about the price. Her husband had seen the danger in her babbling and Helena Domna voiced the thought – which had occurred to me as well. 'So you make decoctions, do you? And the wine was at your store until they brought it here. How remarkable. My son might have some questions to ask you later on, when he has recovered from this unfortunate event. Why, what is it, steward?'

The last words were uttered to an imposing slave who had come the other way, through the side door from the rear – a tall, strong rather handsome man, in a gold-edged tunic and an over-robe which marked him as a servant of some seniority. I recognized the steward that I'd dealt with earlier. I'd thought him impressive, when I'd met him then, but now he was wringing his big hands together in a helpless way, and there was an expression which looked like abject panic on his face. He stood there looking between Minimus and me, as if somehow between us we had let him down, then turned to Helena Domna with a look of pure despair.

'Mistress, I don't know how to tell you. It's a dreadful thing. My master, Honorius – he won't be asking questions of anyone again. And the wedding must be cancelled. He can't sign anything. The fact is, mistress ... I'm afraid he's dead.'

Four

Honorius's mother had no need of face-chalk now. The skin under the white coating had turned as pale as ice, and the colour with which she'd tinged her lips and cheeks looked even more bizarrely artificial than before.

She was clearly shaken, and for a moment I expected an embarrassing display – a rending of garments and beating of the breast, perhaps, accompanied by a theatrically ululating wail. There is a tradition in Roman families, that the death of a member of the household – particularly an honoured eldest son – calls for some such public outpouring of grief.

But Helena Domna was made of sterner stuff. She was a Roman patrician to the core and – in front of mere tradesman like Vinerius and myself – obviously knew how to impose strict self-control. The only outward sign that she had heard at all was a tiny tightening of the corners of her mouth and an involuntary loosening of her fingers on the fan, which fell with a little clatter on the floor. In the sudden silence it sounded very loud.

It was a long moment before she made a move, but then she motioned in silence to the page to get the fan. Immediately, the wine merchant's wife began to keen – not a funerary lament, but a high-pitched howl of frightened misery. 'It wasn't us ... it wasn't ... oh, by all the gods—'

'Maesta, be silent!' Vinerius began, but the words died on his lips. The screen door from the atrium was pushed impatiently aside and a young woman in pink robes came bustling out. It was the pretty girl I'd noticed on the dais earlier, and she was accompanied by a portly female slave.

'Helena Domna,' the young woman said, looking prettier than ever as she came across to us, her rose-coloured stola rustling as she moved. She must, I realized, be Honorius's much talked-of second wife – and a much-prized individual by the look of it. The gown was clearly made of oriental silk, which was worth its weight in gold – literally worth it, ounce for precious ounce. Her voice was pretty too, low and musical, though tinged now with sharp anxiety.

'Helena Domna, what are you doing out here in the hall? Our guests are missing you. Have you dealt with the hitch that you were speaking of? Or is there still a problem of some kind? Oh, but I see that there are visitors out here.' She looked in bewilderment at Vinerius and his wife, and then at the steward and the grovelling page, who was still groping underneath the table for the fan.

Helena Domna stood as if she'd turned to stone, silent as the statue of Juno in the niche nearby.

The young woman's face burned fiery and there was a tremble of fury in her voice. 'My mother-in-law, as usual, will not acknowledge me.' So she *was* Honorius's wife, I thought – or rather, poor thing, she was his widow now. She turned to me. 'You, citizen, can enlighten me perhaps? I think I saw you in the atrium just now, when this red-haired servant came to summon you? What is happening? Didn't I hear mention of an accident? Have they contrived to burn the wedding food, or is it simply a servant who has hurt himself?'

I glanced at Helena Domna, but she was staring at the wall. I forced myself to voice the awful news. 'An accident. A fatal accident. But it was not a slave. It was your husband, Honorius, I regret to say.'

'My husband?'

I nodded.

She pressed her hands against her chest as though to still her heart. 'But how...? When...?' She shook her head, as if in disbelief and then said angrily, 'You knew this, Helena Domna, didn't you? Why did you not come and announce it in the atrium? Or at least send word to me? I would have gone to him at once.'

'Your pardon, lady,' I murmured. 'This must be a shock. But we have only just learned of this event ourselves. When my slave here was sent to summon me, Honorius had been taken ill, but he was still alive. It seems that things have taken a fatal turning since.'

'So he was ill and conscious? And I wasn't told? Did he not call my name?' Her voice was trembling. There was no mistaking, she was shocked and close to tears. Whatever kind of person Honorius had been, I thought, this woman at least was genuinely upset that he was dead. She whirled around to the steward. 'Where is he now? Take me to him. I must see for myself.'

'Livia!' Helena Domna had found her high, cracked voice again. 'Control yourself. Of course you will be able to see him in due time. Since he leaves no son or near male relatives, it will fall to you and me to perform the obsequies – though that is for later, when the body is laid out. But first we must consider what is best to do at once. The house is full of visitors and Pompeia's bridegroom is almost at the gates. It is most unfortunate. We will have to postpone the wedding, naturally – a girl can hardly marry with her father lying dead – but we must announce it with a little dignity and try not to create an unseemly spectacle.'

'Helena Domna—' Livia began.

Her mother-in-law cut her off with an imperious hand. 'Pray, Livia, do not interrupt. I am attempting to formulate a household plan. Of course, I will make the announcement to the guests myself. And since we've offered sweetmeats, we should give our guests a drink. Something safe – the wine that we were drinking yesterday perhaps. It might be watered down enough to go around, with water from the well. Meantime – as I said before – Vinerius can oblige us by sampling all the new amphorae from his shop. The page can take him and show him where they are. And his wife with him – see she tastes them too. If they are resistant to testing any of the wine, we shall know where

52

to look and be certain whom to blame.'

The page looked troubled, but prepared to lead the way. Maesta seemed as if she might protest, but Helena Domna brooked no argument. 'Now! At once! Before I call the watch and have you both arraigned before the courts on suspicion of attempting to murder my poor son.' It was clear that she meant it, and – rather to my surprise – the wine merchants submitted to being led away.

'Helena Domna...' Livia tried again.

'And you, Livia, can call the household guard and have them lock up this so-called citizen.' She seized the fan, which the page had put down on the table top, and used it to motion angrily at me. 'Since he is the most likely suspect in this whole affair.'

I was so startled that for a moment I could not speak at all, but the young widow forestalled me by crying out at once, 'Helena Domna, I understand that you're upset, but by all the gods you can't behave like this. Vinerius could be poisoned, too. Have you considered that? If someone has really been tampering with the wine! And this man is a guest...' Her voice was shaking with emotion and distress.

Her mother-in-law dismissed her with a scornful laugh. 'A guest? You know that he was discovered skulking round the house without so much as an escorting slave? Just before Honorius was taken gravely ill? If anyone had the opportunity to poison my poor son, it was this wretch. What proof has he that he was ever invited to the house? He didn't show the page an invitation scroll and he is not known to me. Do you know who he is?'

Livia shook her head.

'In that case, steward, you can seize him now.'

The steward did not dare to disobey. He put a reluctant hand around my wrist. 'A thousand pardons, lady...' He threw a frightened glance at me. 'He is known to me. This is the protégé of Marcus Septimus, and I am assured that he was properly invited to the feast. This red-headed lad is Excellence's own slave ... or was.' He gestured towards Minimus. 'I can vouch for that. He has been here on his Excellence's business many times.'

Helena Domna seemed to waver for a moment, then she swept all this aside. 'Silence, fool! What difference does that make? A slave is in the service of whoever owns him now – and you can see what kind of man his present master is. The representative of Marcus Septimus? In that dishevelled toga? A sneak thief more likely – taking the chance to steal the wedding gifts. Look at that piece of silver he is carrying. The slave is his accomplice, I expect – used as a way of getting access to the place. It seems quite clear to me. He was prowling unescorted in the house and he's very well informed on poisons, it appears. He could easily have put something in the wine. Who else had the opportunity? Livia, send for the household guard at once and have him put in chains. We'll let Honorius's bodyguards work on him a bit. Whatever the truth is, they'll beat it out of him.'

My mouth went dry. I had seen those bodyguards and the whips and clubs they used. A few moments in their company would have me gibbering and ready to admit to anything they chose – and then no doubt I would be bundled to the courts for sentencing, just at the moment when Marcus was not here! It was likely that I'd never see my wife and son again. As a citizen I was protected from the crueller deaths, of course, but if I was found guilty of this poisoning I would probably be glad to drink a lethal brew myself. And as for what would happen to poor young Minimus! I dared not look at him.

I was still trying to make my tongue obey me, when to my great surprise the younger woman said, in a suddenly clear and quite determined voice, 'With respect, Helena Domna, we shall do no such thing. I'm sure this citizen is what he says he is – the friend of Marcus Septimus. I was there when Honorius agreed to send the scroll. I shall certainly not ask the guards to lock him up.'

Helena Domna looked first startled, then furiously annoyed. She rapped the young woman sharply with the fan. 'How dare you contradict me – and in my own son's house. Mind out of my way there – I shall send for them myself.'

Livia was a smaller woman, and a less imposing one, but she held her ground and stood firmly in Helena Domna's way. 'Steward, please release that citizen at once.'

'But lady, I cannot. I very much regret...' the poor fellow stuttered. 'Helena Domna...' He looked helplessly at Livia, as if for some advice.

'Steward, do I understand aright?' she said. 'Your former master, Honorius, is dead?' She did not turn towards him as she spoke, but raised her head and looked directly into Helena Domna's eyes. 'In that case, tell me, who is mistress here?'

'I suppose that you are, lady.' He looked abjectly terrified, but he let me go.

'You see, Helena Domna? This is my house now. Even the servants are aware of that, and – as I apprehend it – the same is true in law. Honorius bought it with my dowry and it reverts to me – quite apart from any other provision in his will. So understand me, madam, things are different from now on. If there are arrangements to be made, I shall be making them.'

Helena Domna tried to interpose, but this time it was Livia who refused to pause. 'Steward, go to the anteroom at once, and prevent poor Vinerius from poisoning himself, in an attempt to prove his innocence. I don't wish to bring more trouble on this house. If we are to test the wines, we'll do it properly and get the court to send us a condemned criminal or two to see which ones are poisoned, if any of them are. Go quickly, steward, while there is still time.'

The man looked at Helena Domna doubtfully, but all the same he went, leaving the two women alone with me and Minimus.

Livia flashed me a smile. 'I'm sorry, citizen. I must leave you now and go back to our guests. I think—'

But what she thought I never had the chance to hear, because there was a sudden commotion at the outer door: a babble of voices, distant cheers and shouts, followed by the banging of a tambour and a tootling of flutes, over which the doorkeeper's voice could still be heard, 'Don't come bursting in. Let me announce you...' But it was far too late.

The passage to the atrium was already full of shouting, laughing, jostling young men – all in fine togas which proved them citizens – some carrying boughs and instruments and already bursting into raucous bawdy song. 'Where is the bride who is shortly to be wed?' they carolled, crowding from behind. These were clearly the bridegroom's friends and relatives, and they nudged ahead of them a large, plump older man, with a bald head and fleshy red-veined face, who seemed embarrassed by his entourage, but whose incongruous festive wreaths of fresh flowers identified him clearly as the would-be groom himself.

He tried to stop the whole procession as he saw us in the hall, but his attempt to call for order was drowned out by the noise. The singers were oblivious, they were wrapped up in the song, detailing with some relish – and great vulgarity – the more salacious attractions of a wife, and the jostling of the crowd behind him forced the bridegroom forward. The pressure of people in that narrow passageway was such that both the ladies had to step aside and move towards the kitchen quarters at the back, while Minimus and I were pressed against the little table by the wall.

We might have moved backwards into the atrium, but the noisy arrival of the bridegroom's party had clearly reached the guests – and even Roman patience and good manners has limits when there is a wedding imminent. The screen was pushed open, and the guests came thronging out – laughing and clapping and giving the usual suggestive whistles to welcome the groom and his attendant group.

Someone shouted, 'Where's Honorius?' and the chant was taken up. 'We want Honorius, the father of the bride.'

'Do something!' I saw Helena Domna mouth the words, although her voice was lost in the tumultuous din. I looked at Livia and she nodded back at me.

There seemed to be only one thing I could do. I was pressing up against the table all this time, and with Minimus's help, I scrambled on to it, seizing a drum from one of the revellers as I went. I stood and thumped on it, but without much effect, until I glimpsed the doorkeeper hovering uncertainly at the entrance way as if appalled that they'd escaped him and burst into the house. I caught his eye and motioned that he should sound the gong, which he did with such effect that it almost deafened us. It made the very rafters of the passage ring.

It did, however, quieten the crowd. The shouting and singing died uncertainly away, and when I banged the drum again the whole assembly turned and looked at me. People were standing on tiptoe in the atrium to see.

'Citizens, members of the household and honoured guests,' I said. 'I fear that I have dismal news for all of you. Within the last few moments – so recently that news of it has not reached all the household yet – your host Honorius has taken ill and died. This has become a house of mourning, suddenly, and therefore the planned marriage cannot go ahead.'

Five

There was, not surprisingly, a little stir at this: first a universal gasp of disbelief, and then people huddled into groups and started whispering.

The bridegroom, who was standing at my feet, turned to his chief attendant, and above the general murmur of dismay, I heard him mutter in a plaintive tone, 'So what do we do now? All that dowry – I was going to pay my debts. We had a contract...'

'And doubtless will again,' the man hissed back at him, 'once the period of due mourning has been properly observed. Honorius will certainly have left a will, and no doubt has specified a legal guardian for the girl – you can make representations to him later on. They can hardly turn you down, since her father made the match, and you know that her grandmother approved. In the meantime, Gracchus, try to look decently distressed. The fellow would have been your father-in-law, if he'd lived.'

Gracchus sighed and nodded and, glancing up and seeing that I was observing him, instantly put on a mournful face. He turned to his companion and muttered something else, but this time he made certain that no one else could hear.

I had not time to think any more of that, because my attention was drawn by the reappearance of the steward. He came from his errand to the kitchen and storage area, stopped to have a brief word with Livia, and had now started waving frantically at me. I saw him weave his way towards me through the crowded passageway, which was now more thronged than ever with shocked, muttering groups of guests. No one was showing any tendency to leave.

For an instant I lost sight of his tunic amongst the crush – there was little attempt to clear a path for him – until then he suddenly bobbed up by the table at my side, red-faced and panting with his tunic all askew, as if he had been jostling among the milling legs. He beckoned me closer, as if for secrecy and I stooped to listen to what he had to say.

'The mistress says...' he murmured breathlessly, 'to tell them there will shortly be some wine. Vinerius had tasted one of the new amphorae before I got to him, and up till now he's suffered no mishaps. She says to offer that one to the guests, and then we can decently ask them to go back to their homes.'

I glanced at Livia and she confirmed this with a nod, and made a motion with her hands as if shooing geese away. Clearly she wanted me to disperse the crowd.

I held up my hand for silence and banged my drum again. This time the hubbub died down instantly. 'If you will move into the atrium, a light memorial refreshment will be served,' I said. 'Then we must ask you to respect the family's grief and leave the house as soon as possible.'

I had no sooner spoken those words, than I regretted them. If everybody left, how would I find who Antoninus was or even discover exactly what had happened here? I made a swift revision. 'Though I would ask for your assistance in one matter, citizens. Everyone who was present when Honorius left the room, and anyone who went into the rear part of the house would oblige me very much by coming here, and speaking to me very briefly before they leave, to help me piece together what his last movements were.' There, I thought, that should include Antoninus – since I was certain that he'd preceded me into the house – and would also help determine who might have had the opportunity to put something in the wine.

Over the general hubbub I raised my voice

again. 'Then we must ask you to go quietly to your homes – except any actual relatives, of course, who may be wanted to arrange the funeral. The rest of you may wish to offer your respects, but that will be appropriate at another time, and you will be notified of that, when the body has been properly laid out and members of the household have recovered from the shock.'

I had meant to be discreet in asking for information 'before Honorius left the room' but one of the guests, at least, was far too quick for me. No sooner had I finished than I heard a booming voice. 'So he didn't die naturally. I thought as much – I was sure I heard that servant talking about an accident. And, my friend Antoninus, don't go skulking off.'

At the mention of that name I looked around, of course, and picked out the speaker instantly. It was the stout young town councillor that Minimus had jostled on his way to me, and he was accosting a hawk-nosed citizen at the atrium door. The fellow was squirming to get away from him, but the councillor persisted. 'That fellow says he wants to question us. You had a lot of dealings with Honorius, I believe? And you were the last person to speak to him today.'

If so, that was very interesting, I thought. So this was Antoninus – the very man that I was looking for. I looked at him, to make a mental picture of the face, but apart from the nose, he was unremarkable: a man of middle age, medium height and average size, with mousy coloured hair cut in a common style. The sort of man it would be easy to overlook, I thought. I strained my ears to hear his sharp reply.

'It wasn't me who was the last to talk to him. It was that decurion over there. If anyone, Redux, they will want to talk to you. You were related by marriage to Honorius after all – and you made no secret that you bore a grudge.'

Others were turning round to stare at this bad-tempered loud exchange, but the steward stepped forward and put an end to it. 'This way, citizens and honoured guests! The slaves will wait on you.' And he shooed the invited guests back to the atrium, though the bridegroom and his retinue stood by, irresolute, filling up the hall and obviously uncertain if they should stay or not.

People were milling in the passageway making in the direction of the door, when all at once there was a high, unearthly shriek and in the screen doorway the would-be bride appeared. She had snatched off her wedding wreath and was using it like a carpet-beater's flail to force a path into the hall. I was still on the table. She looked up at me. Her eyes were wild and a spot of bright colour blazed in either cheek

'Is it true? My father, Honorius, is dead?' Her voice was shaking and unnaturally high.

'I fear so, lady—' I began, but she interrupted me.

'Then it is my doing. I admit it, citizens. No, slaves, do not attempt to silence me again. I do not care who hears. I did not want to marry anyone. I told my father so, but he would not listen, so I took other means – though I did not expect it to turn out like this.'

She gave a racking sob, followed by peals of wild laughter that were halfway to tears. The crowd fell back, as if instinctively, and two of her handmaidens led her hurriedly away into the private apartments at the rear.

If there had been shock and disbelief before, this unexpected appearance of the stricken bride, and her amazing outburst, produced still more effect and more horror than the news about her father's death had done.

Suddenly, everyone wanted to be gone. Most of the bridegroom's attendants backed away at once, and I heard them muttering excuses at the door. They, of course, were not included in my request to stay, but the important councillors also collected up their wives and began emerging from the atrium. Some – now that there was space within the passageway – went across to Livia and Helena Domna to offer their embarrassed and confused respects, and the steward was immediately called on to go away again and fetch the visitors' servants from the slave quarters upstairs.

No one but Minimus paid any heed to me, as with his assistance I climbed down from my perch. 'You were impressive, master,' he murmured, smoothing down my toga-folds and trying to restore me to some dignity.

'Not sufficiently impressive for this company,' I said, a little sour, though I was secretly grateful for his praise. I felt dishevelled and I'd managed to get a sandal strap undone. 'It is clear that no one is going to stop and speak to me, as I requested them to do.' I handed him the drum and tugged my under-tunic straight.

He looked at me, surprised. 'But surely there is no need for you to question people now. It's clear what happened to Honorius.' He went around and started rearranging the toga at the back. 'Will they arraign her for murder, do you think? Or simply decide that she was maddened by the gods, and confine her to some island exile till she dies? People are already saying that she must be locked away.'

'Who?' I said, stupidly, picking up the precious plate which had been standing on the table all this while.

'Why, Pompeia, of course. You just heard her confess. She said she killed her father, so she must have somehow put the poison in the wine.'

I shook my head. 'I doubt that very much. Oh, she may have killed him, but I don't see how. Certainly not by poisoning the wine. That arrived this very morning, so Helena Domna said, so if it were poisoned here it must have been today. Oh, don't bother with my sandal, I'll do it later on,' I added, as he tried to kneel and tie it up.

He stared up at me. 'What makes you so sure it wasn't Pompeia?'

I laughed. 'If there is one person in the household – on a day like this – who would not have the opportunity to poison anything, it must surely be the bride. We will talk to her handmaidens, naturally, but I'm almost certain we shall find that Pompeia was woken early by her slaves and has been primped and preened continually ever since. I doubt she has had a single moment to herself.'

Minimus nodded brightly, but I found myself wishing I had Junio by my side. I would not have had to explain these obvious facts to him.

'So you still want to talk to people, as you said before?' Minimus seemed positively excited at the thought. 'Can I help you with the questioning? Tell me who you want to interview, and I will see that they are—'

'Citizen?' The voice behind me made me

turn around. It was Gracchus, still wearing the wreath around his neck, although he had taken off the one around his head. 'I have been listening to everything you said. Do I deduce from what I overheard – and from Pompeia's outburst – that Honorius was kill-ed? He did not simply have an accident and die?'

I nodded. 'That seems to be the case. I am sorry if the omens—'

He cut me off. 'By poison?'

'That's the probability.'

He looked me up and down. 'But you don't think Pompeia did it? Did I hear aright? Despite what she just said?'

'If he thinks so, he is probably correct. This man is famous for solving mysteries,' Minimus put in, before I had a moment to reply. 'His Excellence Marcus Septimus has used him several times.'

I was cursing Minimus for his impetuous remarks, but Gracchus looked thoughtfully at me. 'Look, citizen, this is of consequence to me. Pompeia's dowry is a considerable sum – I was promised a forest and another tract of land, as well as quite a quantity of gold. Obviously I cannot take a mad woman to wife – let alone a father-killer – but if you're right, this might be salvaged yet. I heard what you were saying and I applaud your reasoning. What would it cost to have you demonstrate that she is innocent?' He saw me hesitate, and he added urgently, 'Prove that it was someone else, and I will pay you handsomely.'

I frowned. 'But citizen, she made it clear she didn't want to marry you. I should be loath to—'

'Not exactly, citizen. There was nothing whatever personal to me. She simply said she didn't want to wed.' A calculating smile spread across the fleshy face. 'Many new brides doubtless feel the same – it can be seen as a tribute to their delicacy. Of course Pompeia made a public scene, but she is young and had clearly just sustained a dreadful shock, so – if you are right about her father's death – that might be forgiven, if the dowry's right. Naturally she'd never find another suitor after this, so the family – or whoever was named as guardian – would almost certainly agree that I should have her as arranged. Of course the new wedding would have to be a small affair, and probably not in Glevum, though I could accept that.' He seemed to be talking chiefly to himself, but now he turned to me. 'A hundred sesterces if you prove the case.'

I gazed at him. I did not like the man, but a hundred sesterces is a handsome sum.

He saw me havering. 'Come, citizen! You cannot harm Pompeia – if that's what worries you – any further than she has harmed herself. In fact, you might save her from a

69

dreadful fate. The punishment for parricide is always particularly severe. Harsh exile at the very least – or worse. Honorius himself was calling for reintroduction of the sack – the courts might be minded to use it in this case. You know that its use has never been repealed.'

He was right of course. I nodded doubtfully. 'I would be glad on my own account to discover who killed Honorius,' I said. 'Helena Domna thinks that it was me.'

'Then it is agreed.' He gestured towards the owner of the drum. 'Come, Linneus, I want you to witness this event. I promise to pay this citizen a hundred sesterces on condition that he finds the person who killed Honorius, and proves that it was not the maiden Pompeia, and here I pay him one brass *as* as a pledge.' He seized my hand and pressed a coin into it.

'Do you accept this?' Linneus asked me, and I murmured that I did. 'Then I witness that this contract is binding under law. And here is Helena Domna coming this way now. Gracchus can tell her the arrangement you have reached. So if you will excuse me...' He took his drum from Minimus and bowed himself away.

Six

Helena Domna had reached us by this time. 'Gracchus.' She greeted the bridegroom anxiously at once, giving him no time to say anything at all and paying no attention whatsoever to myself or to my slave. 'This is most unfortunate. After such careful plans between the families. First Honorius is taken ill and dies, and then Pompeia makes that appalling scene – I don't know what you must think of her. Naturally, we'll have to release you from the betrothal after this.'

Gracchus gave her an ingratiating smile. 'It may not be necessary to revoke the vows. This citizen has convinced me that the girl is not to blame. I would be willing to take her, if he can prove as much.'

She spun around to me. 'And what do you know about it? The girl is clearly crazed, just as her sister was – what else explains the way she just behaved?'

Gracchus looked alarmed. 'You think it's in the blood? In that case, madam, per-haps—'

Helena Domna realized what her words

71

had done and hastened to recant. 'I don't mean the kind of madness that runs in the family. It's my opinion the two girls brought it on themselves, when they were giggling in their quarters, as they used to do. No doubt looking at the moon through glass – or some other childish game of dare – and failing to wear the proper charms as antidote. Nothing that can't be cured with a sacrifice or two, and a little bloodletting to relieve the brain. Provided that she's really innocent of her father's death, of course, which I sincerely hope – so if the citizen can prove it, we shall all be much relieved. Though how can he possibly prove anything at all? No one knows what happened. Unless of course he poisoned my poor son himself!'

Gracchus put a restraining hand upon her arm. People were queuing up behind us to take their leave of her, and might be listening to this interchange. He dropped his voice as if to warn her of the fact. 'It seems he has a talent for solving mysteries of this kind – and now he has undertaken to work on my behalf. Perhaps, if he succeeds in doing it, we could have a wedding later on? On the same terms as this one, as far as dowry goes? After the funeral, and leaving a due period for mourning, naturally.'

For the first time I saw the glimmer of a smile. She said, with an attempt to drop her strident voice, 'We could hold an appropriate public cleansing sacrifice, perhaps, to lift the evil omens of today, and appease the gods.'

Appease the gossips was what she really meant, but Gracchus merely smiled. 'Then my word upon it, lady. We will speak of this again. In the meantime, I will take my leave.' He took off his wreath, and said in a voice that was intended to be heard by everyone, 'Send this, and my greetings, to the lady Pompeia and tell her I hope she will recover soon. And you will inform me when the body is laid out, I will come to pay homage and attend the funeral.' He bowed his head to us and – acknowledging the surprised and sympathetic murmurs as he passed through the crowd – he followed his friend Linneus out into the street.

'Well!' Livia had detached herself from some departing guests and made her way to join us, the plump handmaiden still following at her heels. 'The disappointed bridegroom has left us now, I see. I am sorry not to have managed to have a word with him. Though I doubt my words would be a compensation for his loss.'

'It may not be a loss yet,' her mother-in-law muttered, grudgingly. 'Thanks to this incomer you think so highly of. He has wormed his way into Gracchus's confidence, now, and persuaded him that he can prove Pompeia innocent – in which case Gracchus

73

will have her in spite of everything. I can't say I approve of the bargain – or of him – but I suppose that we shall have to make the best of it. It would assure Pompeia's future, at the very least.'

Livia turned her pretty face to me. 'Then it seems we owe you gratitude for this also, citizen. As well as your help in taking charge of things.'

Helena Domna scowled at me again. 'I don't know why you sent to ask him to do that. Most inappropriate. One of the family should have spoken to the crowd. You should not have called upon a stranger to dismiss our guests. And look at them – departing straightaway, without a semblance of hospitality. The news will be over the whole colonia by dark. I don't know what Honorius would have said, I'm sure.'

Livia exchanged a meaningful glance with me. 'I'm sure it is his death which will concern them more.'

Helena Domna sniffed. 'And that's another thing. Who is to close poor Honorius's eyes, and do the calling of his name and start on the lament? You and I can't do it, decently – much as I'm sure you'd like to volunteer to do the task yourself. A female! If we were to show such disrespect, I should expect my son to come and haunt the house for evermore. If only my dear brother was still here to act for us. But there are no living male

74

relatives at all, and dreadful as it is, we may have to use a slave.' She looked around. 'But people are waiting to say farewell to us. We'll say no more about this until everybody's gone.' She fixed an artificial smile upon her face and turned away to speak to a departing visitor. Most of the invited guests had left by now – including Antoninus, I observed – and, as she'd said, the few that remained were obviously waiting to say their goodbyes as well.

I raised my brows at Livia. 'But isn't there a relative by marriage in the house?' I murmured, then added, since she was staring in puzzlement at me, 'Somebody called Redux, or something similar? I thought I heard it mentioned.'

From the chill that followed you might have supposed that I had named the hound of hell himself within a house of death, and was myself in danger of bringing a curse upon the place.

Her face turned scarlet and her voice was surprisingly unsteady as she said, 'Related by marriage in a fashion, I suppose. But quite remotely and some time ago. Hardly the person to perform the rites.'

She was so dismissive that I pressed the point. 'But, surely, even a remote connection, in the circumstances...' I trailed off, remembering. 'Oh, but come to think of it, do I recall hearing that there was some kind of grudge?'

She gave me a thin smile. 'Exactly, citizen. And that is family business, so if you'll excuse me now...'

She made as if to turn away, but I prevented her. I could not lay a hand upon her arm – that would have been presumptuous – but I said in an urgent undertone, 'Lady, if I am to help you in this matter, I must know the facts – and I would rather hear them from your lips than have to ask the gossips. Or perhaps Helena Domna would enlighten me...?'

The name – as I hoped – was enough to do the trick. Livia gave me a nervous sideways glance. 'I suppose you'd find out somehow. At least if I tell you, there's some chance you'll hear the truth. Very well. Come into the *triclinium*, where we won't be overheard.'

She waved her maidservant and Minimus aside and led the way into the dining room, where the decorated central table, and the stools and other seating set around the walls were a forlorn reminder of the cancelled feast. She sat on one of the three dining couches for which the room is named, and motioned me to sit beside her on a stool. 'I can't be long, I shall very soon be missed, but I will tell you the story very briefly, citizen. It is not a happy one. Redux was brother-in-law to young Honoria – Pompeia's elder sister and my stepdaughter –

who was executed by my husband for her presumed adultery. Perhaps you've heard the tale?'

I nodded. 'I had heard rumours.'

'I am not surprised. It was the talk of Aqua Sulis for a moon or two. In the old days, of course, when people like Julius Caesar were alive, it was a dishonour not to mete out that kind of punishment – but these are modern times. It was regarded as a very cruel and violent thing to do. Even Redux's brother Miles thought so, and he was the husband in the case.' She picked up one of the roses from the tabletop and – as if her hands were moving without her willing it – began to tear the petals from it one by one.

'Though Honorius was defending the husband's honour as well as his own,' I said.

She nodded. 'Miles didn't want to believe Honoria had been unfaithful – the maids had heard her screaming that she was innocent, and he would have heard her out. But her father wouldn't listen – there was no excuse, he said. He was visiting the house and found her in her sleeping room, apparently, lying on the bed frame half-undressed, with a man who was not her husband hiding underneath. There was only one thing for a father to do in such a case, according to his view. And, of course, he did it. He pulled out his dagger and slit both their throats – "cutting off the bough that shames the tree" he called it – to uphold the honour of the family name. And when there were protests – from Miles among others – Honorius took the matter to the courts, and won. The two men had business dealings – that is why the marriage was arranged in the first place – but it made for awkwardness. They are still obliged to meet. All, of course, kept perfectly polite, but there has been coolness between the families ever since.'

'But this brother, Redux, was invited to the feast today?' I said. I was surprised by the idea of social interaction after such events – if these were Celtic households there would have been a silent feud and people would have avoided each other in the street – but Roman patrician families did things differently, especially when there were business interests to be borne in mind.

Livia had started shredding another rose by now. She still did not seem conscious that she was doing it. 'Miles lives in Aqua Sulis and has taken a new wife. He may have been invited to the wedding feast himself – I'm not sure of that – but he would not in any case have been expected to attend. Redux lives near Glevum so he was asked to come, since my husband has trading connections with them both. Or rather, he did have. I keep forgetting that he's no longer here.' She stacked the torn petals into a little pile and placed them on a ribbon which adorned the tabletop.

The dumpy maidservant was peering round the doorway by this time, and it was clear that Livia had been missed outside, and that we could not continue to stay here for long without her being discourteous to her guests. But I wanted her to make the most of what little time we had left. I leaned forward. 'I can understand a coolness with the husband,' I observed, 'if he was not in favour of the punishment. But why should Redux bear a grudge? It could hardly be said to have affected him.'

She looked at me squarely, as if coming back to life. 'Except that the fellow that was killed that day turned out to be Zythos, Redux's great friend. Redux is convinced that he was innocent and there was some other explanation for his being there – though it is a little difficult to see what it might be. He was there – uninvited and concealed – at night and in Honoria's room. If her father had not happened to call in to say goodnight, it is probable that they would have got away with it.'

She reached out a finger and sent the little tower of torn petals tumbling. 'But, of course, there is no possible redress and – like his brother – Redux has to deal with my husband in his trade so he keeps his feelings strictly to himself. On the surface, anyway. Though I understand he has voiced his opinion to his friends.' She jumped to her feet. 'And that, citizen, is all that I can tell you, I'm afraid. Come – my slave has clearly been sent to look for me. I must go back and make my last farewells.'

I attempted to detain her. 'But how did he get in? This Zythos fellow?' I followed her, as she was walking to the door. It was an important question. A Roman home is not unguarded, like my roundhouse is. A man like Miles would have a doorkeeper and at least a dozen slaves – precisely in order to keep strangers out. So, I persisted. 'Some member of the household must have let him in – unless he used a ladder, or scaled up a wall, and even then he'd need someone inside to keep a watch.'

She was still walking and did not look around. 'I don't know, citizen. Honorius asked the same thing, several times – but all the servants swore they'd never seen the man before.'

'In Aqua Sulis, that is? But you knew him here?'

She whirled round and stared at me. 'And why should you say that?'

I shrugged. It seemed obvious to me. 'He was clearly familiar with Honoria at least. Being a young woman of good family, I don't imagine she had many opportunities to meet young men, unless they were invited to the house.'

She smiled then, a little ruefully. 'Of course. I had forgotten you were skilled at reasoning. And naturally, citizen, you are quite correct. After Honoria's betrothal was announced, we saw him several times. He lived in Glevum, not very far from here, and, as I said, was a friend of Redux – the brother-in-law to be. We liked him very much. He was charming and successful – though a Greek, of course – and there was no hint of a special friendship with Honoria. He was equally attentive to all the womenfolk. In fact, Honorius had hopes of him for Pompeia at one time.'

Poor Pompeia – even a foreigner was good enough for her, since she was thought unlikely to attract a Roman man of wealth; that was very clearly what Livia had meant. The family must have been delighted when Gracchus asked for her. I said quickly, to stop Livia from walking off again, 'So, when your husband found Zythos in Honoria's room he felt especially betrayed? Is that why he exacted such a terrible punishment?'

'Perhaps.' She'd stopped to face me now and had turned deathly pale. 'I was not free to voice the thought while my husband was alive, but I believe that it was cruel and unjust punishment – however much the law entitled him to it. The family was shocked, although we did not dare to grieve or even give her a proper burial. My husband could

81

be completely heartless when he chose. I know that poor Redux was distraught as well – but of course, equally helpless to respond.' She dropped her eyes and went on, in an altered tone of voice, in which it was evident that she was close to tears. 'We'd even invited Zythos here to dine, you know, on several occasions when Redux was a guest. All in Pompeia's interests, of course – not that it was ever mentioned openly. Officially it was to make up the proper number at the feast. Honorius was a stickler for social niceties like that. There must be nine at every table – three couches of three each, that sort of thing.'

'But not today?' I murmured, looking at the single table and the stools around the walls.

She flashed me that little rueful smile again. 'Today was the exception. This wedding had to be at home and there were too many guests to seat them formally. We were going to have the slaves bring little folding tables in. Even then I had a job to talk Honorius into it. He thought it was ill-omened. And perhaps it was!' She paused for a moment at the entrance way and glanced around the decorated room. 'But you can see now, citizen – I'm sure – why Redux, despite his connection with the family, would not be the proper man to ask to close my husband's eyes for him and call upon his soul.'

And with that, she joined the waiting slave and went back to the hall, leaving me alone among the empty chairs.

Seven

I watched her go, but didn't follow her. In fact I deliberately stayed behind and bent down to pick up the scattered petals from the floor, where there was a fine mosaic of the seasons laid at the dining end. It was not my place to do so, in a household full of slaves, but I was half-hoping that one of them would come in after me and I would be able to learn the servants' view of what had happened in this house today. Besides, Livia had given me a lot to think about and I wanted a little time to consider what it meant.

Had Redux somehow contrived to murder Honorius to avenge the honour killing of his friend, when the legal process offered no redress? That much was plausible. But how could he have put poison in the wine? Or had there been some other method of administering it? Perhaps I was wrong in thinking there was wolfsbane used at all – there were other poisons which would have the same effects – though surely only aconite would have killed so instantly?

I was collecting the flower-fragments as I mused, but I hadn't gathered more than one or two of them before I was interrupted by a puzzled small voice from the door.

'Master?'

It was my own slave, little Minimus. I straightened up and saw him standing at the entrance to the room, clutching the ill-fated wedding platter in one hand, and my cloak in the other. When he saw what I'd been doing he put those down at once and came across to pick the petals up himself.

'You should have called me, master, not scrabbled on the floor,' he chided, collecting up the scattered remnants in a trice and rising, flushed and panting, to put them in my hand. 'I knew you must be in here but I couldn't see you from the door. I brought your belongings. Everyone has left. I'm sorry, master, no one at all has stayed behind as you requested them – most people didn't even stop to drink the wine. After Pompeia's outburst they were all eager to be gone.'

I nodded and put the broken petals on the tabletop. 'Antoninus among them. I am aware of that.'

I must have sounded sharp, because he looked chagrined. 'I didn't see him leave. I'm sorry if I should have prevented him from going. I thought of asking people to stay back to talk to you but I wasn't sure who you would want to question. I did approach one citizen – that decurion that Honorius spoke to last of all – but he said you wouldn't need him now, because there was no mystery. I suppose he thought that with Pompeia saying what she did...?' He made a little helpless gesture with his hands. 'I could hardly compel an important man against his will.'

'It can't be altered now.' I picked my cloak up from the stool where he had put it down, and shrugged it round my shoulders in a careless way. 'But I would like to have had a word with him, and Antoninus too – and a man called Redux who was with him in the hall. I suppose I shall have to try to find out where they live.'

'Redux the trader, are you speaking of?' Minimus brightened up. 'I know where you can find him, master – or I think I do. He has a warehouse down beside the dock, trading with the ships from Hibernia and Gaul. I was talking to his slave upstairs, before the steward came to tell us that Honorius was ill.'

I looked at him with sudden interest. Perhaps the boy was not so useless after all. 'A warehouse full of what?' I said aloud – wondering if Redux dealt in wine at all.

Minimus was proud to show off what he knew. 'Everything from Glevum roofing-tiles to Celtic woollen cloth. Anything that's cheap from the locality. He buys it in when there's a glut, and keeps it for a while, then either sells it on again when prices rise or exchanges it aboard the trading ships for things you can't get here, like pickled anchovies and olive oil or even foreign slaves.'

'And so makes a profit?' I was struggling to fasten the cloak around my neck.

He rushed across to fix it with a shoulder-clasp. 'Making a small fortune out of it, I hear. At least till recently. But according to the slave that I was talking to, Redux had a partner who died quite recently and since that happened things aren't going so well. He doesn't have the instinct that his friend had, it seems, for knowing what to buy and when to sell. But he's still got the warehouse. I could show you where, I think. The slave was boasting about how big it used to be, and how it was sited right beside the docks.' He fussed about me, settling my cloak-folds neatly into place with a care that my poor garment scarcely merited, then standing back to admire his handiwork.

'Since you have brought me my cloak so diligently, you could take me there before we leave the town.'

'Immediately, master, if you wish to set off straight away. Or I'm sure the offer of refreshment will still stand. Most things, of course, are being put away until the funeral feast – the sweet cakes and the wedding dishes that the kitchen had prepared – but you could still have fruit and watered wine before you leave, if you desire.'

I realized that he would not have dreamed this offer up himself – nor taken the initiative to bring the cloak to me. 'Helena Domna sent you?' I enquired. 'To hint to me that it was time to go?'

He grinned. 'In fact it was the lady Livia,' he said. 'Though only when she came out to the hall and found out that her mother-in-law had already organized the slaves and had them starting to clear the atrium. She had even sent the steward out to fetch the embalming women and arrange the bier – and of course she hadn't consulted anyone at all. Her daughter-in-law was not best pleased, I fear, but Helena Domna insisted that she'd been forced to act because the household needed to begin the mourning rites as soon as possible, otherwise it was a dishonour to the corpse.'

'That was really a rebuke to Livia, I suppose,' I said, 'because she was with me and wasn't there to make the arrangements for herself?'

'Exactly, master. But of course, it all needed to be done and there wasn't much the poor lady could do except agree. Though she said to tell you that you'd be welcome to come back, once Honorius's body is prepared for burial and laid out in the atrium in state.'

I nodded. 'A good many people will be calling then, no doubt, to pay their homage and help with the lament.'

'Oh, and the chief steward will be starting that, and closing the eyes and calling on the soul. I had to promise that I would tell you that. She seemed to think that you would want to know.'

'In the absence of a suitable male relative,' I said thoughtfully. It was a confirmation that Redux had not been approached for the task.

'But doesn't Livia have a guardian under law?' Minimus enquired. 'You'd think Honorius would have named one in his will. She doesn't have three children so I thought she needed one. And – come to think of it – since Pompeia hasn't married after all, won't she be requiring a legal guardian too, now that her father's dead? But perhaps there is no will. I know there was talk that Honorius was going to call for witnesses and nominate Marcus as a beneficiary. I heard it talked about when I was serving them one night.'

I picked up my silver platter. 'Oh, there is a will, all right,' I said, remembering suddenly what Marcus said to me. 'Though whether it's a new one, is another thing. Honorius was about to change the one that he had made, but I don't know whether he'd had the new one witnessed and ratified or not. In fact, that might have a considerable bearing on the case. If he hadn't, then he might have been murdered to prevent him doing so. If he had, then it would be interesting to know who would benefit by the later will, and therefore have a motive for removing him. And in that case, I suppose, as residuary heir, Marcus might even be the legal guardian...' I went on, then trailed into silence as I realised the full force of this.

Marcus was a senior magistrate, and to be legal guardian was scarcely onerous to him. It was usually a titular appointment anyway and generally regarded as a compliment. But Marcus was at this moment on his way to Rome, and I was officially his representative; I did not like where this was leading me.

I was still thinking about this when Minimus piped up. 'So do you wish me to lead you to this warehouse straight away, master? You can hardly talk to the family now, in any case, since they are preparing for the funeral.'

I nodded. I had spoken to Livia anyway, I thought, and that was probably the best that I could hope. Helena Domna was unlikely to cooperate with me, and though I would have liked to have had a word with some of the household staff, it had been made fairly clear to me that it was not convenient and it was time for me to leave. A pity. I could have asked somebody about the will, perhaps.

I sighed. It would have been quite different if Marcus had been here – he would simply have declared that they must talk to me – but as it was I had no proper authority. I turned to Minimus. 'Since I am working on Gracchus's account, I should have liked to have a moment with Pompeia if I could, but I don't suppose it will be possible.'

He shook his head. 'I doubt it master. Her handmaidens have taken her into her sleeping room and I know they have instructions not to let her out. And the older ladies will be changing into mourning clothes by now, so I doubt we shall see anyone from the household as we leave – except the page, of course. He is already waiting outside the door to see us out.'

And indeed he was. He stood in the now empty vestibule, where only a trampled wreath and an abandoned flute lay on the floor to show where the enthusiastic wedding guests had been. Through the open door of the atrium I could see a group of slaves, engaged in stripping the wedding flowers from the tables and the statues of the gods, while others stood ready to replace them with funerary wreaths. The *imago* of Honorius's father had been brought from whatever cupboard it usually occupied and was already standing by the altar on a plinth, and no doubt Honorius's own would follow it, when the funeral arranger had made a mask of him. Typical of this old-fashioned household, I thought, that these ancient customs should still be carried out here in the provinces when one heard that these days they were not always observed in Rome.

Even as I paused to watch the servants at their work, Helena Domna came into the hall. As Minimus had predicted, she had changed her clothes and now wore a long tunic of a sombre hue, with a dark net veil covering her hair and a gold chain set with fine jet beads around her throat. The most startling change, however, was the difference in her face. The careful chalk-paint and bright red lees had gone, and the sallow skin was almost colourless, except for the ashes she had rubbed upon her brow. There was no attempt to hide the wrinkles now, and there was no longer kohl around the eyes. She looked what she was: an ancient woman who had lost her son – and for a moment I felt a surge of sympathy.

There was no alteration in her manner, though. As soon as she saw me her mouth snapped firmly shut and it was through pursed lips that she addressed me. 'Citizen? Are you still here? I thought that you had left.'

'I was hoping, madam, for a word with you. I wanted to check on Honorius's movements just before he died—'

She interrupted me. 'Citizen, do not be so absurd. We women were all in the atrium with the wedding guests throughout. You saw us there, yourself.'

As there was no possible reply to that remark, I simply forced a smile and muttered that I'd hoped to speak to Pompeia at least. 'If I am to do as Gracchus hopes and prove her innocent. But I understand that that's impossible.'

Perhaps it was an instinct for contrariness, or perhaps it was the mention of Gracchus that made her say, 'Who told you that it was impossible? It is entirely possible, if I give you leave. I am the child's grandmother, after all – unlike Livia who has no blood-ties to the girl – and I still have some rights in that regard. If I say you may see her, then you may. Though you may not get a lot of sense from her. I have agreed that Maesta should provide a sleeping draught for her, made from the juice of poppies. She has just returned with it. I don't know if Pompeia has yet taken it or not, but if you hurry you may find her before she falls asleep. You may leave your servant here, and I will find you a female slave to take you to the place.'

It was so unexpected that I almost gawped, but I collected myself sufficiently to say, 'I appreciate your assistance, lady, very much.'

She no longer had her fan, otherwise she

would have rapped me with it I am sure. 'Then you will repay me by doing what you are employed to do, and seeing that my granddaughter gets married after all. Convince the world she didn't kill her father, despite her outburst here. Though how you can do this without showing that she's mad – which is no help to anyone – I confess I cannot see. However, Gracchus thinks you'll do it, and if you prove him right I shall be as pleased as he is. So...' She clapped her hands and at once the dumpy maidservant appeared. 'Pulchra, show this citizen to Pompeia's sleeping room. He has some questions he wants to put to her.'

'Madam...' Pulchra looked as if she had something to impart, but Helena Domna waved the words aside.

'Quickly, before Maesta's poppy juice begins to take effect.'

Pulchra sketched a bob towards her and then said, 'In that case, citizen, if you would follow me?' And she led the way towards the inner door. As we went through it I heard the grandmother's shrill voice ordering the page to move the basket of unwanted walnuts from the floor.

Eight

I was in a hurry as I strode into the court, but I did take a moment to look around at it. When I was previously in the house, laying the mosaic in the hall, the final building works were not complete – especially in these private quarters at the back – so I was interested to see what had been done. It was obvious even then that it was to be very grand, but I was not prepared for quite how grand it actually was – a piece of conscious ostentation on the owner's part.

It was built like a country villa, although it was in town. The sleeping quarters were not upstairs, as they were in the rest of the fine houses in the colonia; here the extra story over each wing of the house was given over to the slaves – one area each for male and female no doubt, and accessed in each case by external stairs. When I had previously been working at the house, the servants had been housed in a wooden shed at the back, where I could now glimpse a brand-new kitchen block. It had been divided off behind an ornamental gate with another building (presumably a stables) beyond that – as though space and valuable land were of no account at all.

The bedrooms for the family were ranged around the court – the courtyard garden which backed the atrium and in which the guests had been milling earlier. It was a lovely place: full of flowers and ornamental shrubs, a fountain and so many fine statues that it took your breath away. No sign of anything so mundane as plants that one could eat, which is what most country houses used such gardens for.

But the most arresting feature was the verandaed colonnade that ran around the garden on both sides, and linked the private quarters with the front part of the house. It was crammed with life-size marble statues of all kinds: gods and goddess and figures from the past – I spotted Romulus and Remus and their wolf – all lined up and looking down on one. It should have been attractive, but it was the opposite: oppressive, as if a hundred eyes were staring down at one.

I marvelled at what must have been the cost of all of this. Most of the work was of such quality it suggested workmen and materials specially brought from Rome. I realized for the first time what a compliment it was to have been asked to contribute a pavement here myself.

'Citizen?' I realized that dumpy Pulchra

was waiting up ahead. I had forgotten for a moment that we were hurrying. As I hastened after her she gave a knowing smile. 'Impressive, isn't it?'

I grinned, and fell into step beside her as she led the way, under the watchful gaze of stony eyes. 'Honorius must have spent a huge amount on all of this,' I said. 'I knew he was successful, but I didn't know how much. And such works of art...' I indicated a particularly handsome statue of Minerva in a niche.

She gave a small derisive snort. 'It was his weakness – perhaps the only one. That Minerva you're admiring is just the latest piece. But this was all done with my mistress's dowry, of course. I thought everyone in Glevum was aware of that. It would have been a poor thing for him if she'd ever wanted a divorce, though – Minerva bless her – she showed no signs of it.'

I nodded. 'Otherwise by law he would have had to give it back. Or most of it, at least – unless she was proved unfaithful or immoral in some way.'

That caused her some amusement. 'Livia? Believe me, citizen, he'd never have found that kind of an excuse. I should know, I was with her all the time. She could not have concealed that sort of thing from me. In any case, he was very fond of her – insofar as that pompous icicle was fond of anyone.'

'So, it was a fairly happy marriage, then?'

She paused an instant to raise her brows at me. 'If you say so, citizen.'

'Meaning that it wasn't?' I enquired.

She folded her arms across her ample breast. 'Now, I didn't say that, citizen. She was content enough. I don't believe she loved him – who does, nowadays? – but, as I said, he was fond of her. He actually indulged her, in all kinds of ways – not like his former wife, from what I hear, poor thing. So if you are thinking that she might have murdered him, I suggest you think again. Besides,' she added, with a wicked grin, 'if she was going to poison anyone, it would have been Helena Domna, I am sure. That woman was the source of any discontent my mistress may have felt. But hush...'

She stood aside to let a bunch of women past – stout red-faced women in coarse working tunics, each carrying a covered basket. They gave off a faint smell of oil and herbs and myrrh and something more unpleasant which I could not quite define. Obviously these were funeral workers come to prepare the corpse, and Pulchra gave them a superstitiously wide berth, as if their very presence might imply a curse.

We watched them as they skirted round the court from the back gate and went into what was clearly the master's sleeping room, since it had a fine door and pavement and a shuttered window too. They shut the door behind them and Pulchra looked furtively at me, then dashed to the fountain in the court to rinse her hands and face as if she were scrubbing off the dust of Dis itself.

'You know what they say, citizen,' she apologized, shaking the purifying water from her hands. 'The funeral women are a warning that the fates are watching you.'

I was impatient of the interruption. I had been rather hoping she might say something more about the family. I have long believed that servants know more than anyone about what is happening in a house and what the personal undercurrents are – though very often they are too loyal to tell you anything.

I tried to prompt her. 'Was Helena Domna actively unkind?' I urged, as she walked slowly back to me.

Pulchra, however, had decided it was time to be discreet. 'It is not my place to comment, citizen. I really couldn't say.' She wiped her fingers on the hem of her tunic as she spoke. 'Perhaps you should ask my mistress that herself – I see she is coming from her sleeping quarters now.'

I looked across and saw that this was true. Livia was emerging from the room next door to where the funeral women had gone in. Clearly, like most Roman couples of high birth, she and her husband had adjoining rooms. Just as Helena Domna had done earlier, she too had changed into her mourning clothes: a stola and tunic of the deepest black, and a long dark veil to shroud her face and hair – though it was so finely woven that I could see through it from here. But where Helena Domna had looked crushed and old, the dark clothes simply emphasized how fair and attractive the young widow was. She was accompanied by a pair of junior female slaves.

She saw us and came hurrying across the court at once. 'Citizen Libertus, you are still here, I see. Come to see Pompeia?' She stretched out her hands, as if in greeting – though she looked a little startled when I took them in my own. Perhaps it was not fitting, given who we were, and the fact that we had never met until today.

I let them go, embarrassed. 'Your mother-in-law has kindly given me permission,' I replied. 'And we are in haste. Pompeia has been given a sleeping draught, I understand.'

She gave a bitter laugh. 'I would have suggested that you came to her myself, but I did not think that my mother-in-law would sanction it. Nor would I have given the girl a drug to make her sleep, but – until my husband's will is read, at least, and there is a proper guardian – Helena Domna has the final say in what becomes of Pompeia, since she is the only living blood relative she has.'

I was in a hurry, but I could not lose the

opportunity to ask, 'Honorius has appointed a guardian for the girl? I heard that he was planning to amend his will.'

'You heard?' She looked surprised, then nodded. 'I suppose it was no secret – all the household knew – and of course, there were seven outside witnesses as well. And I can see it might be relevant. It's true, he had made another will quite recently, disinheriting his elder daughter and her heirs. He has made a good provision for Pompeia, I believe. I don't know all the details – I am only a woman after all, and he rarely confided his business plans to me – but Honorius knew that I was carrying his child, and he assured me that we two were well provided for. And the house would revert to me in any ca—' She broke off, interrupted by the sound of running feet, and the little page came hurtling down the colonnade from the direction of the passageway.

He was so intent upon his headlong dash, he almost rammed straight into us, but when he saw us he skidded to a halt. It looked as if he were about to turn and try to skirt around the other way, but at that moment the chief steward came pounding after him, his face as red as fire and already out of breath.

He gestured to the handmaidens who were still loitering at the rear. 'Well, girls, don't just stand there. Seize that page for me. The little wretch is trying to run off and escape.'

The girls looked startled and set off half-heartedly, but Livia had already reached out a hand and had him by the shoulder. The page did not resist.

'A thousand pardons, madam,' the steward panted, coming up and taking charge of the boy. 'He's got it in his head that he's likely to be flogged. Afraid that Helena Domna is going to punish him, because he wasn't at his master's side – fetching those dratted walnuts from the store.'

Livia looked very gravely at the boy. 'Of course, there will be no such punishment,' she said. 'As I was just saying to this citizen, I understand the house and contents have been left to me.'

'So you will inherit most of the estate?' I said. 'All these works of art and everything?'

She smiled. 'Not exactly that. It is left in trust for us – the child in particular – if we survive the birth. There is a legal guardian appointed until the child – if it is male – should grow to be of age in which case he inherits my husband's whole estate. If it is a girl she shares it all with me. Pompeia has her own provision, which is separate.'

I glanced at the unhappy little page. 'And Helena Domna?'

Livia gave the faintest of triumphant smiles, which the flimsy veil did not entirely obscure. 'She is not named at all. In this will, anyway. My husband did not expect her to outlive him, I suppose, and she has a little money of her own in any case. Of course, I shall tell her she is welcome to stay here – until she can make more suitable arrangements somewhere else.'

I should not care to be a witness when that interview took place, I thought. 'Is she aware of this arrangement?'

That little smile again, then she dropped her voice, as if the statues might be eavesdropping. 'She will find out soon enough – when the will is given its public reading on the steps of the basilica. Of course, that won't be till after the funeral – and the provisions won't apply till then. A pity, or we might have had our legal guardian close the eyes. As it is, it will be the steward, I suppose.' She nodded to the fellow, who bowed and left – still clutching the tunic collar of the little page.

'Do you know who is nominated to be your guardian?' I said, when they had gone. 'It isn't Marcus Septimus by any chance?'

She shrugged. 'I don't think so, citizen. Marcus may be residuary again, in case arrangements fail, but Honorius will have named a proper guardian, I'm sure. One of my husband's council friends, I expect. Or it might be Gracchus possibly, since Honorius expected him to marry Pompeia, and that would make him part of the household, so to speak.'

Gracchus as guardian? After what I'd overheard about his debts? Having the management of a substantial legacy might make a considerable difference to him. Enough to make him think of homicide? I shook my head. Why would he be so anxious to marry Pompeia, I thought, if he could have the use of the money anyway?

'He might still join the family – if I can clear her name,' I said.

It was Pulchra who seized my meaning instantly. 'And – excuse me mistress – he had better go at once, if he is hoping to do anything of the kind.' She had put her hands upon her hips again and was almost chiding us – more like a *paedogogus* talking to a child than a handmaiden addressing the mistress of the house. 'If Pompeia takes that potion she will be fast asleep and he won't be able to get any sense from her.'

Livia laughed. 'You will have to excuse Pulchra, citizen. She's been with me many years – in fact she was my wet nurse when I was very small – she stayed to be my nursery maid and has served me ever since. But sometimes she forgets that I'm no longer two years old. Honorius has had her punished quite severely once or twice, and Helena Domna thinks that I should sell her on. But I would be lost without her.' She patted Pulchra's arm. 'I really believe that she'd do anything for me.'

'And can you wonder?' Pulchra said. 'You see how kind she is.'

Livia, however, ignored the flattery. 'She is the only servant I brought with me when I wed – my husband already had a household full of slaves. Like those who helped me change into my widow's clothes just now.' She gestured to the two girl slaves, who were still loitering by Romulus and Remus at the rear.

Pulchra scowled. 'And a poor job they have made of it, as well! I don't know why you used them, madam, and didn't wait for me. I'd only gone out to see the sweet cakes stored – because you asked me to.'

I was beginning to get anxious to get to Pompeia by now, but I could hardly interrupt Livia, who was saying, with a little laugh, 'Pulchra, this is the same outfit that I wore to Helena Domna's brother's funeral last spring, and you seemed to think that it was satisfactory then. Helena Domna has her own, of course, though I shall need to arrange some mourning tunics for the slaves. I've sent the spare ones to the fullers to have them cleaned and dyed, while the sewing girls have orders, as soon as possible, to stitch dark bands round the hems of the ones that are in use. Your own included, Pulchra.'

Pulchra sniffed. 'I'm perfectly capable of doing mine myself – and I'll alter that stola for you at the same time. Later, perhaps, when I've put you into bed. I'm sorry to say it, mistress, but you really need it done – you don't want everyone in Glevum guessing you're with child, when otherwise it doesn't need to show.'

Even the veil could not disguise that Livia had turned pink. 'You see what I put up with, citizen? And I was the one who thought her beautiful and nicknamed her Pulchra when I was very small!' She turned towards the slave and said with mock severity, 'But, Pulchra, I am a Roman matron now, and a widowed one at that. If you don't show a little more respect, I shall be obliged to do as Helena Domna says and put you up for sale.'

Pulchra had the grace to look utterly abashed. 'I'm very sorry, mistress. I only thought...' She stopped and then went on in an altered tone, 'I'd better take this citizen to Pompeia's room at once.'

Livia gave a nod. 'Very well. Then come and find me in the atrium afterwards. I'll want someone to go down to the forum later on to see the silversmith. I've had a lock of the dead man's hair cut off, and I want a mourning locket that I can wear it in. Oh, and you may alter my stola later, I suppose, since you're so anxious to. Though it will scarcely make any difference to the gossips, I'm afraid. The news that I am carrying a child will be all over Glevum once the will is read.'

The plump face fairly beamed. 'I'll do that, mistress. This way, citizen.' And, moving the bar that they had pushed across the door, she led the way – at last – into Pompeia's sleeping room.

Nine

The girl was lying face down on the bed, still in her pathetic wedding clothes, with one of her servants standing over her.

'Come on Miss Pompeia, just a little sip. You don't want to have them hold you down and force it down your throat.'

The slave girl held a cup which she was evidently hoping to put to her mistress's lips. But Pompeia's face was resolutely buried in the pillow which she was lying on. She was obviously crying, though she made no noise – the heaving of the saffron veil gave evidence of sobs.

'It's all right, Pompeia, it won't do you any harm. Only make you sleep for just a little while. And it won't taste nasty, I can promise that – not like the mixture that I gave you for your warts.' The voice from the corner took me by surprise. I looked over and saw Maesta sitting on a stool. I had been so interested in the figure on the bed that I hadn't noticed that she was in the locked room too.

I looked around me now. There was nothing much to see. Except for a table and the stool – neither of which looked as if they properly belonged – there was nothing in the sleeping room except the bed, at all. No rugs, no cupboards, no chests of clothes – no sign of perfumes, combs or jewellery.

I turned to Pulchra. 'This is Pompeia's room?' I asked her, in an undertone.

She whispered back. 'It used to be her mother's room, in the last days of her life. They put Pompeia here because it's easier to bar – there is nothing of her own in her old room anyway. Everything is packed and waiting at the gate. It was due to be taken to the bridegroom's house, of course, once he had walked her in triumph through the town.'

I nodded. I could imagine that. If we ever saw a bridal possession in the street Gwellia invariably wanted to stop and watch. You could always tell the house that they were heading for – the threshold would be hung with greenery and draped in fresh white cloth, and once the new bride had anointed the doorposts with symbolic oil and fat and tied a piece of woollen fillet round each one of them, the groom would pick her up and carry her inside to prevent her from tripping on the step. All this to prevent bad omens for their future life, but Gracchus would now have to take the decorations down – and as an augury, I thought, that must be even worse.

I did not voice these dreary thoughts, however. I spoke to the servant with the drinking cup. 'Pompeia's things will be brought back, no doubt?'

The slave girl nodded. 'As soon as the immediate arrangements for the funeral have been made. She will need to change into some different clothes, even if she is not to help with the lament.'

The figure on the bed gave a convulsive sob at this. The servant made another attempt to give the girl the cup, which almost resulted in the liquid being spilt, and that brought Maesta hurrying over from her perch.

'Can you persuade her to drink it, citizen? If Helena Domna comes and finds her still awake, she'll send for the steward and make him force it down her throat. It could choke her if she struggles, and then they will blame me. My husband will be furious that I suggested this at all. He says that we are in quite enough trouble as it is – if it does turn out that there was any poison in the wine.'

I looked at her. She was quite dishevelled

now. Her rich wine-coloured stola was hanging all awry, the greying hair was straggling from its fashionable combs and her stout face had taken on a mottled purplish tinge – which rather matched her under-tunic and her leather shoes. The haughty, sour expression had deserted her and she looked terrified.

'Helena Domna knows that I have come to speak to her,' I said, 'so she will not be displeased to learn she's not asleep.' But I took the cup and motioned the slave to move away.

Pompeia seemed to sense that I had taken it away. She raised her head a little, and looked round at me.

'I don't want to speak to anyone. I want to be alone. Just go away – all of you – and leave me here until they come for me.'

'Who is going to come for you, Pompeia?' I enquired.

She rocked back on her knees and scowled up at me. Her face was red and swollen under the saffron veil, and the pathetic bridal plaits had been torn undone. She looked so miserable and angry that I felt sympathy for her.

'I suppose they'll kill me, after what I've done. Or send me to some island and leave me there to die.'

'But what have you done, exactly?' I kept my voice deliberately gentle as I spoke. 'You said you killed your father, but I don't believe you did. I don't see how you had the opportunity today.'

She seemed almost disappointed at my cool response. 'I made it happen – and that's all there is to that. So let them come and get me. I don't care any more. In the meantime, you don't have to stand there watching and gloating over me. And I'm not drinking anything that woman has prepared. How can I be sure that it isn't poisoned too? Somebody clearly wants our family dead.'

'So it wasn't you that put wolfsbane in your father's wine?'

She gave a shivering sniff and glared at me. 'Well, of course, I didn't do it personally. Where, by all the gods, would I get wolfsbane from? And when did I ever have the chance to do anything alone? But – I am telling you – it was my fault all the same.' Her voice was coming in little gasping sobs.

'You mean you paid someone to do it?' Pulchra's voice was sharp.

Pompeia flung her a look that would have withered stone, and said, with the same little catches in her breath, 'I had no money. How could I do that?'

I had a flash of sudden insight and bent very close to her. 'I think I understand,' I murmured softly. 'You put a curse on him, or something of the kind?'

She looked at me with a kind of gratitude.

'I knew it would come out somehow, though I vowed I would not tell. But now you know. It's illegal, isn't it? You can be put to death for using supernatural means to kill someone like that?'

I took a deep breath. 'That depends on circumstance,' I said, though she was right in principle of course. The use of magic to procure a death was still potentially a capital offence. Marcus – ironically – had mentioned it to me, not very long before he went abroad. The law had fallen into abeyance more or less in recent years, but the Emperor's increasing willingness to see threats everywhere had meant that there had recently been talk of it again. Ambitious councillors and magistrates throughout the Empire – including, unsurprisingly, Honorius himself – had actively argued in favour of reviving it.

I turned to Pompeia. 'It's a question of whether you used spells and sorcerers.' And whether it could be proved that there was a deliberate human agency instead, I added to myself.

She shook her head. 'Nothing of that kind, citizen. I called upon the gods. I made a secret, special sacrifice and made a vow to Venus that if she heard my prayer, I would remain a virgin all my life. I didn't want to marry like my sister did, some business contact that my father had picked for me. Or be

111

like poor Livia, bullied and tormented by a mother-in-law who made her days a living misery. I prayed to all the gods that they would deliver me – and so they have done. In this dreadful way! So you see, citizen, it is exactly as I said. I deserve whatever punishment the courts reserve for me. I was responsible for my father's death.'

There was shocked silence and then Maesta said, 'Well, there you are then. Best if she drinks that potion I made, and it will give her oblivion at least. Have them bring a slave in, if she doubts that it is safe, and have him take the draught. She will see it only makes you sleep. I have another dose of the same mixture in this phial.' She produced a woven basket from underneath the stool – it had been hidden by her skirts when she'd been sitting there – and took out another little bottle. 'I was going to leave it here, in case it was required. They can give her that one, if she would prefer.'

Pompeia turned her tear-stained face to me – she had obviously adopted me as her protector in all this. 'Don't let them, citizen. How can I be sure that the mixture is the same – or that the poor servant won't be murdered too?'

'I don't think so, Pompeia. I am here to witness what is happening, and they could not give you poison without my knowing it. Besides, there is a different proposition I

112

could make. We'll put a little of this poppy juice into another cup, and Maesta herself can have a sip of it.'

Maesta looked startled. 'And if I fall asleep?'

I shrugged. 'What does it signify? You were staying here to see that the potion took effect, and you were to be locked into this room with her until it did. If Pompeia goes on refusing to touch it in this way, it might be quicker if you simply had a sip yourself.' I didn't add that I was interested to see her reactions for myself. Maesta's skill with herbs might be important yet. Someone had poisoned Honorius, after all – although it seemed that Pompeia had not – and who better than the vintner's wife to have access to the wine? Though, admittedly, it was hard to see what her motive might have been. I would have to talk to Maesta – and her husband – later on.

For the moment, though, Pompeia was my chief concern. I turned towards the girl. 'If Maesta agrees to taste it, then I think that you should drink the rest. It would be good for you to sleep. You do not want them to call a medicus and have him declare you mad, or worse still call the guard and have you dragged away. I am not surprised you hold yourself responsible for this – by your own admission, you called on the gods to help you to thwart your father's plans. But you did not curse him, or ask them to strike him dead. I don't think any court could find you guilty – particularly when someone else set out to murder him. And there is no law against praying to the gods.'

She gave a little groan. 'You really think so, citizen? I made my vows in private – there is no proof of what I said.'

'It may be that the gods have a sense of irony, but I think this murder was by human hand. I don't believe your prayer was really answered, anyway. You wanted to be delivered from this marriage, I'm aware, but it was really the married state you wanted to escape – and your grandmother's still hoping to find a groom for you.' I didn't add that Gracchus was employing me, and was prepared to take her as a wife himself.

I had rather expected that she would be relieved by my reassurance that she was innocent, but instead she looked appalled. 'But my vow to Venus! I promised on my life...'

I grinned. 'Ah, that is where you are very fortunate. Or you made a very clever bargain with the gods. If you are given in marriage your prayers have not been heard – in which case you are not bound to keep the vow. If you remain single, it will keep itself.'

For the first time I saw the flicker of a smile, and was amazed how it transformed her face. It wasn't pretty – it could never be that – but it softened markedly, though there was still a hint of fierce determination in the eyes. Perhaps I should not have been surprised at that – most girls would simply have embraced their fate, not tried to enlist the aid of goddesses. Perhaps she had inherited a little of her paternal grandmother's strong will and stubbornness.

'Very well. If you will undertake to speak on my behalf, I will drink the potion, if Maesta tastes it first. But I don't want to marry, you can tell them that – especially not someone who just wants my settlement. And if they try to force me, I'll find another way. I'll hide the balance scales – someone has to hold them at the ceremony or it will be so ill-omened they won't let it proceed. Or better still, I will refuse to say the words. They can drag me to the altar, but they can't make me speak.'

She might just dare to do it, too, I thought. And without her uttering the ancient formula 'where you are Gaius, I am Gaia', the marriage would not stand. I wondered what Gracchus would say if he knew about all this. Refuse to pay me for my efforts, probably – though my contract only said that I must prove her innocent.

'No one will expect you to marry anyone, at least until the mourning period is complete,' I said. 'And surely even marriage is better than slow death on a barren island, or permanently being locked up in your room, which is what will happen if they think that you are crazed.'

She shook her head. 'I didn't expect my father to be dead,' she muttered. 'I hoped ... I don't know what I hoped. Honorius being prepared to change his mind, or some other miracle like that. But I would not have chosen to kill him, citizen. It only puts me into Helena Domna's hands – whoever my guardian is, she will have the final say – and I am no better off than I was before. It would have been better if Gracchus had been struck. Or my grandmother herself.'

I stifled a smile at this heartless list. 'Would that have saved you?'

'I think it might have done. Livia would have spoken for me, I am sure, if I had begged her to. She was quite kind to me, and she was the one person my father listened to. He could not deny her anything at all – not like my poor mother who was virtually his slave.'

This was a new insight into Livia's married life. I glanced at Pulchra, but she was staring at the wall with that look of martyred patience waiting slaves adopt.

Pompeia gave a sigh and bounced herself upright. 'But what does it matter now? It is all a dreadful, messy irony. Go on then, citizen. Let Maesta taste the sleeping draught and I will drink the rest. Perhaps it would be better if it killed me anyway. And it can't taste any nastier than the last one that she made.'

I made a mental note to speak to Maesta soon. I remembered how Helena Domna had pounced upon the fact that Maesta had a certain gift with herbs when there was first concern about Honorius's health – as if the idea was quite new to her. Yet it was evident that Maesta had made several cures for members of the household here at different times.

She saw me looking at her and burst out at once, 'I made that decoction particularly strong – as Helena Domna instructed me to do – and no doubt it will affect me even with a sip. But I will take it, citizen, if you insist on it – though I would be glad if somebody would let my husband know what has happened and why I've not come home. Oh, I wish I'd not suggested it. I thought Helena Domna would be pleased and not blame us for the problems with the wine. I even hoped she might become another customer. And now look what I've done. But I suppose there is no help for it.' She reached out her hand to take the cup from me.

Pompeia surprised us, by saying in a sober tone of voice, 'If she is prepared to drink it, that is good enough. She would not do it, if there were poison in the cup.' She looked at me. 'I'm sorry, citizen. I have caused a lot of trouble for you and everyone, I can see that

– but when my father died suddenly like that, you can see that I supposed that somehow I had been responsible for it. And when I learned that he'd drunk something poisoned, I was afraid myself. I would not put it past my grandmother to order me a draught to save the family the shame of having me arraigned. You know what she and my father thought about the honour of the house!'

I nodded. When I thought about it, I could understand. In her position I might well have thought the same myself. I handed her the cup.

Maesta stepped forward. 'Half of it will do, now that she is calm. I made it very strong...' But it was far too late. Pompeia had already swallowed every drop.

Ten

Maesta looked from me to the girl in some alarm. 'She shouldn't have done that, citizen. I made it very strong. It was intended to calm her frenzy as well as make her sleep.'

Pompeia gave her a beatific smile. 'Well, for once, it didn't taste too bad. And you need not worry. It's having no effect – I thought from what you said I'd be fast asleep by now.' But even as she spoke her speech was slowing down and I thought I noticed the telltale lack of focus in her eyes.

I turned to Maesta sharply. 'What did you put in that?'

Maesta was wailing in that keening tone again. 'Nothing, citizen – or nothing that you would not ordinarily expect. Just the root of mandrake and white poppy juice, though I did add a few wild poppy heads as well. Wild poppy is a sovereign remedy for frenzies of all kinds, especially hysterias proceeding from the womb. Galen says—'

'You have read Galen?' I was incredulous. 'How did that come about?' Galen had been physician at the court when Commodus's father Marcus Aurelius wore the imperial purple, and his works had been admired throughout the empire. But a copy of a book like that was very rare indeed – even an extract was a hugely expensive luxury. It could take days for an amanuensis to copy out the text – even if you could find a version that you could copy from – and a skilled scribe would charge you dearly for his services; and then there was the price of ink and bark-paper, or even costlier parchment, to take into account. 'I know the public medicus in Glevum has access to a scroll, but I would be surprised if there was a private copy in the whole colonia. And how many vintner's wives could read it if there were?'

Maesta was wilting under my questioning and her former pompous manner had all but disappeared. 'My family were not always merchants,' she explained. 'Grandfather was a surgeon with the army, long ago, but he had only daughters so the tradition lapsed. He came to live with us when he was very old. He used to terrify us children with his tales – how some poor soldier had his guts ripped out and grandfather covered them in olive oil and put them in again then sewed the wound with grass, and how the patient had lived for days and days.'

She looked at me to see if I was satisfied, but I did not smile. 'I'm surprised he taught a girl.'

She shook her head. 'He didn't – at least not directly, citizen. Grandfather kept his instruments and things until he died and then my father sold them in the marketplace. But we still had his herb box and a piece of rolled-up bark where he'd copied some of Galen's work. The theories were amazing: how there is blood, not air, in all the arteries, and how the four humours teach us what herbs to use as cures. I was always interested in that sort of thing – more fun than the weaving and spinning I was taught – and I used to sneak it out and look at it by oil light when I was supposed to be asleep.'

'But you could read it?' Not many women of her age and class were as literate as that, even if they were Roman citizens. I had assumed until this moment that she had learned the use of herbs the way most women learned them – at their mother's knee – but it seemed she had a much more systematic grasp.

She smiled defiantly. 'My father didn't have me taught to read, of course – we were not wealthy enough to have a private tutor at home – but I learned from my brothers when they went to school. They hated it – the teacher would beat them every day – but I would make them read the tombstones by the road outside the town, and I would copy them till I could do it too. I soon worked out how letters represented sounds.'

I confess that I was quite impressed by this account. Maesta obviously had a lively intellect. I would treat her cures in future with more respect, I thought.

I was going to ask her a little more about all this – in particular what other herbs she had provided for this house – when I was interrupted by a sudden clatter behind me from the bed. I whirled around. I had almost forgotten Pompeia's sleeping draught, but it had clearly taken dramatic and complete effect. The girl had drooped back on the pillows, fast asleep, and the rattle was the metal goblet falling from her hand on to the floor. Pulchra was already on her hands and knees retrieving it from underneath the bed.

Maesta walked over to the sleeping girl and raised one eyelid up. Pompeia made a little groaning noise and stirred but did not wake.

Maesta nodded. She was visibly relieved. 'She will be all right. She is still half-conscious though it was a heavy dose – the sort of thing my grandfather would use before he wanted to cut off a limb. But Pompeia is a big girl, and it was not too much – though I could only guess what quantities to use.' She nodded to the slave girl who'd been there when I arrived. 'Keep a close watch on her. She will sleep all night – until past noon tomorrow, if I am any judge – and she may be very thirsty when she wakes. See that a jug of water is kept beside the bed.' She went back to the stool and picked the basket up. 'And now, I think, I may fairly claim my fee. My patient is sleeping – as I claimed she would. So if someone will escort me to Helena Domna now, I will take my payment and then I will go home. My poor husband must already be wondering where I am.'

I nodded. 'Pulchra can take us both,' I said. 'My business here has been concluded too. I need to go back to the atrium and collect my slave.' And I could talk to Maesta on the way, I thought. I wanted to ask her more about that wedding wine and perhaps, if I could work around to it, whether her

122

husband had any grievance against Honorius – or, indeed, if she had any quarrel of her own. I would have to word my questions very tactfully, of course, but it occurred to me that she was a great deal more likely to talk to me in the present circumstance than if I had simply called on her at home. I knew that her husband held me in contempt.

Pulchra, who had picked up the cup by now, put it on the table and came across to us. 'Of course, I will escort you to the atrium at once.' She opened the door to let us both pass through, and I stood back to let Maesta lead the way. As I did so, I saw Pulchra signal with her eyes. It was obvious she wanted something.

'What is it Pulchra? You wish to talk to me?'

I was speaking softly, but she placed a finger on her lips and shook her head. She indicated Maesta, who was by now outside, and already in the act of turning round to say, 'Is there some problem? I have no time to waste!' The vintner's wife was smoothing down the dark-red stola as she spoke, with small impatient gestures, and the old sour look was back on her face.

Pulchra looked urgently at me, and feeling that I must offer some covering excuse, I muttered, 'I was wondering if we should replace the bar across the door.'

Maesta managed a tight-lipped smile at

this. 'It will not be necessary now. I have told you, citizen, she will remain asleep and anyway it seems the frenzy may have passed.' She turned away and set off towards the atrium, obviously impatient to be on her way.

My heart sank. Maesta clearly felt more confident again, now that she was no longer anxious about her sleeping draught. Or perhaps it was the strong smell of lavender which had restored her to her old disdainful self – a group of slaves was busy in the central area cutting swathes of aromatic branches to lay around the corpse. Whatever the reason for the change of mood, I thought, it was unlikely I would get much more information out of Maesta now.

I tried. I attempted to fall in beside her as she walked, and said conversationally, 'You have provided decoctions for this house before?' She only walked a little faster and did not answer me, so I pressed the point again. 'You were talking about something you gave Pompeia for her warts?'

She flounced and I thought for a moment that she'd ignore this too, but then she muttered, 'Nothing that any seller of simples would not have given her. Bruised leaves of hartshorn to lay upon the place, and a weak decoction of briony and wine to cleanse the liver and drive away any evil humours from within. I'm not sure she ever took that, after the first dose – it is quite fierce and bitter, and Pompeia is strong-willed. But the hartshorn alone was enough to move the warts. Pompeia had been afflicted by them from a child.' She was striding along the path around the courtyard all this while, but brought herself up short and stopped to glare at me. 'Is all this important, citizen?' She stood aside to let a slave pass with a pail.

'Maesta,' I said gently, taking the liberty of addressing her by name, 'there has been a poisoning in this house today. It is important to know what potions we might legitimately find.' I saw her redden with embarrassment. I risked another question. 'By the way, who paid you for all that? It wasn't Pompeia – she told us that she had no money of her own. And it was not Helena Domna – she was quite surprised today to learn that you had any skill with herbs. So who was your customer? The lady Livia?'

Maesta paused beside the statue of Minerva in the court, sniffing the wreath of herbs that now encircled it. She would not meet my eyes. 'I don't know what business all this is of yours, Citizen Libertus. You are a pavement-maker, not a member of the council or one of the town watch.' She brought herself up short, and glanced at Pulchra who was standing at my side. 'But others will doubtless tell you, if I do not. So since you ask me, you are quite correct, I have served this

125

household several times before – both the lady Livia and her predecessor too.' Her voice softened. 'Many's the love potion that I made for her, poor lady, while she was alive – but she could not get her man to drink it, so it did no good.'

Pulchra was standing as no slave should stand, with her arms folded across her ample chest, openly listening to every word of this. When she caught my glance she amended this at once, and adopting a properly submissive pose, she said in a careful, polite and docile tone, 'Your pardon, citizen. But if you wish to know about decoctions which might be in the house, I believe my mistress has a tonic in her room at this moment – provided by this lady, if I recall aright. It is supposed to relieve the morning sickness and make the child grow strong, but it smells disgusting – that is all I know. And it tastes so nasty that she has to wash it down with watered wine. The mistress opened a new phial of it this very day. I could fetch it for you, citizen, if you would like me to.' She dropped her voice. 'That was what I wanted to tell you, citizen. Since there was poison – I thought you ought to know.'

The vintner's wife seemed unconcerned by this, though I noticed that her cheeks were still ablaze. She was still striding through the statues towards the atrium as she said, 'Vulvaria – stinking arrach – it is a well-known cure. Send for it by all means. No harm could come to anyone from drinking that. Now, are we going to be announced in the atrium, or not? My husband will be expecting me at the shop by now.'

There was something so urgent in the way she turned her back, and abruptly tried to change the subject, that it made me wonder what else she had to hide. 'One more question, madam. Those are the only potions you have ever provided in this house? You never concocted anything for the eldest girl, or – of course – for Honorius himself?'

The back of her neck had turned to mottled red. 'I don't know on whose authority you ask me all these things, but since you'll hear it from the slaves, no doubt' – she turned and glared at Pulchra with such malice that it took me quite aback – 'I suppose I'd better tell you, though it was years ago and couldn't possibly have anything to do with what happened today.'

I glanced at Pulchra, but she was staring at the ground. 'What was it you provided, Maesta?' I enquired.

She hesitated. 'It was something I once did for Honorius himself – well, not exactly for himself. He paid me to supply him with hemlock for the jail – a dose for some prisoners who were condemned to death but were permitted to choose the form of execution. You know the sort of thing?'

I nodded. It was not uncommon. It is a privilege awarded by the courts to those of higher rank – and sometimes lesser prisoners, who would otherwise die a long and painful death – to bribe the guards to bring them poison and get it over with. Was hemlock the poison that had been used today? I had thought of wolfsbane, from what Minimus had said, but I am not an expert on these things in the way that Maesta was – and I hadn't been a witness to the death myself. Hemlock was a possibility – it too can produce that drunken look that Minimus described. 'Hemlock?' I said, thoughtfully. 'And Honorius approved? It does not sound like the sort of thing he'd be in favour of.'

She nodded. 'He told me that it was right to be severe but within the law one could be merciful. Even a famous Greek philosopher took hemlock, so he said.'

'When did he ask you this? Some time ago you said?'

Now the news was out, she had relaxed again. 'Oh, years and years ago – when his last wife was alive. I think he found out that I'd been supplying her – all those wasted love potions which she'd paid me for – and he came to see me on his own account one night. Vinerius was very angry when he heard – he doesn't really like me selling herbs at all: says a proper Roman wife stays home and tends the house, though he is happy enough to see the money that I make from it. Honorius, in particular, paid very well indeed. He used the hemlock, but there was a problem with one of the subjects, I believe – a tax inspector for the Roman court – who did not die at once, but recovered and had to be thrown to the beasts. The poison should have worked – it was a massive dose – and at the time I could not account for it, but I have found a reason since. I understand that it is possible, if you take tiny doses of poisons every day, in time they will not harm you. You have heard of Mithradites – the ancient king of Pontus who invented *mitraditium*, the antidote to almost anything?'

I nodded. It was a famously ironic tale. 'The one who drank small doses of poison every day, to prevent assassination by his enemies?'

'Exactly, citizen, but it worked too well. And when he was taken prisoner, and tried to take his own life by poisoning himself, it didn't kill him and he had to fall upon his sword.' Maesta shook her head. 'I explained it to Honorius, but I think he still blamed me. At all events, he never asked me for anything again.'

'Who could have known what you'd supplied him with? Anyone in the household?'

She looked bewildered. 'No one, I don't think. Helena Domna didn't live here at the time – she still lived with her brother, though she stayed here quite a lot; Livia, of course, wasn't married to him then. His wife and daughters might have known, I suppose, but it was my impression that he kept it strictly to himself, and did not even tell the council what he'd done – as if he was ashamed of showing weakness with regard to punishment.'

'But it was Helena Domna who employed you today?' I said.

'It was, but I suggested it myself – offered to bring something to calm Pompeia down and make her sleep.' She gave that unexpected moaning wail of hers. 'Vinerius was furious when he knew what I had done – while we were rushing home for me to pick up the remedy, he swore and blustered at me all the way. He says that my herbs bring suspicion on us both, and we'll be lucky not to be dragged before the courts and put to death – especially if there turns out to be a problem with the wine that we supplied. He means it, too – told me to prepare a lethal dose for us in case. And of course I haven't done it – I didn't have the time before I came back here with this, and anyway I haven't got the herbs in store that I could do it with.' She seemed to have forgotten whom she was talking to, but now she pulled herself together and finished breathlessly, 'Really, citizen, I have said too much. Vinerius always accuses me of gossiping. If I am not careful he will take a stick to me. I must get my money and go home as soon as possible.'

If I feared a beating when I got home, I thought, it was the last place that I would want to hurry to, but I am not a woman.

I said severely, 'Very well. I have finished with questioning for now, but tell your husband I shall be calling at the wine shop very soon because I am looking into matters for the family.' It was almost the truth, I told myself. Gracchus would be part of this household very soon. 'In the meantime, Pulchra, you may announce us now. I believe your mistress is in the atrium? And I think my slave will be waiting for me there.' I gestured to the door which opened from the atrium to the court and which had been closed off since the guests had gone. 'And perhaps you could find out where Helena Domna is – Maesta and I both need to speak to her before we leave.'

Pulchra sketched a bob and scurried off, to come back an instant later. 'I am wanted elsewhere in the house, but I am sent to tell you to come in.' With that, she ushered us into the atrium. But it was not the lady Livia who was awaiting us.

'Ah, there you are, citizens.' It was Helena Domna, leaning on a stick and supervising the dozen or so slaves who were arranging wreaths and sweeping the ornamental floor

131

where the wedding dais had stood, though that had been completely dismantled and removed. A purifying sacrifice was already being made on the household altar, by the look of it. The air was thick with the smell of burning herbs and a shapeless female servant was wailing on a lyre.

'I'm afraid Livia has gone to light the candles round the corpse of my poor son. The funeral women will almost have finished by this time, with their washing and anointing rituals, and they will be bringing in the body for the lament to start. You have been a long time with Pompeia, both of you. Maesta, I am not altogether pleased. From your promise I expected swifter results. And as for you, citizen, I was about to send my page to fetch you back.' She waved her free hand to waft the smoke away.

'It appears that your granddaughter did nothing criminal, merely called upon the gods, and thought that she had somehow brought down a curse,' I said. I was about to explain about the sleeping draught, but Helena Domna interrupted me.

'Well, that is satisfactory – though there's no time for details now. I am wanted elsewhere and, so it seems, are you. There has been a message for you. Your slave has taken it.'

'For me?' I was astonished.

By way of an answer, she gestured to the

corner of the room, where Minimus was already scrambling to his feet. He had been resting on his haunches, in the way slaves do when they are engaged in that everlasting waiting which they seem to do. I sympathized – I have been a slave myself – but the boy was hastening over to apologize.

'I am sorry, master, I did not see you come. There has been a note.' He still had the silver platter in his hand. There was a folded writing tablet resting on it now, and Minimus offered it to me as he spoke, bowing very slightly as he presented it.

'That's a striking writing tablet,' Helena Domna said. 'I wonder where it's from?' It was indeed a very pretty thing, with ivory covers part inlaid with gold, and tied with a piece of finely woven silk. Her voice had taken a peculiar edge and I wondered if she hoped that I would make a gift of it.

However, I did nothing of the kind. I simply took the tablet and undid the ties, then read what had been scratched on the wax surfaces inside. 'It is from that fellow Antoninus,' I said. 'Asking me to meet him at his apartment in the town. There is something of importance that he thinks I ought to know.'

'"And which might be of profit to us both",' Helena Domna read, craning unashamedly to have a closer look.

Minimus had got that eager expression on

his face. 'So, master? Are we going there straight away?'

'Around the ninth hour this afternoon, he says. That's when the sun is halfway down.' I handed him the writing tablet, which he slipped into a pouch inside his tunic top, while I did a little calculation. The hours were shorter at this season of the year – daylight was simply divided into twelve – but if we called on Antoninus at the suggested time there would still be almost three hours before they closed the gates. 'We should just have time to get home without a long walk in the dark. Very well, we'll go and see him, but we'll visit Redux first.'

I looked around for Helena Domna to make my due farewells but she had turned away and was paying Maesta some money from her purse, so we waited until she'd finished before I took my leave.

Eleven

Minimus was almost hopping with excitement as the pageboy led us back down the passage and to the entrance. The prospect of helping me investigate this crime obviously thrilled him half to death.

I wished I could feel enthusiastic on my own account, but without Marcus here to lend me his authority I could not well interrogate important councillors – or even insist that members of this household talked to me. I had faintly hoped that I might see Pulchra in the hall, in case there was something else that she hoped to say to me, but there was no sign of her or anybody else. From the interior of the house there came the smell of burning herbs, and I realized that purification of the corpse was under way. It would not be long before the body was brought to lie in state and the formal lamenting and homage would begin. Already I could persuade myself that I could hear the steward's distant voice raised in a faint and ululating wail.

The household was plunging into mourning and I would not learn much more from here – until the corpse was decently disposed of, anyway. I could only hope that Antoninus had some helpful news for me, otherwise there was no chance of earning Gracchus's fee. It was not enough to argue that Pompeia was innocent, I knew: after that confession she would be arraigned for sure – it only took one witness to bring a formal charge – and I had to discover who the real culprit was.

The lugubrious doorkeeper greeted me with a faint, mocking grin. 'You have your cloak already, citizen, I see.' He opened the door and stood by to let me out – adding as he did so, in an undertone, 'Though your slave need not have been in such a hurry to collect it earlier. You are the very last to leave. And you didn't have to worry about the rituals, after all.'

This reminder of our earlier conversation made me pause. 'You know Antoninus, don't you?' I said thoughtfully, remembering how he had reacted to the name.

The same result. He stiffened and his friendly tone grew colder than the Sabrina river at Janustide. 'Perhaps I do. What is it to you, citizen? There is no law that says a slave can't have acquaintances.'

He had said 'acquaintances' not 'friends' I noticed, though perhaps I should not place too much importance upon that. Most slaves don't strike up friendships with aspiring councillors. 'I wondered,' I said, 'if you might know where he lives. I've been asked to call on him today, and I know he has an apartment somewhere in the town. Not far from the temple of Jupiter, I think, but that is all I am certain of. I was hoping for directions. I thought that you might help...?'

He was so relieved that it was almost comical. 'Oh, is that all, citizen? That's an easy one. It's not very far from here. Go to the temple, take the second block along and you'll find him on the first floor above a cobbler's shop. There's a public staircase leading from the street, because there are lots of people living on the top floor overhead, but if you go up there and knock the door his slaves will let you in.' He grinned again. 'Got to be careful while you're waiting, though – the upstairs lodgers throw things down the steps, slops very often. Jealous of people who have braziers and fancy togas, I suppose. It's pretty cramped and miserable in those attics, I should think, and you can see from the street that the roof is falling in. But the landlord doesn't bother – they still have to pay the rent.'

'I shall find it, thank you for your help.' I slipped him a few coppers and went out into the street. Minimus followed, and we were about to walk away, when a sudden realization made me whirl round to the doorkeeper again. 'So you have obviously visited the place yourself, my friend?'

It caught him off his guard. There was of course no 'law' (as he would have put it) to prevent him visiting, but it was not usual for a doorkeeper to walk around the streets – far less to call on somebody of Antoninus's rank. And if Honorius, for instance, had visited the place he would generally be accompanied by a page or personal slave – not by the man employed to guard the door.

He stammered and turned pink. 'I had a business errand to perform. Something from this household that I had to take to him.'

'Something that Antoninus had left behind?' I asked.

He shook his head and frowned, but there was a glint of grim amusement in his eyes. 'Something of the kind. I don't think I actually saw it at the time. I'm sorry, citizen, I can't remember now.'

'Perhaps Antoninus will recall the incident. I'll ask him when we meet.'

A pause. Then: 'How well do you know Antoninus, citizen?'

'I have never met him. He has asked for me. He says that he has important information to impart.'

'Then I hope you have deep pockets, citizen.' There it was again, that hint of mockery. 'Have you discovered why he sent for you, in particular?'

'Because I have been asked to look into Honori...' I began, then trailed into silence. The doorman had a point. I was certainly enquiring into this, but how could Antoninus possibly have known? It was a personal arrangement between Gracchus and myself: true it had been witnessed by his friend Linneus, when we were standing outside the atrium, but Antoninus had not been anywhere near us at the time. Or had Gracchus and his friend been spreading the news around the town?

If so, it was against his interests, I thought. There was no reason why anyone outside the family should think that I had a special interest in investigating this – and that was what I was relying on. I didn't want people put too much on their guard. No one is ever truly frank and free in what they say if they think their gossip might be used against them later on, or taken as testimony against someone else. And if the murderer was from outside the house, which now seemed possible, better that he – or she – continued to believe that since Pompeia had confessed, no one was looking for anybody else. I wished I had thought to say as much to Gracchus earlier.

'I wonder how Antoninus heard the news?' I said aloud.

The doorkeeper raised one eyebrow half an inch. 'I see that you are learning what kind of man he is.'

I bridled. 'Indeed. And I intend to learn a little more. My patron, Marcus Septimus asked me to talk to him. Antoninus wishes to become a magistrate and hopes that my patron will support his claim.'

'I see!' He was looking sceptically at me. 'Then visit him by all means, but be on your guard. He can be a difficult man to satisfy. He does not only deal with wealthy and important men, you know.' And to my astonishment, he leaned forward and gave me a confidential wink as though we were conspirators in some unspoken way.

I was wondering what I should reply to this, when I saw the pageboy coming down the hall. 'Doorkeeper! You are to come and have the dark bands sewn around your hems. I am sent to keep the door for you till you return. And go and see Helena Domna in the atrium on the way – she has an errand for you when you are relieved. She wants to hire additional musicians for the funeral.'

'Why me? I've already been on duty here since dawn! Isn't there another slave that she could send?'

The pageboy grinned. 'She's got all the other servants running round with herbs and things, ready to put the master's bier into the atrium, and the steward is standing by to start up the lament. I offered to go for her, but she said you'd know the place, because you went there when the former mistress died. And she is waiting for you, so you'd best be on your way.'

The older man gave me a lugubrious shrug and turned away.

'I don't know what he's looking glum about,' the pageboy said, watching his colleague walk away. 'He'll get a tip, no doubt, from the musicians' guild, as a reward for bringing trade. Not that he'll need it now. He'll get his promised freedom from Livia, I expect, now that she won't have her husband to convince. Honorius has been half-promising for years, but never found it quite convenient.'

'Leave the household? What will he do then? He doesn't have a trade.' I meant it. It's no light matter for a man to live without the certainty of food and shelter every night.

The pageboy grinned. 'Oh, he has money. Quite a lot of it – I saw him counting it the other night. He's been saving for his slave price for a long time now, and wears it in a little leather bag around his neck.' He gave a giggle, like the little boy he was. 'The other servants joke that that's what makes him stoop! He'll have enough to rent a room and perhaps set up a stall. Isn't that what every slave aspires to do?'

I nodded. That was exactly what I'd done myself. I slipped the pageboy a small coin (he looked grateful, too!) and hurried off to join Minimus in the street.

My slave looked at me sideways. 'What was that about, master? It took you quite a time. I thought we were hurrying to visit Redux now? There is some way to walk and it is already long past noon.' It was obvious that his enthusiasm hadn't dimmed.

I nodded. 'Then we must set off at once. Though it is not certain that Redux will be there – after all, he was expecting to be at a wedding feast all day.' I saw the young face fall. 'But we might learn something. You can lead the way.'

It was indeed a long way to the dock, especially as Minimus confined us to the streets. There was – as I knew – a much quicker route than this, through the putrid alleys and byways of the town, in the marshy area where the floods had been and where ruined buildings lay abandoned in damp, dismal courts. But that was the domain of the outcast underworld, the thieves and maimed and homeless, the 'ghosts' who haunted the night-time streets and lived on what more fortunate people threw away. I knew this, because I had briefly lived among them once, but today I was happy to walk the broader streets, though from this direction even those were not as wide and clean as in other, more salubrious parts of town. Figures lurked in doorways, watching us, and I had to tell Minimus to take my cloak from me, wrap the silver salver in it and at least hide it from view. Carrying it openly in this area was asking to be set upon and robbed – though a bulky parcel might well have the same effect, I thought.

We hurried on past greasy hot-soup kitchens and public wine shops – all open and busy with jostling customers, even at this time of day, with more people swaying and vomiting in the street outside. Girls in scanty costumes and in various poses smiled at us from lurid pictures painted on a pair of doors nearby, advertising the delights which might be had within, and as we passed an archway an actual girl appeared, lifting her tunic up to flaunt her scrawny knees and giving us suggestive gestures with her eyes. I hurried Minimus past before she spoke to us, and almost stepped into a pile of stinking muck, washed up in the last flood and simply left to rot.

I was much relieved to reach the busy dockside on the riverbank. There was more activity than a beehive here, and with a louder buzz of noise. A large ship from somewhere was unloading goods – its sail furled and its owner supervising the gang of dockyard slaves carrying the heavy sacks down creaking, wobbling planks on to the shore, while their overseer shouted at them that they were too slow and threatened to encourage them with lashes from his whip.

From the safer streets at the other corner of the dock, donkeys and handcarts were appearing to take away the goods. The air was full of oaths and curses and the sound of bartering.

It was a world where Roman law and order ruled again, and when a surly soldier asked where we were going, I told him and he pointed out the place.

'Redux's warehouse? It's right over there. And that's his foreman steward with the handcart and the slave. After a bit of this cargo, I expect. Salt, for the most part, from the salt pans further south – so it's to be hoped his warehouse is still dry. Hey!' He thumped his baton on a cask near by. 'You! The fat one with the cart! You've got a visitor. This citizen would like to have a word with you.' He looked at the parcel wrapped up in the cloak. 'Are you returning goods?'

I shook my head. 'I want to talk to Redux, that is all. Something that happened at a wedding feast.'

'You won't be the first that wants to talk to him. There has been a bit of trouble down here, once or twice.' He cleared his throat, importantly. 'So, if you have any difficulty, you get back to me. We don't want the kind of problem we had here yesterday – people trying to knock down the door, and fighting in the street. Very nearly had someone in the dock – and it interrupted trade. One of the captains nearly missed the tide. We had complaints from several quarters at the time. That's why they're posting one of us down here, to see that nothing of the kind occurs again. Now here's the foreman – but remember what I said.' He tapped his nose, to signal secrecy, and turned away to watch the docks again.

The fat foreman had left his cart and slave beside the gangplank on the dock and was trundling up to us. 'What is it, citizen? You want something with me? I can't spare many moments. I got work to do. My master wants me bidding for any extra salt – the last few sacks they fill are sometimes tinged with sand, but they bring them up to see what they can get for them.' He was a big man, more fat than muscular, but bulging in his orange tunic – and he did not look pleased to see us. I have seen battering-rams that looked more welcoming.

'It was your master that I was looking for.' I tried to summon a disarming grin. 'Is he in the warehouse?'

'I couldn't tell you that.' There was no answering smile. 'Who is looking for him, citizen?' he said.

So Redux was there, I thought privately. Aloud, I said, 'I am a citizen – as you can see, my friend. I was a guest with him at a wedding feast today – but there was an unfortunate incident and the ceremony had to be

145

postponed. I hoped to speak to Redux at the time, but he left before I could have a word with him. He will know me, I am sure of that.' Of course he would, he had seen me standing on that table in the hall. I did not mention that I'd never met the man.

The fat man put both thumbs underneath the belt that tied his tunic in, hitched it upwards over his ample stomach, and sniffed impressively. 'I don't know if the master is here or not, citizen. Give me your name and I will go and see.'

'I am the citizen Libertus,' I replied. 'The representative of His Excellence Marcus Septimus. This is his slave who is accompanying me. Perhaps you would care to tell your master that.' That was a formula that ought to do the trick.

He had small, greedy, beady eyes with fleshy eyelids, like a pig, and he was squinting suspiciously at the pair of us. But his tone became decidedly more civil as he said, 'Your pardon, citizen.' He ran a hand across his jowly chin. 'Of course I'll tell the master – when I get a chance. I'll go and look for him. Though of course I can't answer for whether he'll be there.'

'Master?' Minimus whispered urgently to me. 'If we can't see Redux, perhaps we should move on. It must be almost the ninth hour by now.'

I glanced at what I could make out of the

sun. It was clearly nearing the last quarter to the west. 'Perhaps you're right,' I told him. 'We are not succeeding here. I'll leave a message for Redux and come back another day. Antoninus will be expecting us.'

That name had a charm which my patron's name had lacked. The beady eyes looked furtively at me. 'Did you say Antoninus, citizen?'

I nodded. 'I have business with him at his apartment later on.'

'Then I'm sorry to keep you waiting out here, citizen. Though perhaps you wouldn't mind explaining what you've got in there?' He gestured towards the parcel that Minimus still held, and from which the corner of the salver was now peeping through.

'It is a piece of silver, fashioned as a tray,' I said, 'though I don't understand what business that might be of yours.' Then, conscious of the soldier still on guard nearby, and fearing that I should be accused of stealing it, I added hastily, 'It was to be my patron's wedding gift at that marriage earlier.'

'I see.' He nodded. 'Well, I'll go in and see what I can do for you. But I can't make promises. You'll have to wait and see.' And with that he lumbered off towards the warehouse door, leaving the handcart in the charge of his sleepy-looking slave.

I gave that individual a tentative grin, but he looked away and pretended to be engrossed in the unloading of the salt, so there was nothing we could do but wait and hope the fat foreman had helpful news for us.

Twelve

We did not have long to wait. A moment or two later our fat friend appeared again, puffing and panting, and gestured us to come.

'Come with me, citizen, if you would be so good.' He led the way towards the warehouse door, and as we stepped inside I realized for the first time what a huge place it was – it looked big enough to put an entire ship inside. It was built entirely of stone, though there were rough wooden partitions dividing it inside, and the place seemed half-empty, vast and echoing.

The foreman paused beside a pile of bulging sacks inside the door. 'The master said I was to show you in. He's in his office, at the other end, but he wants me to go back and see about the salt. So, citizen, if you could find your way down there yourself?' He spoke as if Minimus was invisible.

He hovered a moment, as if he were expecting a tip for this, but I had none to

give him so I turned and walked purpose-
fully down the centre aisle. What Minimus
had told me earlier was correct, I saw: Redux
obviously traded in all sorts of things. As we
passed the different partitioned areas I
noticed crates which had been opened and
were half-unpacked: salt fish, potted dormice, Samian ware – and they were only the
goods that I could see. And on the far side of
the aisle there was a pile of British capes
obviously waiting to be traded on. It was
impressive. Most importers deal in one
commodity alone.

Redux's office was behind the partition at
the end. He had abandoned the toga he had
been wearing at the wedding feast – it was
neatly folded and lying on a stool – and he
was sitting at a wooden desk in his tunic-
sleeves, surrounded by wooden writing tab-
lets and bark-paper scrolls. But he still looked every inch the councillor he was – the
under-tunic was wine-red and of elaborate
design, with fine embroidery at the neck and
hems, and the shoes that he was wearing
were of softest red leather, with little silver
tassels on the toes.

He rose to greet us as we came into the
room. He was every bit as large and rounded
as his foreman was, and one might have
thought it was the pattern of the house, if it
were not for the skinny slave that leapt up
from the floor, where he had been mixing

ingredients for ink, and hustled to bring a folding stool for me.

Redux extended a fat hand, with a heavy ring on every finger, and motioned me to sit. 'Citizen! Of course I recognize the face. I saw you at that ill-fated wedding earlier. What a dreadful business for poor Honorius. You were the one who made the announcement, I believe.'

I sat down gingerly. It was a flimsy stool. 'I was asked to do so by the family,' I said, anxious not to sound as if I were too involved. 'Though I do not know them well. I happened to be in the passage when the news arrived, that's all – and it was easy for me to gain the attention of the guests.' This did not sound convincing even to myself.

It did not convince him either. 'And to ask questions of people afterwards?' he said.

I had forgotten that he had shown himself to be sharp-witted then, and able to make deductions other people missed. 'At the time I was looking for an explanation,' I replied. 'But...'

He looked at me wryly. 'Ah, of course. And then the girl confessed.' I was sure from his ironic tone of voice that he didn't believe it any more than I had done, but he rubbed his hands together and went on affably: 'Well, citizen, what is it that I can do for you? My foreman tells me you may have something that you wish to sell.'

'Sell?' I was astounded, and then I saw the direction of his glance. 'Oh, the silver salver. That is not for sale. It was to be my patron's present at the wedding feast. He is Marcus Septimus, whom I expect you know. I was only there because he couldn't come. I shall have to return it to his house as soon as possible.'

'I see.' He gave a peculiar little smile. 'Would you permit me to have a look, at least?'

'By all means.' I was a bit surprised, but I could see no reason to deny him the request. 'Show it to him, Minimus.'

The boy stepped forward and unwrapped the tray. Redux took it from him and examined it. He then took it to the lighter area by the window space and scrutinized its every detail, turning it over and rapping it, then weighing it thoughtfully in his hand. 'It's a fine piece,' he said, after a little pause. 'I could give you a handsome price for this.' He named a sum which made my eyeballs bulge. I had not supposed it to be worth so much. Marcus had simply picked up the nearest tray to give to me – a minute earlier he had been eating figs off it.

But there was only one answer I could make, of course. 'I have told you, it is not mine to sell.'

He smiled. 'And yet you bring it into this part of the town – where it could so easily have been stolen in the street. Who is to know it wasn't? Or that it won't be, as you are walking back? That would be a dreadful pity, wouldn't it?'

He was still smiling blandly, but it could have been a threat. I thought quickly. 'I shall ask that soldier on the dock to look after it for me, and deliver it to the guardhouse when he is relieved. My patron is friendly with the commander there, and, of course, I will ask for a receipt, and hand it over in front of witnesses. Perhaps you would care to be one of them?' I said.

'Ah.' He walked over and handed the salver back to me. 'An honest man, I see. A pity – it is a handsome thing, though I don't quite know where I'd have found a customer just now. I know who would have been very interested but – unfortunately – he is dead.'

'Your friend Zythos, I suppose?' I said, secretly pleased to have recalled the name.

He frowned at me. 'I was speaking about Honorius, of course. He had a weakness for all works of art. He spent a fortune on them – that whole house is full of lovely things. I delivered him a new one, just a month or two ago – a statue of Minerva, very finely done. You must have noticed it if you were in the house – even if you don't know the family very well. Though, frankly, I don't know that I'm convinced of that. Who told you about Zythos otherwise? Someone must have done! You have never been a customer of ours that I'm aware.'

I was struck again by the fellow's speed of reasoning, and was wondering what I was going to say to this, when to my surprise Minimus spoke up.

'Your pardon, citizen, but I can answer that. I was the one that told him about your partner's death. I was put in the attics this morning at the wedding with this slave of yours, and we were exchanging stories about what our masters did. So I gave my master a full account, of course, when he decided we were coming here.'

All eyes had turned now to the skinny slave, who by this time was looking cowed and terrified. 'It is quite true, master. My foolish tongue again. I was boasting about what a great trader you had been, and I might have mentioned Zythos in the course of it. I beg your forgiveness if I spoke out of turn.'

I thought he might have earned himself a flogging for his words, but his master, if anything, seemed smugly satisfied. He only cuffed the boy around the ear, and said, 'You boast too much. I've told you that before, but there isn't any harm done here, I don't suppose.' He came back to sit down at the desk and rested his fat chin upon his chubby fingers. 'So it was servants' gossip? I apologize.'

I privately called on all the gods to bless the skinny boy. 'I assure you I had never heard your partner's name until today,' I said, 'though I was very sorry to hear about his death, of course.'

Redox straightened his embroidered tunic cuffs and leaned back on his chair – which was a handsome, black, three-cornered one, obviously of foreign origin. 'You heard how it happened?'

I swallowed. How was I to answer that? 'Rumours, that is all.'

'Rumour could not be more gruesome than the truth. And it is no secret. I sometimes think the whole of Glevum knows. He was executed on suspicion of adultery – with my own sister-in-law Honoria, in fact. Her father killed them both.'

'So Miles is your brother?' I asked, as if I had just worked it out myself.

He inclined his head.

'Your only brother?'

He gave a sour smile. 'The only family I have. I lost all the others to the plague in Gaul. Unless you count Zythos. He was almost a brother to me, too.'

'But now you have lost him, too?'

He nodded and suddenly there were angry tears in those intelligent brown eyes. 'And for nothing, citizen. There was no immorality with young Honoria, I am convinced of it. I know that it looked very bad for him, being found half-naked where he was – but I'm sure there was some other explanation for the facts, if he had been given a chance to offer it. And Honoria was screaming that she was innocent, I know – Miles heard her from the other room. Of course Honorius had murdered Zythos by that time, and so he had to kill the girl as well, or he could have been indicted for the death – the law demands he must kill both of them.'

I nodded. 'Then he could call on the protection of the court, because he was protecting the honour of his family name?'

'And the so-called honour of our family too. I'm sure that's why he acted as he did – he did not intend to kill Honoria at first, but it justified the murder of my friend. To say nothing of the fact that he got her dowry back intact, which would not have happened if she'd simply been divorced. My brother would have been awarded at least a half of it, and if he had managed to prove unfaithfulness – which I don't believe in any case – he would have got it all.' He looked squarely at me. 'Honorius was very familiar with the law. I don't believe he genuinely thought that Zythos and his daughter were having an affair, and I am perfectly certain they were not. But they are both as dead as if it had been true.'

He paused as though the memory was too painful to pursue, then snapped his fingers at his slave – who didn't wait for further instruction but disappeared at once and returned a moment later with a tray, bearing a jug of wine, a dipper and a cup.

'Slaves, you may leave us,' Redux said, and both of them retired. The trader poured out a little wine and was about to swallow it, when he recalled his manners. 'Will you take a little of this with me, citizen?'

I shook my head. I am not a great enthusiast for wine in any case, preferring a honest mug of ale or hot mead, and this afternoon in particular I wanted a cool head. 'Thank you, citizen. I was offered a little refreshment at the house.' I hadn't taken it, of course, and in truth I was beginning to feel rather thirsty now, but Redux had a quick and able mind and if I wanted to learn anything from him I needed all the advantage that I could obtain.

'Are you quite sure, citizen? You could take some home with you. I can find a small amphora that I can put some in.'

I shook my head again. 'Thank you, but I have a long walk ahead of me. Too far to be carrying even a small amphora, I'm afraid. But you enjoy your wine, by all means.'

He drained the wine then, and put down the cup. 'Then, citizen, what is it that you want from me, in fact? You did not want to sell the silver tray and you have shown no interest in my merchandise. But – though I am delighted by your company, of course – I do not imagine that this was a social call.' He poured another drink. 'You mentioned Antoninus to my foreman, I believe. Do I take it that he sent you here?'

I was so astonished that I could only gape.

He took a gulp of wine. 'Oh, come now, citizen, don't look so innocent!' He wiped his thick lips on his pudgy hand. 'You must have had some object in calling on me here. I thought at first you'd come to sell, otherwise I might never have asked you to come in. Then I thought you might be sent here by the family, to arrest me for the murder of Honorius – I'm sure the lady Livia believes that it was me. She was aware that he came to see me in this office yesterday, and her doorkeeper saw me outside the house last night.'

'I didn't know that...' I began, but he held up his hand.

'But though I gave you every opportunity – spelled it out to you that I had a possible motive of revenge and sent my slave away – you made no attempt to lay hands on me yourself, or to call that soldier I saw you talking to. Not even when I purposely demonstrated that I sometimes trade in wine.'

'And how easy it would be to put some in a small amphora, too, which you could have taken to Honorius last night,' I said, as the realization slowly dawned on me.

He turned the goblet slowly in his hand. 'Exactly, citizen – I knew you'd see the implication of that offer, given time. Yet you made no accusation, and you do not do so now. And there are no hordes of well-armed slaves or guards outside, waiting to be called in to drag me to the courts – I looked out through the window while I was examining the silver salver in the light. I told my foreman to be on watch for them and he signalled to me that the dock was clear.' He put the cup down suddenly and leaned forward on the desk. 'So I ask myself, citizen, what was it brought you here? It must be Antoninus. How much does he want?'

Thirteen

To say that I was thunderstruck would be understating it. I could not have been more startled if the statue on the desk had suddenly transformed into Jupiter himself. I found my mouth wide open like a actor's mask, designed to portray the emotion of surprise. In other circumstances it would have been quite comical. 'I don't know what you mean,' I gasped at last. 'I'm not his messenger. I have never spoken to Antoninus in my life.'

He looked at me coolly, and with faint disgust. 'Citizen, I warn you, I am not quite as stupid as you seem to think. Nor as unprotected. I see you are unarmed. However, I have a sharpened dagger in this drawer, and my foreman keeps a large club just beside the warehouse door. Also, a large number of the slaves that you saw working on the dock outside are mine. Strong fellows, all of them. I lease them to the overseer as extra lightermen when I'm not using them myself, but if they get a signal they will come at once, armed with any implement they can lay their hands upon.'

'And that's what you would have done if I'd attempted an arrest?' I said, through lips which had suddenly gone dry.

A faint smile played around the chubby face. 'Of course. What did you expect? That I'd go quietly and let them drag me off and lock me in some fetid cell until Livia brought some trumped-up charges against me in the court? I would have made at least an effort to defend myself, if only long enough to make my own escape. Livia could not have brought a charge against me then.'

I nodded. 'You have to produce the person you accuse before the magistrates, or there is no case.'

'Exactly. So I would have called my slaves.

And don't think they wouldn't come. I have had occasion to call upon them once or twice before, when someone has tried to cheat me out of what I owe. They are quite effective, when they are asked to be.'

I remembered what the soldier had told me about the rumpus yesterday, and flinched. It had not occurred to me before that I might be in danger here. 'But I did not come to arrest you, citizen.' I realized I was bleating rather like a sheep.

'So I observe. And you did not come to trade with me, and you swear that Antoninus did not send you here. I am not a trusting man.' He examined his fingernails, which were carefully manicured – by some personal slave, I suppose. 'And if you do not tell me – clearly and at once – what you came here for, I will whistle for assistance and see if my servants can persuade you to explain.'

There was no doubt this time that it was a threat. I quickly decided that honesty was the safest course. 'I did come to see you about the death today, but not at Livia's behest and not because I suspected you of it. I wanted more information about Honorius, that's all, preferably from someone outside the family, who might be relied upon to give a balanced view. I knew that you'd had business dealings with him in the past.'

He was looking unconvinced. 'And why should you bother to ask anyone at all? You tell me you didn't especially know the family?'

'That's true. But my patron used to use me to investigate such crimes – it has become a sort of habit with him, I suppose – and Gracchus got to hear about my reputation in this field. He is paying me to find the murderer and prove Pompeia innocent.' I paused and glanced at him. 'I hadn't intended to tell anybody that – I wanted them to assume I was a simple citizen, wanting to talk about a crime I'd witnessed, that is all.'

He finished the wine slowly and pushed the cup away. 'You know, I'm inclined to believe you, citizen. I think I've heard of you, by reputation anyway. A protégé of Marcus Septimus, you say? Are you that pavement-maker who once foiled a plot against the state?'

I bowed my head. 'The Provincial Governor was good enough to say so, citizen.' I felt so weak and giddy with relief, I would even have been grateful for a sip of wine.

But that was not to be. He folded his arms and went on scrutinizing me. 'Marcus was praising you in the curia one day. A fine mind under a humble exterior, he said. Only a pity that you weren't a richer man, because you would have made a useful councillor yourself. Would you agree with that assessment of yourself?'

I could only smile wryly at this analysis.

161

'My wealth, or lack of it, is largely in the hands of His Excellence himself, since he feels it would "insult" me to pay me for my time, but these assignments inevitably keep me from my trade.' I paused. I was afraid this sounded rather critical – which could make for serious trouble if Marcus heard of it – and I hastened to add quickly, 'Though of course he has always given me gifts in kind instead – many of which are very generous.'

Redux gave an unexpected hoot of laughter at my words. 'Presents, eh? Well if I know Marcus, they are gifts which rarely require him to reach into his purse. Rather like that wedding salver, in fact.' He raised one eyebrow at me.

'A very handsome gift,' I said, refusing to be drawn.

Redux surprised me with his response to that. 'Loyal as well as honest? You impress me, pavement-maker. So tell me something else. Why should Gracchus employ your services? I hardly imagine that he wants to wed Pompeia after this? She isn't such a girl as would make one desperate ... Aaah!' He leaned back in his chair again and slapped the desktop with a triumphant smile. 'Gracchus is desperate for that dowry, isn't he? I'm only guessing, but I'll wager he's in debt.'

I nodded, mentally acknowledging the

man's intelligence.

I realized that Redux was looking expectantly at me. 'Well, am I right?' he prompted. 'Gracchus is in debt? Or don't you know the answer?'

'There may be something of the kind, I think. In fact, from something that I overheard, I'm sure of it. Of course he didn't say as much to me.'

'I knew it!' He clapped his pudgy hands. 'Well, there's a wonder! Gracchus inherited a fortune only months ago. I wonder how he managed to squander it so fast? Fine living? Or prostitutes? Both of them perhaps. Or betting on the chariot racing on the sly? It only takes a little to get a man in deep. Those moneylenders in the forum are quite merciless.'

I took a risk. 'You don't suppose that Antoninus has got his teeth in him as well?'

That shook him. The triumphant manner faded in a trice and Redux glared furiously at me. 'What do you know about Antoninus? I warned you, citizen...' His hand was already moving to the drawer.

I managed to forestall him by leaning forward and saying peaceably, 'Oh come, citizen, what else am I to think? I don't know anything about Antoninus, except what I deduce – that he clearly has a hold on you, and probably on several other people in the town. You asked me earlier: "how much does he want", and that set me thinking, even at the time. It might have just been business – his setting a high price for something you required – so I tested you with that suggestion about Gracchus I just made. And now I'm sure I'm right. After your reaction, what else could it have been? You would have worked it out yourself if you'd been in my place.'

I meant it, but the flattery did its work on him. 'I suppose it's possible.' He was still scowling, but his hand moved from the drawer. 'My foreman said you mentioned Antoninus in the yard.'

'Only because he asked me to call on him today – sent a message saying he has important news for me. That is the only communication with him I have ever had, and I have no idea to what it might relate. I know it sounds absurd. But my servant has the writing tablet, you can read it for yourself. I assumed it was something about the poisoning.'

He seized the jug and poured out the last remaining drops of wine, then drank them at a gulp. He hadn't used the dipper at any point, I saw. He was still frowning. 'But why should Antoninus send a note to you?'

'I have asked myself the selfsame question, citizen. I wondered if Gracchus had mentioned me to him, and he'd hoped to impress me for my patron's sake. He has asked Marcus to propose him to the council, I believe. His Excellency told me so himself, before he left. Though I don't know what "important information" Antoninus has.' I felt myself colour. 'I even wondered if he intended to offer me a bribe.'

A derisive hoot of laughter, louder than the last. 'Antoninus, offering a bribe to you? I doubt it, citizen. Does an eagle condescend to catch a fly? More likely the information is concerning you, and he is going to propose that if you put in a word for him to Marcus Septimus he will desist from telling your patron what he knows.' He shook the jug hopefully above the empty cup, but there was not a drop.

'I see...' I said, thoughtfully, searching in my mind for what I might have done. I could not think of anything particular just now, but there are always small infringements which a man can make – not wearing a toga in a public place, or spitting too close to the statue of the Emperor. Or had I said something unwise about my patron, as I had done just now? 'Antoninus would have made it his business to find out that sort of thing?'

'Literally his business, pavement-maker,' Redux said. 'You clearly have the measure of the man. Antoninus claims to be a fellow trader, and he is too – in a way – but most of his business is the opposite of mine. Where I buy cloaks and dormice and sell them on again, he trades in information, but keeps it to himself. At least, one hopes he does. What's more, he requires a handsome fee for doing nothing – as it were – and it is a very successful business in all kinds of ways. If times are poor, he simply requires his customers to pay him more than once. You can't do that with potted dormice, citizen. Sometimes he even puts the price up, the second time around. And – as a rule – his clients simply pay. They're not usually in a position to complain to the authorities. And, of course, if he does offer normal goods for sale, the same people will pay him anything he asks.'

'Extortion,' I said thoughtfully. Marcus would be very interested to hear of that.

'Or bribery, if you prefer to think of it that way. A mutually profitable arrangement between friends, is how he talks of it. Either way, it's clever – though not a pleasant trade. And don't ask me where he gets his information from. I only wish I knew.' He shook the jug again, and I realized for the first time that he was becoming slightly drunk.

Otherwise, perhaps, I would not have dared to ask him, as I did, 'And what is it that he knows about you, citizen?'

For a moment he looked tense, and then he slowly smiled. 'You'd hardly expect me to tell you that. You are clever, pavement-maker, I concede. You've already got far more information from me than I meant. But I've paid Antoninus money to keep my secret safe, and I'm certainly not about to share it openly with you. In any case, it is a purely private matter, nothing to do with Honorius's death.' The plump face creased into a humourless, wry grin. 'Although, of course, I'd always be likely to say that, wouldn't I? You will simply have to take my word for it. And that is all I'm going to tell you on the subject, citizen.'

'You don't think Antoninus will tell me what it is? It might be the very information he was going to offer me.'

That troubled him a moment, but not for long. 'I doubt that, citizen. But I tell you what I'll do. I'll accompany you to Antoninus's dwelling place myself, and whatever he has to tell you, he can tell us both.' He could see that I was about to refuse his company, and he tapped the desktop sharply with his fingertips as if to remind me of what was in the drawer. 'It might be to your advantage, citizen, to have me come along. If he has found out from Gracchus that you're investigating this, I wouldn't go there wholly unprotected if I were you. Especially if he turns out to be in any way involved.'

'And you think he might be?'

'Nothing would surprise me, where Antoninus is concerned. He did have business dealings with Honorius – and I happen to know that he was there last night. I think I mentioned that I called round there myself, and I saw Antoninus skulking in the street, though he did not see me and I didn't speak to him – for reasons obvious. I generally try to avoid Antoninus in public if I can.'

I frowned. 'But surely Honorius was a stickler for the law, and is famous for living a life beyond reproach? Antoninus couldn't possibly have had a hold on him?'

Redux stood up and went across to where his toga was. 'I don't know, pavement-maker, I honestly don't know. A man who makes a public show of high morality is always very vulnerable if he does do something wrong, especially if he is a well-known councillor, and urges harsh punishment for other people's crimes. On the other hand, Antoninus does sell some proper merchandise as well – he would not last very long if that were not the case – and it might be clever for him to engage in simple trade with someone as well known for probity as Honorius.'

I got to my feet. It was clear this interview was almost at an end, but there were things that I still wanted to ask him while we were alone. I hastened to agree with the last thing he'd said – that often makes people more inclined to talk. 'I see what you mean,' I said, respectfully. 'It makes Antoninus seem respectable so people are not ashamed to be known to deal with him.'

He nodded. 'And apart from his victims, nobody would guess where he really gets his money from. A sort of double bluff, like men who play at dice honestly declaring what numbers they have rolled – until the moment that they choose to pounce.' He raised his fingers to his mouth and made a whistling sound – rather as I've heard Marcus summoning a dog.

The skinny slave came running from the room next door. 'You want me, master?'

'Help me with my toga.' He raised his arms and let his servant wrap the garment on, folding and tucking until just the end was left. Redux took that and draped it round his arm – suddenly the very picture of wealthy elegance. 'I am going to accompany this citizen into town – just as soon as I have fixed the price of salt. Fetch my foreman and have him come in here.'

The slave said nothing, but bowed himself away. Redux went over to the desk and took out a small knife in a leather case. 'In case I should be called upon to dine,' he said, giving me a wicked little smile. 'I wouldn't dream of carrying a weapon in the streets. That would be illegal.' He attached the knife case deftly to his belt where it was hidden by his toga-folds. 'But enough to give Antoninus pause, if he tries to threaten us. If he has one weakness, it is cowardice.'

'If Honorius had a weakness...' I was still following my earlier train of thought. 'What do you guess that it would be?'

He shrugged, and began to rifle through the tallies on his desk. 'I don't know, citizen. Works of art, perhaps? The lady Livia? His family honour, even – he has killed for that.'

'So, to protect his mother?'

He was scratching something on a tablet with a stylus now. 'He might be persuaded to do something foolish, I suppose. But I'm not sure of that. She was always domineering and wanting her own way, and since he defied her and married Livia, relationships between them have been distinctly cool. And I don't think she's forgiven him for Honoria's death – whatever she may say about that publicly. Honoria was her favourite grandchild after all.'

'And what about Pompeia?'

That hooting laugh again. 'Oh, the would-be bride? She was the younger daughter and of no account. Everyone ignored her, except Honoria, and after her sister's execution she was heartbroken. Helena Domna never spoke to her, except to use her like a slave – order her about and find fault with what she did. Livia was quite kind to her in a vague, general sort of way, but she would do the same for a beggar at the gate – it wasn't for Pompeia in particular. I rather think that's what prompted the child to make that

170

pathetic so-called "confession" when her father died – and don't pretend that you were taken in by it. What did it turn out to be – she'd called down a curse on him?'

'Not even anything as definite as that. She had simply appealed to the gods to be released.'

He smoothed out what he'd been writing, with the stylus. 'Well, there you are. Unless you think she made a point of confessing to all that, to disguise the fact that she had secretly poisoned her father all along? I don't think she has the subtlety for that. I think she wanted some attention for a change – and I'm not surprised.'

'She might have been better getting married then.'

He looked up from his task. 'Not to Gracchus, pavement-maker. Not if she wanted to be of some account. Gracchus likes his wine and dancing girls and doesn't care who knows – a wife is just for breeding in his view of things. I think Pompeia knew that – she is not a fool. I used to tell Zythos that he would have a chance with her, but he wasn't interested.'

Zythos. Again there was that suspicion of emotion at the name. I made a sudden guess. 'You encouraged him to marry? But surely, you were attached to him yourself.'

He had turned the colour of his tasselled shoes. 'Who told you, citizen?'

'Your own tone of voice.'

He turned away from me and stared out of the window hole towards the dock. 'Is it so obvious? Well, citizen, there is no shame in it. He was so beautiful he was loved by everyone: pages, married women, councillors – they all flung themselves at him. I could not expect to have him solely to myself – and besides he was a Greek by birth. They have a different philosophy from us – men for pleasure, women for the race.'

'Not unlike Gracchus's attitude in fact?' I said, ungraciously.

'Except that Zythos would always have been charming to a wife, and Gracchus is a boor. Pompeia would have been ideal for him in many ways – she can be amusing when she puts her mind to it – but, as I say he wasn't interested. I rather think he may have had his eye on someone else, but – for once – he wouldn't tell me who.' He stared at something imaginary in the sky. 'I found a poem he had written on a tablet, once: "To my fair-haired beauty." I think that at last he had truly lost his heart. It was not to me.'

'And it was not Honoria, you are sure of that?'

'As certain as I can be. Although Honoria was by far the prettier of the two, she was still dark and dumpy – like her father was.'

'Of course.' I remembered the swarthy councillor as I had seen him once on the steps of the basilica.

'And she had his temperament – all prim morality. She would never have demeaned herself, as she would think of it. She was devoted to my brother – and he was fond of her. As these things go, it had worked out very well. Besides she'd just announced she was with child, and Zythos regarded that as sacrosanct. He would never have forced himself upon a woman – I am sure of that – especially a member of my family. More likely he was after one of the maids, that night, or one of my brother's little serving boys.'

'So what was he doing in Honoria's sleeping room?'

'I imagine that he found himself surprised, felt that he'd dishonoured me and my family by the act and simply rushed into the nearest room to hide. And then Honorius came in.' He snapped the tablet shut. 'But we will never know. If there was an explanation, Honorius would not hear. But, enough of that. Here comes my foreman. It is time to buy some salt, and then I'll come with you and we'll pay that little call.'

Fourteen

I collected Minimus, who had been crouching inside the warehouse door – playing knuckle bones with the skinny servant by the look of it – and we followed Redux and his foreman out on to the dock.

The purchase transaction took a little time. It was clear that the foreman had already half-agreed a price, but when Redux appeared there was a flurry of further haggling, with a lot of raised voices and emphatic gesturing. I retreated to a safe distance with my slave and settled down to wait.

'Did you discover anything useful, master?' Minimus enquired, when we were out of earshot of the rest. 'I was sorry not to be able to assist you in your questioning.'

It seemed a pity to deflate the boy by admitting that I hadn't succeeded in asking Redux much. 'I've learned a lot about Antoninus, for one thing,' I replied. 'Not a pleasant character, by all accounts. Redux has offered to accompany us there – he knows the man well, and he may be of help.' I didn't mention daggers.

Minimus grinned at me. 'And after all, Redux is not himself a suspect, I suppose?'

But of course he was, I thought. And I must not be seduced into forgetting that, just because he'd pointed out the facts himself. Redux had both the motive and – as I now knew – the opportunity, since he had been to Honorius's house the night before and could obviously have taken a little wine with him – as a gift, perhaps, just as he'd suggested that I take some with me. Or he could have slipped poison into something else – it had not been proved that it was in the wedding wine.

But would he have shown me how easy that would be, if he had really done it? I shook my head. Redux was sharp enough to have outlined a case against himself, knowing that I would reason exactly in this way. He had even mentioned the strategy of confession as a bluff – although in relation to Pompeia, of course. I looked at Minimus. 'I have not entirely ruled him out,' I said, and gave the boy a sketchy outline of my reasoning.

He beamed at me. 'Then, master, I have something which might interest you.' He held out a small glass phial with no lid on it. 'I didn't know if it was useful, but thought you would be pleased to have it anyway.'

It was quite empty. I turned it upside down but not a drop came out, and when I gave it an experimental sniff I could not really detect anything at all. I was about to dip my finger in the neck and see if I could recognize the taste, but Minimus – who had been almost bouncing with excitement during this – put out a hand and stopped me doing so.

'Don't do that, master. It may do you harm.' He sounded gleeful, rather than alarmed.

'What was in it?'

'Wolfsbane, master. The slave was using it. He mixes it into the ink, he says, to stop the rats and mice from nibbling the writing on the bark. His master always keeps a stock of it in his office for that use.'

I took my finger out of the phial as quickly as I could. 'And how did you get hold of this?'

'I beat the slave at knuckle bones and claimed this as my prize. He had lost the stopper so it wasn't any use, and I pretended that I was going to put some ink in it and try his little tip. He was quite relieved. He only had a single *as* in cash and he was afraid I was going to ask for that.' He grinned. 'So, I suppose you could say I paid an *as* for it. But I thought you would be interested to know about the rats.'

I beamed at him. 'You did well, Minimus. Here, give that to me. Redux might not be very pleased to know that you have taken it.' I put it inside my toga as I spoke, securing it in the large pouch-purse attached to the belt of my tunic. 'And wrap that tray securely in my cloak. I'm going to give the package to that soldier over there and have him take it to the gatehouse when he is relieved, and hand it to the commander of the guard. That way we won't get robbed. I'll go and do it now, in fact, while Redux is busy with his bargaining.' I left my servant waiting and went over to the guard.

The soldier was reluctant to take responsibility at first, argued that it was hours until his relief was due and it would be impossible to look after my package till then, but when I mentioned Marcus his demeanour changed. 'Oh very well, citizen. I'll see what I can do. There is a party from the barracks coming down here very soon – the army are taking a little of this salt. They'll bring my relief and I'll go back with them. I presume there will be a small reward?'

'When the salver is safely at the villa,' I replied. 'In the meantime...' I looked around. I was prepared to forgo the formal witnesses – I didn't want Redux noticing the phial – but I had forgotten the necessity of getting a receipt. I had nothing to write on, and in the end I had to call on Minimus and smooth out the note that Antoninus had written to summon me to him. I didn't have a stylus either, but I found a piece of stick and manage to scratch a statement using that.

The soldier glanced at it and scratched his initials where I'd left a space. I wasn't convinced he'd read it properly – or even that he could – but it would have to do. I was confident that he would see the parcel safely to the guardhouse at the gates, if only to lay his hands on that reward. I thanked him and put the tablet in my pouch as well – to Minimus's visible dismay. 'I'd better keep this now,' I said to him. 'In case I have to produce it at the gatehouse later on.'

I looked around for Redux, and saw that he was busily engaged, waving his arms about and arguing. So when a pie seller sauntered past us, his tray upon his head, I fiddled in my purse to see what coins I had. The smell of hot pastry made my stomach groan and reminded me that I hadn't eaten anything since shortly after dawn. I found enough to buy a couple of his remaining wares. They were tough and greasy, but I wolfed mine down, and Minimus was happy to tuck in as well, though he told me that he had eaten bread and curd-cheese at Honorius's house – it was the custom to offer something to the slaves of visitors, while their masters enjoyed more lavish hospitality downstairs. Only, of course, the feast had not occurred.

I was further tempted by the sight of a dairy woman coming down the dock, offering not only slabs of cheese but dippers of milk from the little metal cup chained to the handle of her pail. But I had spent all my money so I could not buy a drink. We contented ourselves with plunging our mouths and faces under the spout of the public fountain on a street corner nearby.

We got back just in time. The bargainers had reached agreement finally – based on a price of hides and cloaks it seemed, because the foreman and the slave were fetching piles of each from the warehouse even as I watched. Redux came over, with an expansive smile.

'Barter, citizen?'

My puzzlement amused him. 'Always rather more flexible than gold – it clears my warehouse, and besides, it is much harder for the taxman to assess.' He beamed. 'And we are all satisfied with the bargain we have reached, I think. Now, shall we call litters to Antoninus's house? It is a little way to walk and it is getting late. You wanted to be there by the ninth hour, so my foreman said, and it must already be rather more than that.'

I made a face at him. 'I don't have money for a litter, citizen. I came out ready for a wedding feast, with just a little money – and I used most of that to tip the doorkeeper.' I did not confess to the purchase of the pie. He was already looking rather pitying as if an empty purse was never part of his experience.

I thought for a moment he might volunteer

to bear the charge for me, but he simply nodded. 'Very well. There isn't a litter anywhere in sight, in any case. I'll send my slave back to my rooms to fetch some other shoes – these are expensive but they're rather soft to walk in on the streets. He can catch us up. In the meantime, let us make a start. If we keep to the main roads it should be fairly clean. This way, citizen.'

He led the way across the dock, in the opposite direction from the way we'd come, where a wide street led directly into town, though the stones of the roadway were deeply grooved with carts. The pavements on each side were particularly high, to save pedestrians from walking in the dirty water, I suppose, on occasions when the river overflows its banks and – in drier times like these – from the animal droppings and squashed vegetables which are the inevitable refuse of the town. Even on the pavement Redux was picking his way with care, obviously anxious about his fancy shoes.

He was still pleased with his bargain, and he chatted about that – how the Romans were building concrete drying pans to improve the quality of salt, and how the price was still remaining high – as we hurried past shops and drinking places not so different in kind from what we'd passed before. Except that the soup kitchens and tavernas here were prosperous and clean, and if (as was likely) some offered girls upstairs, the advertisements for their services were much more discreet. But then we moved into the area where the copper workers were, and conversation became impossible. Not only was the street crammed with their merchandise, so that we had to walk past it in single file, but from the interiors incessant hammering went on. I wondered how the other little businesses survived the noise, squeezed into tiny premises between the coppersmiths, but they seemed oblivious. There was a busy fruit stall, a flower seller with a cart, a shoemaker in a narrow doorway stitching boots, and a baker pulling fresh loaves from an oven as we passed.

I stopped to wait for Redux, who had fallen a little way behind. He was looking more uncomfortable at every step, and clearly it was not entirely the shoes. The plump face was red and glistening with sweat, and it occurred to me that he rarely walked at such a pace – certainly not for any distance, anyway.

He lumbered up to us, flustered and out of breath. 'I'm sorry, citizen. I can't keep up with you. In these shoes anyway!' He stepped into the gutter as he spoke, to avoid a carpet stall which was spread out across the pavement, and narrowly avoided a rotting cabbage in the road. 'I don't know where my slave has got to with those stouter ones.' He looked helplessly up and down the street as if the boy might suddenly appear by sorcery.

He looked so unhappy that I took pity on his plight. 'Look, there is a litter in that alleyway. Bringing someone for the shoemaker, by the look of it. I'll send Minimus to catch it, if you like, and you can get them to take you to where Antoninus lives. It isn't very far now, so you can wait for us. As you can see, we won't be far behind. And if your slave turns up with your other footwear in that time, we'll bring him with us. You can change shoes when you're there.'

He seemed to hesitate. 'Well, if you're quite sure, citizen? It would be a relief. I'm afraid I've stained the leather of this one past repair. Will you be able to find the place all right? I'll stand outside it on the pavement till you come.'

I sent Minimus at once to catch the litter before the slaves went dashing back to town looking for other customers. He came back a moment later. 'They've contracted to take the lady home again, when she has finished with the shoemaker, so they must hurry back, but they will take you quickly if you are ready now?'

Redux was still puffing but he looked relieved. 'In that case, citizen, I will see you there. It isn't above a half a mile or so from here, at most. If it weren't for these shoes I could have walked it easily...' He broke off as the litter-bearers trotted up to us, and put the litter down for him to sit in it. They got him seated, fixed a price, and then they bore him off.

I grinned at Minimus. 'I wonder they did not ask him double price. He must be twice the weight of some other customers. Of course those slaves are trained to move at quite a pace, but if we hurry we can nearly walk as fast. We don't have Redux to carry, after all. It may even be possible to keep them in sight, and then we shall know exactly where we're going.'

Of course it wasn't quite as easy as all that. There were donkey carts and street sellers and stalls to dodge around, and even a fortune-teller trying to accost us as we passed but we hurried on and, only a little later, found ourselves in the centre of the town, close to the forum and the temple of Jupiter which was next door to it.

'Second block along,' I said, recalling my directions from the doorkeeper. 'On the first floor, above a cobbler's shop.'

Minimus looked doubtful. 'Two blocks in which direction?' he enquired. He looked around. 'I can't see Redux waiting anywhere.'

He spoke too soon, for even as he framed the words the man himself appeared at the doorway of a building a short way further on. He seemed to be in some measure of distress, staring first up and down the street and then behind him in a frenzied way as if the furies were pursuing him. Then he began examining his clothes, dabbing at his toga and his handsome cuffs. I remembered what the doorkeeper had said about the slops and could not suppress a smile, although Redux looked almost on the verge of running off.

Then he caught sight of us and gave a frantic wave. We hurried up to him.

'What happened, citizen? I thought that you were going to wait for us out here,' I began – and stopped.

If he had been red-faced before he was bright scarlet now, and I was almost fearful that he was going to burst. He was breathing so hard that he could barely speak. He reached out and put a hand upon my arm, as if he needed the support.

'I just went up to tell his slave that you were on your way, but the door to his apartment was open, citizen. Of course, that's not uncommon. When he has private business of the kind that we discussed, he always made a point of sending all his slaves away. I put my head around the door and called – but there was no reply. So I went in...' He shook his head. 'It isn't any use.'

'Antoninus refused to see us? Or he wasn't there at all?' I asked, feeling rather foolish to have brought the poor man all this way, and caused him such exertion for nothing after all.

Redux surprised me. 'Oh, he was there all right. But...' He shook his head again. 'On second thoughts, citizen, I think you'd better come and see him for yourself.'

Fifteen

Once inside the building I could see at once what Honorius's doorkeeper had meant about the stairs. The flight which led up from the street was adequately broad as far as the first floor but above us the steps were narrow, steep and treacherously dark, and the whole stairwell smelt atrociously. As I followed a breathless Redux up to Antoninus's door, I was uncomfortably aware of people overhead coming to peer suspiciously at us from the gloom, though nobody actually threw any slops on us.

There were other inhabitants of the upper floors jostling against us as we climbed the stairs. A stout woman struggled past, carrying a heap of turnips in her skirt, while her thin children dragged up a branch of firewood – though there were clearly neither hearths nor chimneys in the rooms above,

185

and cooking fires in tenements like these were officially against the law. As we reached the turning our way was almost blocked by a bunch of skinny, toothless, old men squatting in the corner, bickering at dice; they scarcely looked up or moved to let us past.

The door to Antoninus's apartment, when we came to it, looked particularly imposing by comparison. It was large and thick with a hefty lock and, although Redux had warned me of the fact, I was half-surprised to find it currently ajar. Even so, it was not the kind of entrance that one walked through unannounced, and I was about to knock discreetly when our companion, who was scarlet and panting from climbing up the steps, leaned past me, pushed the door wide open and said breathlessly, 'There is no point in doing that, citizen. There are no slaves to answer if you knock, in any case. Just go inside. Antoninus is in the other room.'

I did as he suggested: went in and looked around. The apartment was impressive, a spacious entrance hall which opened into a sort of central room, with what was clearly a bedroom and study beyond that. There was a handsome central table with a bowl of fruit on it, and a massive wooden chest against the further wall. On the right-hand side, so small that it seemed merely a recess in the wall, was a little dining alcove, complete with a wooden trestle and a couch. Antoninus had obviously been lunching recently – there was a platter with a hunk of bread and crumbs of cheese on it, a pot of what was clearly garum on a tray, an empty drinking cup and an equally empty wine jug standing on the floor.

On the left was a narrow passage to the rear, which I guessed led into spaces used for slaves or stores. If there was a kitchen area it was out of sight, but more likely Antoninus sent out for more elaborate meals, or wangled invitations from his friends or guilds. Even braziers were a danger in a block like this.

However there was one heating the corner of the room, beside an altar table with the household gods displayed. I went over to it, thinking to warm myself while I was waiting to be summoned by our host, since there was nowhere obvious for a guest to sit.

There was still no movement from the other room. From my new position I could glimpse it through the half-open door. It was obviously some kind of study area: there were several wooden racks containing scrolls in pots, while other – perhaps less-regarded – manuscripts were neatly stacked on top, beside half a dozen little oil-lamps and a water clock festooned with jet and gold around the base. It appeared that Antoninus liked expensive things. It seemed too, that he had seen and admired Redux's foreign chair, because there was one exactly like it, pulled up to the bench which its owner was clearly using as a desk. He was leaning intently forward on it now, for though the open door obscured the greater part of him, the edges of his toga were clearly visible. There was another brazier standing quite close to him in there.

I was preparing to give a warning cough to remind him we were here, but something in his slumped attitude – combined with Redux's obvious alarm – finally warned me of what I should have guessed before.

I glanced at my companions and rushed into the room. 'Dear Jupiter!' I cried.

He was sprawled across the desk, his hands outstretched and his face and upper body in a pool of seeping black. I thought for a moment it was drying blood, but it was only the contents of a bowl of ink that he'd been working with, and which his dying gesture had upset and spilled. The blood was quite a different colour, though there wasn't much of it – apart from the thin stream that had trickled down his arm from the knife stuck into his back.

I turned to Minimus who had followed me inside and was staring at this spectacle with wide and stricken eyes. 'Go at once and find a member of the town watch, if you can – or even a soldier from the garrison. You might find one off duty in the wine shop opposite.

Someone in authority should know of this at once.'

The little slave glanced up at me. His skin had taken a pale and greenish hue and he looked as though he was close to being sick. The adventure of helping me with questioning had obviously dimmed. 'You think that he is dead?'

At any other time that would have made me smile. Antoninus was as dead as it was possible to be. 'It rather looks like it.'

'The same hand that killed Honorius, you think?'

I shook my head. 'We can't be sure of that – at present anyway. You go and find that soldier while we take a closer look.'

Minimus nodded gratefully and disappeared at once.

'What do you expect a closer look to tell you?' Redux said. He had been hovering at a distance all this time, as if reluctant to come nearer to the corpse. 'Surely he is dead, and there's an end to it. But I suppose you are the expert on these things, pavement-maker. What do we do now?'

For want of a more intelligent reply, I raised the ink-stained head and taking the ink bowl, which was made of burnished brass, I held it closely to the lifeless lips. 'No breath at all,' I was saying smugly, when I stopped in some surprise. 'There's still a little warmth in him – that might be because of the brazier perhaps – but he's still pliable. He cannot have been dead for very long.'

I turned to the brazier, where the coals still glowed but were covered by a pile of recent ash. Somebody had been burning something and not long ago. 'Did you touch anything?'

Redux shook his head. 'He was like this when I got here. And, in case you were about to ask me, that is not my knife. Mine is still here.' He gestured at his belt.

It had not occurred to me to wonder about that, although his sharp assessment made me think I should have done. I tried to make amends by asking briskly, 'All the same, it seems that someone came here fairly recently and ran a dagger into him. And set fire to some documents. Another of his so-called clients, do you think?'

Redux shook his head, but he did not speak and I noticed that his hands were trembling. He attempted to disguise the fact by gathering some of the scattered scraps of bark paper, and laying them fastidiously beneath the window space. 'We might as well collect the rest of them,' he said. He had contrived to turn his back towards me, I observed.

'And you didn't see anyone suspicious on the stairs?' I said.

He spread out another sheet of writing and said, in a more collected tone of voice, 'Not that I noticed. Should we make enquiries of the neighbours, do you think?'

'I doubt they'll talk to us.' It was true. I walked over beside him and looked through the window, but there was nothing to be seen, only the usual gaggle of slaves and tradesmen going about their business in the town. We were not far from the temple and the forum area, and the streets were busy with commerce at this time of day, including Vinerius, whom I noticed haggling with a man – a tall stooped figure that might have been Honorius's lugubrious doorkeeper. 'If I had worn my working tunic, I might have had a chance, but our togas are a serious barrier in a place like this.'

He nodded. 'Then we'll leave questions to the authorities, since you have called them in. No doubt they'll have the means to get a story from any witnesses – though whether it will be the truth or not, is quite another thing.' He pretended to be rapt in examining a scroll. 'It is only to be hoped that they don't start suspecting us – though as citizens we should be safe from actual torturers.'

It was not a happy notion – but of course he was quite right, especially as Marcus wasn't here to speak for me. I was beginning to wish I hadn't been so quick to call the guard.

He put down the bark paper and picked up another sheet. 'It might help if we could find a list of clients anywhere. I suspect he kept one, but I haven't found it yet.'

So that was what he had been looking for! It was an interesting notion, and I joined him in his task. The little scraps were scribbled on in various different ways, but nothing that looked like an appointment list. There were columns of figures, a fragment of a note, something that might have been a bill. Not all in the same ink or writing, I observed. I picked up the last one, and placed it on the pile.

'Of course it might not have been a client after all,' Redux said. 'It could have been a stranger – a robbery, perhaps. We cannot be certain that there's nothing missing here.'

I shook my head. 'Not a stranger, I am sure of that. It is clear that the killer was admitted freely to the house. There is no sign of a struggle, or forced entry anywhere. Antoninus was sitting calmly at his desk. Besides, would any thief leave precious objects like that water clock? And why burn documents if you're a passer-by? So either a client, or someone with a key. I presume Antoninus had some family? And I think you mentioned slaves – someone will have to question them as well.'

He nodded. 'No family that I know of, but he did have slaves. There are two of them: a pretty little chap that Antoninus uses as a personal attendant and a pet, and a burly fellow whom he keeps in case of trouble, I suspect. But, as I told you earlier, he sends them both away if he's doing business of the kind we spoke about. They will not come back till dusk, I expect.'

'And who would know that?'

'Any of his clients.' Redux refused to look me in the eyes.

'So when you come to see him, who comes to let you in? He doesn't leave the door ajar in this way normally?'

He shrugged. 'Of course not. You have to knock and wait. He'd let you in himself. I think he would peer through the key-space to make sure it was you. And he always insisted that you sent your slaves away. He said it was essential for proper secrecy. But it's very unsettling when you're used to having them – it makes you feel exposed and unprotected. Which is exactly why he did it, I expect.'

'So anybody could have come this afternoon, and expected to find him unaccompanied?'

'Any of his clients, that is, who knew that he had a private appointment at this time.' He patted the collected bark fragments into a single roll and tied them with a ribbon lying on the desk. 'Which is odd, when you think about it, wouldn't you agree? Because you tell me that you had no arrangement till you got that note, and that was after the wedding was postponed. But he would have expected to be at the feast all day, and he would have made no other appointments for this afternoon. So who might have known that you were coming here and that Antoninus would therefore be conveniently alone?'

'Just what I was about to ask, myself.' The voice was unexpected, and I whirled around to see a Roman soldier standing at the door. A legionary tribune by the look of it, a youth in decorative armour, fancy cloak-clasps and expensive boots and a look of self-importance on his handsome face. He was standing in a swaggering attitude now, one hand on his baton and the other on his sword, looking down his long and narrow nose at us, while Minimus cowered behind him and glanced nervously at me.

'I found this soldier in the wine shop, master, as you said...' he began, but was silenced by a heavy cuff around the ear.

'I was talking to these citizens,' the tribune snapped, in Latin that was absurdly cultured and refined.

I gave an inward groan. When I had sent Minimus out to fetch the guard I had not envisaged this. I'd expected some humble auxiliary from the Rhineland, perhaps, anxious to earn an honest copper coin or two by taking charge, not an arrogant young aristocrat sent out from Rome for the customary short spell in the army before a senatorial seat – an imitation officer with a career to make. Such youths may never see a battle in their lives and generally had scant respect for lowlier citizens – especially not for ancient Celts like me.

He proved my fears by marching to the desk and lifting Antoninus's head as I had done, beneath the chin but with his baton rather than his hand. He let it fall again with an unpleasant thump, and then he turned to me. 'You, in the scruffy toga, you heard what I said. From what I overheard you were expected here and the household slaves have all been sent away. What was your business with this citizen?'

'I'm not completely sure.' Even as I spoke, I knew it sounded lame. 'I simply got a message asking me to come. Here' – I fished into my tunic – 'read it for yourself...' I was about to hand the tablet to him before I remembered I had scratched out the message and written over it, and now I had no proof that I'd been summoned here.

I explained this to the tribune, but he looked unimpressed. 'I believe you, citizen, of course,' he said, with just the degree of courteous mockery that told me he did nothing of the kind. 'I just hope that my superiors will do the same. I will have to ask you to accompany me, of course.'

I blanched. 'But it's the truth,' I stammered. 'I'm sure this citizen will vouch for me...' I turned to Redux.

But he refused to look me in the eye. It was clear that I was going to get no help from him. He shook his head. 'I never saw the note. Libertus simply told me he was coming here, and I accompanied him because I knew the way. I'd had dealings with Antoninus in the way of trade – I'd even spoken to him at a wedding, earlier today. In fact, this pavement-maker was a guest as well, but the feast was cancelled because the father was found dead.'

The tribune looked scathingly at me. I was not surprised. If Redux had intended to cast doubt on me, he could hardly have chosen his words with greater skill. 'I see. And you are a friend of this so-called pavement-maker, I presume? Though you seem unlikely acquaintances, from your form of dress.' He looked at my companion's fancy tunic with disdain.

Redux fussed daintily with his embroidered cuffs. 'I had never seen him till the wedding feast. Though he was conspicuous there. He took charge after the host was dead. Then later he called on me at my warehouse at the docks. I was not expecting him.'

'And you? Where did you go when you left the feast?'

'Directly back to work. I'm sure the overseer at the dock would vouch for that. He hires my slaves when I'm not using them, and he was surprised to see me back so soon. The pavement-maker did not come for quite a little while.'

'So, there would have been time to have called here on the way.' The tribune turned back to me again, less supercilious and more threatening now. 'I'm afraid, citizen, that you'll need better witnesses than that – unless you are proposing to rely upon your slave? I'll take him away and have him questioned if you like.'

Minimus looked stricken and I shook my head. Of course, the boy would vouch for me, if I was called to court, but a servant's unsupported testimony is of no account. It is assumed that he will dutifully support his master's report of everything – indeed he would be likely to be punished otherwise – so such slaves are generally handed over to the men with whips and brands to ensure that the truth is tortured out of them. I prayed for Minimus's sake it would not come to that.

It may have been the gods that gave me an idea. 'Helena Domna!' I said suddenly. 'She knew that a message came for me at the house, and she knew what it said. She insisted on looking at the note.'

'Helena Domna? The mother of Councillor Honorius?' Even the tribune was visibly impressed. 'I have heard tales of him.'

'Ex-councillor Honorius, now,' Redux put

in at once. 'He was the one who was found dead today. It is generally supposed that there was poison in his wine.'

The officer made a thoughtful pouting movement with his lips. 'And this citizen just happened to be there?' He turned to me. 'Let's have a look at you.' He took his dagger out and held it casually in the region of my heart while with his other hand he moved my cloak aside and ran his fingers round my toga belt. I knew, in a sinking moment, what he was about to find. I was here, not only without proof that I had been asked to come, but with an empty poison phial hidden in my clothes. If I were investigating Antoninus's death, I thought, I should be very interested in me.

'Aha!' The tribune produced the little bottle with a smirk. 'And what might you have been carrying in this?'

I explained how I had come by it. It was embarrassing, since Redux had not known that I had taken it. Besides, it was clear that the soldier did not believe a word.

'Is this true?' he said to Redux. 'You use poison in this fashion and keep it in this phial?'

Redux shrugged. 'It's true that I do add wolfsbane to my ink – as many people do – but why he has this bottle I have no idea, or even whether it is really one of mine.'

The soldier nodded. 'And there's another

thing. I notice that you are carrying a knife.'

Redux looked shaken and turned pink again. 'For dining, that is all.' He moved his hand towards the wine jug on the shelf, as if he would like to pour a reviving glass of it, but then withdrew it as the tribune glanced at him.

The soldier smiled grimly. 'Of course. Yet this man, who has been attending the same feast, does not seem to have one. Unless it is the one the victim is carrying in his back? And, citizen, if I were you I wouldn't drink that wine.'

Redux looked momentarily appalled and ran his hands across his chest. 'Why ever shouldn't I? You don't think...?' He gestured towards me.

The tribune gave a self-important smirk. 'I have seen a body or two that have been stabbed before. And I can tell you this, it isn't easy to stab someone in the back just once and have them die so instantaneously. It's hard to be sure you have hit the vital place. Not unless the killer has a special skill with knives, or the victim conveniently sits quite still for them – as at first sight it seemed this fellow did. Or unless the blade is poisoned, naturally.'

Redux looked at him with dismay, and pushed the wine jug surreptitiously away. 'You think the blade was poisoned? But who on earth would do a thing like that? And where would they get the poison from?' He was gabbling.

'I don't know, citizen. Unless they were using it to protect their manuscript from rats?' He smirked and put his blade away. 'But I do know this. It's possible that both of you have had a hand in murdering this man. I'll have to ask the pair of you to come along with me. And we'll have your servant too. Now, will you come quietly, or shall I send for help? I have sent for reinforcements to come up anyway – and I think that I can hear them in the stairwell now.'

It would have been hard to miss them – the clattering of hobnail sandals as a quartet of soldiers took the staircase at a run, and a moment later they had burst into the room.

'You two' – he indicated a couple of them with his hand – 'keep a watch here until arrangements can be made about the corpse. You others, search the building and find out if anyone was spotted coming in and out of here, except our fine friend and the pavement-maker here. I'll take them into custody meanwhile.'

'Take us to the garrison, if you take us anywhere,' I said, suddenly having visions of being dragged off to the jail. 'The commander knows me, he'll tell you who I am.'

'May be true, sir,' the eldest soldier said. 'I believe I have seen this citizen before.'

For the first time the tribune looked less

than confident. 'The garrison? Well, if you say so, citizen. It can't do any harm. But if it proves to be some kind of trick, believe me you will wish you'd never been born.'

'Perhaps you could send to Helena Domna, while you're taking us,' I seized on the little advantage that I seemed to have. 'The commander would wish you to call the witnesses.'

He hesitated, visibly this time. Then he turned to Minimus. 'Very well,' he said. 'You can run back to Helena Domna's house and tell them what has happened and what we need from them.'

Minimus glanced nervously at me. I nodded and he needed no bidding after that. He had disappeared before the tribune had the chance to say, 'If you know the commander, I suppose it's different. I won't take you at sword point, but be sure of this – if either of you make any move to run away at all, I'll run you through. I am the quickest sword in all the garrison – I used to practise with the emperor for his displays of skill. And it wouldn't be a nice quick death, like this poor fellow had. So, if you are ready – let's be on our way.'

Sixteen

The appearance of a troop of Roman soldiers in full uniform cleared the staircase as surely as a pail of water will get rid of dogs. Not even the ancient dice players were there to see us leave, though no doubt there were unseen figures still watching from above. Still, our exit was less ignominious than it might have been.

The tribune was as good as his promise, too – he did not draw his sword, although the way he marched us down the street, with himself between us and a half a pace behind, made it quite clear that this was not a pleasant social stroll.

The streets were busy at this time of day – everything from egg-women to imperial messengers – and we attracted a good many frank and curious stares. But no one hemmed us in. When people suspect that you are under guard, they tend to pass by on the other side, and give you as wide a berth as possible, as if you have some terrible disease which they might catch. Today was no exception, and though the streets were thronged with traders, shoppers, slaves, animals and groups of wealthy councillors emerging from the baths, the crowd seemed to open up miraculously to allow us through.

So it didn't take us very long at all to walk across the centre of the town and turn down the wide and handsome thoroughfare towards the southern gate, where the garrison commander had his headquarters.

Redux had begun by trying to look bored and casual, but the tribune forced us to maintain a brisk and steady pace and it wasn't long before the warehouse keeper was out of breath again. Scarlet and panting, he leaned on a wall, begging to be allowed to rest, but the young officer was keen to show his power. He threatened to march us at sword point if Redux stopped again, much to the entertainment of a scrawny boy, who was sweeping up the street.

'I'll put you in this bucket, citizen, and carry you,' he mocked, waving the stinking pail of manure: droppings from the animals which had been driven to the forum market earlier that day, which he was doubtless picking up to sell. 'Can't have a fine gentleman like you marched off like a common criminal.'

Redux flushed more than ever and struggled on again, though he was getting more out of breath at every step. I was finding it difficult to keep up, myself.

So there was no chance of any conversation on the way, and when we reached the gatehouse finally it was a huge relief to be allowed to stop. Though even then there was no rest for us. The tribune gave the password and the guard let us in. We were marched into the courtyard where troops were forming up, for some sort of route-march by the look of it. We huddled in a corner and were told to stand and wait, while the tribune sent a passing soldier scurrying upstairs to let the commander know that we were there.

'Give him a report. Say it's from the tribune who arrived here yesterday. Tell him two suspects await him in the yard. Arrested in suspicious circumstances at a murder scene. Between them they have daggers and an empty phial – both of them are common tradesmen and though they're citizens, I doubt that either of them was of Roman birth. Tell the commander that – and that one of the wretches claims acquaintanceship with him. I'll have them guarded, until he sends for them.' And with that he disappeared into a guardroom opposite, where I saw a centurion get up at once and offer him a seat, even before the door had time to swing closed after him.

It was a long wait, standing in the dusty wind, but we were not permitted to sit down, or squat, or even lean. As surely as we did so, the centurion came out and rapped us round the legs with his confounded stick. Obviously he'd been detailed to keep his eye on us. I tried to have a word to Redux as we stood – to ask why he had not spoken up in my defence – but our guard saw me whispering and rapped my legs again, bellowing that I had not been told to talk. In the end there was nothing for it but to stand there and endure.

After what seemed like an eternity, a different soldier came clattering down the stairs and announced that the commander was awaiting us. I was about to take him at his word and climb the steps, when the tribune reappeared – obviously anxious to be seen in charge. He drew his blade and ordered us to precede him up the stairs, while he urged us onwards with sword pricks from behind.

We were escorted past the lower office and up the steep stone steps. I had been in the commander's office once before; a spartan room with just a desk and stool, and no other ornament of any kind at all except a shadowy statue of a deity set into the stone wall, though two large wooden doors led off into other rooms beyond. It smelt of damp and lamp oil and Roman soldiery – that peculiar aroma which the military have: a mixture of leather, sweat and perfumed oil, and the goose grease and metallic earth they clean their armour with.

The commander was writing something as

we came into the room, his armour gleaming in the light of an oil lamp set beside him on a stand. He did not look up. 'Well? There has been some disturbance, do I understand? But it's a civil matter, isn't it? Why has this come to me, and not simply to the lock-up in the town?'

The tribune stepped forward and took his helmet off. 'In the name of his Imperial Divinity Commodus, the blessed, the pious, the—'

The commander did not wait for him to list the whole array of honorific titles that the Emperor had recently bestowed upon himself. He looked at his subordinate with the impatience of a man who had been a tribune once himself. 'Oh, get on with it, or we'll be here all day.'

The tribune looked affronted, but he could not protest. The commander still outranked him and had seen action too, though instead of retreating back to Rome and politics he had stayed on in military service for the love of it. (Marcus said it was because life in the senate had become so uncertain and corrupt.) He opened his mouth, but nothing sensible came out.

I answered for him. 'That was my suggestion, commander, I'm afraid. I appealed to your authority. I'm sure my patron would have wanted it.'

'Indeed?' He was scattering powder from a

horn on to the ink, and then blowing it gently to dry off the writing. He had not glanced at us. 'And who exactly might your protector be?'

'Marcus Sept—' I began, and then he suddenly looked at me.

'Great Jupiter! Libertus! Are you here again?' But it was not unfriendly, and I thought I saw the glimmer of a smile. He was as lined and weathered as I'd remembered him, and the air of intelligence shone just as brightly from his eyes. 'And there is talk of murder, once again, I hear. You seem to attract troubles, like moths around a flame. What is it this time?'

The tribune gave a self-important cough. 'That, sir, is what I was hoping to explain. Permission to report?'

The commander nodded though he looked resigned, folding his arms across his breast-plate with a sigh.

The tribune adopted a dramatic stance and began reciting in an officious tone of voice. 'I was off-duty near the marketplace when I was accosted by this pavement-maker's slave...' He gave a potted description of events. 'So I brought these two in for questioning. I did not believe their version of what they were doing there.'

The commander listened carefully and heard him to the end. Then he turned his stool round so he looked at me. 'You will swear that you just happened to be passing, I suppose?'

I shook my head. 'Antoninus had actually asked me to be there. I hadn't met him face-to-face before, but he wanted me to come to him and specified the hour. I had a message from him, saying so, but I scratched it out to use the wax again.'

'Let me see.' He rose and walked towards me with an easy stride. He was no longer young but he was strong and powerful, with the athleticism born of daily sword practice in the yard. He made the young tribune look quite feeble and effete.

I handed him the wax tablet and he looked at it, turning the ivory over and over in his hands. 'This is a pretty thing,' he said, and it was obvious that Redux thought so too.

He was looking at it so greedily I thought he was about to offer me a goodly sum for it, but all he said was, 'Foreign workmanship.'

The tribune stepped forward. 'It's only a receipt, sir. I looked at it before. Something about a salver. Nothing relevant.'

The commander cocked an enquiring eye at me, and I explained. 'I would expect the man to have delivered it by now,' I said. 'I asked the man to bring it to the gatehouse here. It belongs to Marcus Septimus. I could not take a risk. This man' – I indicated Redux – 'could vouch for that at least. He himself was warning me about the risk of thieves. At one time he even wanted me to sell the tray to him.'

Redux was still staring at the tablet fixedly, but he pulled himself together and said sullenly, 'I thought that's what he'd come for. But it is the truth. He did have a salver when he first arrived and he may well have given it to the soldier as he claims – that's what he said that he was going to do.'

'You doubted it?' The commander didn't give the tablet back to me. His face had creased into a slight frown.

'At the time, I did. When he refused to sell, and I learned where he was going, I thought he was going to use it to pay Antoninus. If Antoninus knew his clients couldn't pay, he would sometimes agree to take goods instead of cash – though he valued them at much less than their market price, of course – and that tray is very much the sort of thing he always liked. But it seems Libertus really did arrange to send it here – certainly he wasn't carrying it when we went through the town.'

The tribune swaggered forward, all pomposity. 'Well, that should be easy to determine, shouldn't it? We could summon the gatekeeper and ask if it's arrived.'

The commander looked from him to me and back again. 'Or better still, tribune, you may run downstairs and enquire. And I do mean run, please. I want an answer soon. I'll go on questioning these gentlemen.'

The tribune looked mortified, but there was no appeal from a senior officer and he was obliged to troop downstairs and act the messenger for me, as if he were merely some humble new recruit. We could hear him panting – moving fast in armour is an acquired skill.

'Impudent young puppy! His father has pulled a string or two in Rome to have him found a posting – and what is the result? Puts on some fancy armour and thinks it gives him leave to come here and advise me on how to do my job. Do you know he tried to countermand an order yesterday? If it wasn't for his youth and family, I should have him flogged! But I'll teach him a lesson or two before he leaves.' The commander seemed to be talking to himself, but I knew that the explanation was addressed to me – in case I told Marcus later, I supposed.

I nodded. There did not seem to be anything to say.

'However, he has brought this case to me and I suppose that I must deal with it as best I can.' He had been pacing up and down the room, but he stopped in front of Redux and looked thoughtfully at him. 'Now, I know you, Libertus, though I must confess I find your story this time rather thin – but who is this would-be purchaser of precious silver goods, with a taste for finery and fancy cuffs?

And what was he doing at the dead man's home with you?'

The question seemed to be addressed to me again, so I replied explaining how Redux had been showing me the way and how he got to the apartment first.

'So, he had the opportunity to be there on his own?' The commander was still talking exclusively to me, as though Redux was a mute, and Redux was doing little to prove the opposite.

I nodded. 'Though, to be just, it wasn't his dagger that was sticking in the corpse.'

That roused Redux into speech at last. 'I did not kill Antoninus!' He sounded drained and sad. 'He would have deserved it, he was cruel and devious, and getting rid of him would be a service to the state. But I did not do it. When I got there, he was already dead. I can't prove that, of course, except I scarcely had the time – and you can see for yourself that there's no blood on me. Surely you would have expected it, if somebody was stabbed.'

The commander looked thoughtful. 'That isn't always so. When a knife is left inside a wound, it doesn't always spurt. Though the tribune seems to think that it was poisoned anyway and it killed the victim instantly. Was that your impression? Did he look as if he'd made an effort to defend himself?'

Redux shook his head. 'I don't know anything about such things. You'd better ask Libertus, he's the expert, I believe. I am a simple trader, and that takes up all my time.' He sounded petulant.

'Yet you accompanied Libertus halfway round the town, when – by your own admission – you'd gone back to work?' The commander folded his arms across his breastplate again. 'Were you not afraid of losing trade while you were out?'

Redux had the grace to look very much abashed. 'I was supposed to be at a wedding anyway, today. No one was expecting to find me at my desk.'

'Or Antoninus either?' the commander said. 'It's a riddle, isn't it? Yet somebody must have known that they would find him at his home – and, what is more, that he would be alone. Now who could possibly have known that – except the pair of you? And Libertus, I am including you in this.'

Seventeen

For the first time since we had reached the garrison I felt a surge of fear. When I had suggested that the tribune bring us here, I knew the commander would remember me – as indeed he had – but I thought my record (and my patron's name) would have protected us from unpleasantness. But it was clear that this was no token interview. The commander had been sharp with Redux, certainly – subjecting him to pointed questioning and generally making his suspicions clear – but somehow I hadn't expected him to take that tone with me.

That last remark had shown me how badly wrong I was. The commander was harbouring serious doubts about my involvement in the day's events – and I could not blame him, on the face of it.

I swallowed. We could still hear the soldiers down below, forming up and rattling their javelins on their shields. It was a sound designed to be threatening and unnerving to the enemy, and it was certainly successful in unnerving me.

I was seriously wishing I'd consented to the jail – where a bribe or two, and an appeal to rich acquaintances (like Gracchus for example) will usually secure one's comfort overnight – and buy the time to send for witnesses. But if I could not persuade the commander of our innocence, I had no illusions about how unpleasant the next few hours might be. He was not a man to shirk his duty, as he conceived of it. If he could treat a tribune with conspicuous disdain – a young man of patrician birth, with the protection of the Roman army at his back – how would he treat those under suspicion of a heinous crime?

'Well, Libertus?' the commander said again. 'What have you to say? It seems to me to be unusual for a wealthy citizen to be alone with no attendants when expecting guests.'

That was true, of course – and all I could do was offer an excuse. 'Redux tells me that the dead man always sent his slaves away whenever he had private business to conduct,' I blurted, knowing that I sounded like the schoolboy telling his tutor that the dog had gnawed up his homework on his copy-tablet.

The commander turned to Redux with an unsmiling face. 'So you have had dealings with the man before?' I had forgotten how acutely perceptive he could be. 'And what was his business exactly, citizen?'

Redux said nothing. I could have shaken him. This was no moment to evade the truth.

The commander thought so too. 'I advise you not to be obstructive, citizen. I have means of dealing with people who refuse to answer me. And understand that I can find the information anyway, in time, simply by making enquiries elsewhere. And we have soldiers searching his documents right now. So, have you anything to tell me about him, citizen?'

Redux had turned even redder than he'd been when he was out of breath. He gave me a look which said – as clearly as if he'd spoken the words aloud – that this was my fault for having insisted that the tribune brought us here. He turned to the commander, and said reluctantly, 'I hear he made a business out of making threats. Obtaining information that was dangerous to a man in public life, and demanding money not to pass it on.'

The commander went back to his stool and picked up the writing tablet again. 'So he sent you this, Libertus, summoning you to him? But you have rubbed the message out? I think I shall keep this tablet for a while.' He put it into a compartment in his desk. 'And you have no idea what he might want with you? Some kind of "private business" as your friend might say, since

Antoninus had sent away his slaves?'

It did look suspicious when you thought of it like that. The rattle of the javelins had stopped abruptly now, and in the sudden silence my words seemed very loud. 'He was looking for promotion to the council, I believe. He may have wanted to ask me to put in a word for him, once he discovered I was Marcus's protégé. That's all that I can think of, I swear on all the gods. Or perhaps he had some information about someone else, which he was hoping to pass on to me – for a reward, perhaps.' My throat was dry and I was gabbling.

Redux gave a bitter little laugh. 'You could not have afforded his prices, citizen.'

The commander was instantly on his feet again. 'So you know what they are? You must have paid them, Redux, to know a thing like that. Antoninus obviously had some kind of hold on you. I think you'd better tell me what it was about.' Redux said nothing, and the commander came and stood within an inch or two of him. 'I assure you it is easier for you to tell me now, than make me send for someone who'll persuade it out of you.'

It was a threat and Redux looked appalled. He took a step backwards. 'But I'm a citizen!'

The Roman followed him, standing even closer than he was before. 'But Antoninus was a candidate for local government and

Honorius was a senior magistrate. If these deaths are connected, it is a state affair. The law permits extraordinary measures in such a case.' He stressed the word 'extraordinary', and my blood ran cold.

Redux was as pale as he'd been red before. In the last few moments all his fire had gone. He looked beaten and defeated. He took a deep breath. 'Very well,' he said. 'I suppose it hardly matters now, in any case, since both men are dead. It was something concerning Honorius himself – a little business deal that I had made with him. I sold him a statue – it was very fine. The thing is, it was not quite honestly obtained – and Honorius may have known it, but he went ahead anyway.'

'It was stolen?' The commander sounded shocked – not at the idea of theft, I guessed, but at the idea of Honorius conniving in the deal.

Redux swallowed. 'Something of the kind. Naturally it wasn't shipped here in its proper form. It was covered in a rough clay cast that looked like something else – a sort of clumsy copy of the original. I had no part in that side of things, of course. I simply arranged for it to come from Rome, and Honorius bought it from me in the normal way. Of course it was a risk, and the price reflected that. When he got it home he took the coating off and revealed the marble that was underneath. I saw it in the inner courtyard at his house today.'

I nodded. 'I think I know the one. Minerva, isn't it? I marvelled at the craftsmanship when I first noticed it.'

Redux gave me a murderous glance. He clearly blamed me for our predicament. 'I told him it was dangerous to put the thing on show. Anyone with half an eye could see the quality – and naturally the statue has been missed from Rome, though admittedly it is unlikely that they'd seek it here.'

'Where did it come from?' the commander snapped. 'Not the Imperial Residence?' He sounded as if he could not believe the import of his words.

'I don't know and I didn't want to know,' Redux protested, but it was clear he did. 'Zythos arranged it when he was in Rome. I just sold the statue as it was when it arrived and no one can prove that I did otherwise.'

It was my turn to groan inwardly by now. Stealing from the Emperor was a capital offence – and Commodus had perfected some interesting deaths for people who had recently offended him. One bald man, for instance, who had spoken out of turn had been smeared with honey, had worms stuck to his head, and been tied to a post and pecked to death by crows – or so rumour had it. What would he do to someone who had stolen treasures from his house?

The commander had more pressing

questions on his mind. 'And Honorius knew its provenance?'

'I think he must have done, to pay that price for it – though I have no proof of that. But somehow Antoninus managed to find out that I had made the sale. And he demanded a huge sum from me – far more than the profit that I would have made, in fact. I had to pay, of course. The Emperor has spies in this colonia, as he does everywhere. If the stolen statue could be traced to me...' He trailed off, obviously realizing the awful truth of this.

'But how did Antoninus come to learn of it?' the commander's voice was grim.

Redux shook his head. 'That's what I'd like to know. I'm not even certain exactly what he knew, except that the statue had been shipped from Rome – and that Zythos had been responsible for arranging it. He had some paper that proved it all, he said – and if I refused to pay, he threatened to take it to the magistrates. He would never let me see the document close to, though he held it in his hand and used to taunt me with it when I went to visit him.'

'And you couldn't find it when you searched the papers on his desk today?' I said.

I think that Redux had half-forgotten me. He whirled now with sudden fury on his face, and I thought for a moment that he would lay hands on me, but all of a sudden his shoulders drooped and he said, sullenly, 'You realized that I was doing that? Well, I won't deny it. I did look for it. But it wasn't there – nothing that could possibly relate to any part of it.' He looked discomfited. 'I wish I'd had the chance to look inside the scroll jars, too – though it was only written on a little piece of bark.'

'Like the ones that he was working with?' I said.

'Exactly. But when I first got there and found him lying dead, I was too shocked to think of anything like that. I didn't think of searching through the items on the desk until you were with me – and then I couldn't do it openly, of course.'

'So it wasn't you that burnt things on the brazier?' I asked.

'I didn't know that anybody had. I suppose you might be trusted to notice such a thing.'

'Answer the question,' the commander snapped, and I was coward enough to feel relieved. I'd become part of the interrogation now.

Redux gave a shamefaced shrug. 'I might have thought of setting fire to it, if I had found it, I suppose – but I was far too slow. I told you, I didn't even manage to locate the document.'

'So it must be still there somewhere?' the commander said.

Redux's plump face looked ashen now.

'That's what worries me. I could not find it, even though I searched. I hope it hasn't fallen into someone else's hands. Though probably it wouldn't mean a lot to anybody else. It can only be a note or a receipt, I think – unless he managed to find something indiscreet that Zythos wrote, perhaps to a shipmaster or even to the thief. But I can't imagine why that would mention me, I didn't know anything about that end of it. Yet the document would ruin me, so Antoninus said. I only wish I knew exactly what it was.'

'I shall have my soldiers search the premises, and bring everything to me.' The commander rose abruptly to his feet. 'From what you tell me, an examination of his records should prove educational – perhaps about a number of people in the town. As for you—'

But he got no further, a sudden clatter of hobnails on the stairs, and the tribune appeared looking flushed and cross. 'Permission to report? The salver that you speak of has just been brought in now, and the soldier who brought it wants to speak to you. He refuses to part with it without seeing the receipt – he said there was promise of a fee for it. And there is another person asking for you at the gate – a woman with two slaves. The witness that this pavement-maker called on, I believe.'

The commander nodded. 'We'll see the

woman first. You can show her up and tell the man I'll see him afterwards. As quickly as you can.' And the tribune, to his chagrin, had yet another ignominious descent downstairs to make.

Eighteen

I had expected to see Helena Domna at the door but it was Livia who was shown into the room. She wore a long, dark-hooded cloak over her mourning robes, and beneath the hood the veil was double draped across her face – as befitted a new widow in a public place – so one could not see her features; but despite the drapery, the plump little figure was unmistakable. She was accompanied by her pageboy, and by Pulchra too – their tunics now bearing a dark band around the hem and neck. Minimus came in behind them, slightly out of breath.

'This is the person that I spoke of, sir,' the tribune said, as though the slaves did not exist at all – which I suppose they didn't in his view of things.

The commander nodded. 'Thank you, officer. I will call you if I need you. Wait below.' And the poor fellow had to trot all the way downstairs again, looking as discomfited as a chastised child. I could almost feel a little sorry for the man.

Livia stepped forward, and lifted up the veil as if in this dim light she found it difficult to see. The action revealed that she had smeared her brow and hair with dust and ashes, as good widows did, but her face was still attractive, though it was strained and white. In fact, she looked so visibly distressed that even the commander was moved to a kind of awkward gallantry.

'Madam citizen!' He smiled encouragingly at her.

She gave an uncertain little smile in return, then bowed her head as modesty required. After a moment she said in a small voice, 'Gentlemen, I understand that you have asked for me, and so in obedience to the law I've come – though I am in mourning for my husband, as I am sure you know, and by tradition I should not leave the house.'

Pulchra tutted. 'The poor lamb only had an open litter too – all she could find in time – though perhaps it's just as well. It meant I saw her passing, in the marketplace. It shocked me, dreadfully.' She glowered at me. 'I hope it's important, now you've dragged her here. With her husband lying dead! You've only got to look at her to see that she's upset.'

'Hush, Pulchra!' It was obvious that Livia

was very close to tears. 'I'm sorry, citizens. My servant means no disrespect to you. I'd sent her to the silversmith to buy this locket ring' – she held out her hand for me to see the ring that she was wearing on the fourth finger of her hand, the one that sages say connects directly to the heart – 'and when she saw me she insisted on accompanying me here.'

I found it somehow touching that she should wear a mourning ornament like that. Granted that it was becoming the custom nowadays, that ring had been almost the first thing that she'd thought of sending for.

I smiled at her, and it seemed to give her heart. 'So citizens, what is it that I can do for you?'

The commander said formally, 'Libertus will explain.'

She turned to me. 'Of course, I will help you in any way I can, but I am sorry I must ask you to be as swift as possible. I must return to take my place at the lament.'

She sounded so tearful I was instantly contrite. 'I'm truly sorry to have dragged you here at such a time. I had expected to have Helena Domna come, if anyone. I was hoping that she would agree to testify on my account. There was a writing tablet which arrived for me today, while I was in your home. Your mother-in-law saw it, and read the message too – so she could have confirmed my own account of it. But I'm not sure you can. I hope we have not taken you unnecessarily away from the rituals which you should perform.'

'My mother-in-law was not available,' she said. 'She has insisted on being the first at the lament, and of course it was impossible to interrupt her there. She will not be pleased to find I've come here in her stead, but perhaps I can offer the confirmation your require. I did not see the message, but I heard of it. Would that be evidence enough?'

I shook my head. 'The real question is about what was written in the note. You see, Antoninus had invited me to visit him today and actually specified the time that I should come. I was found in what looked like guilty circumstances at his apartment, shortly after his dead body had been found.'

'No one told me that.' Suddenly she was standing very still. 'But it is certain? Antoninus is dead?'

I nodded. 'And not long before I got there, by the look of it.'

'I see!' She looked wildly around the room, and then composed herself. 'It seems there was a curse upon our wedding feast! Well, citizen, at least I can confirm what you said about the note. Helena Domna made a point of telling me that Antoninus had invited you. You were to call on him at the ninth hour she said – and of course that was after the wedding was postponed, so you could not have planned beforehand to go and murder him. Is that what is required? I could even identify the writing tablet that was used, I think. I understand it was unusual, and my mother-in-law described it vividly to me.' She gazed around the guardroom as if to look for it.

The commander shook his head. 'That will not be necessary. You have said quite enough to verify that Libertus was telling me the truth. I do not think we'll need to detain you very long. Just one question more. Can you confirm that your wedding guests were not required to bring a knife?'

She shrugged dismissively. 'They would not have needed one. Our household makes a practice of supplying them. Why do you ask that? Did Antoninus have one with him when he died?'

The commander raised an eyebrow at me. 'In a manner of speaking, you might say so,' he observed.

Any irony was clearly lost on her. 'Well, I suppose he would have eaten when he got home again. Few of our guests remained to take refreshment after my poor husband died – and Antoninus was amongst the earliest to be gone.' Her voice was wavering,

'Then...' The commander gestured to the door.

She pulled the veil across her face, as if to

leave and beckoned Pulchra to accompany her. Then all at once she seemed to change her mind. She whirled around again. 'Oh, Jupiter! I suppose, I shall have to tell the truth. It will only come out in questioning, if you speak to anyone. I was very foolish, I can see that now. But now he's dead!' She clapped both hands against her face. 'Oh gentlemen, I'm very much afraid that I occasioned it...' She tailed off, and then said in some distress, 'I'm sorry, citizens.' She looked as if she were ready to collapse.

The commander took her arm and led her to the stool, poured out a little of his own jug of wine and lifted the pewter goblet to her lips. It was not until she'd raised the netting from her face and taken a good swallow that he spoke again. 'You occasioned it, you say? What do you mean by that?'

She shook her head. 'I think I might have...' She reached for the cup herself and took another sip. 'You know he had private dealings with my husband, I suppose?'

I saw Redux stiffen, and he glanced at me. He was thinking about that statue, that seemed very clear. 'What about?' he asked.

She shook her head. 'He never told me that. I only know that quite a lot of coins were changing hands and they would spend a long time closeted alone. Antoninus was always spoken of as though he was simply an ambitious friend and he always brought a gift of some kind when he called – as people do when they want patronage – but I tell you, citizens, I didn't trust the man. My husband always seemed terse and preoccupied whenever they had met.' She took another furtive swallow of the commander's wine. 'I sometimes wondered if Antoninus was actually a spy, whether for the Emperor or Honorius himself. He used to call on my husband very late sometimes.'

'As he did last night, for instance,' I put in quietly. I was not sure where this was leading, but I was interested.

She put the wine cup down and looked at me, surprised. 'I don't know how you know that, but indeed that's true. I tried to find out what he'd come about, but he would not say. They were closeted together for an hour or two, and I confess I stood outside the door and tried to listen in, but I could only catch a muttered word or two. Then my mother-in-law found me and I had to go away. But he was there – and that's the point, you see.'

The commander glanced at me. 'I don't see at all. What has all this to do with how he died?'

'Well, when he came it seems he brought some garum as a gift – the most expensive kind that you can only get in Rome. The usual present for my husband, I suppose. I found a small container of it in his room

228

today and knew at once it was not one of ours.'

'You didn't mention any such amphora earlier,' I said rather sharply, 'when I was asking about your husband's death?'

She seemed to feel that I had been severe, because she rose and went to gaze at the goddess in the niche – as if to ask forgiveness from the deity. When she spoke her voice was quavering. 'I did not really know of it, until you'd left the house,' she said. 'Helena Domna found it, and mentioned it to me. With all the preparations for the wedding feast today, I had not been in the room, but she went in to get some grave goods from his private chest to lay around his bier. She brought it out to me.' She paused again.

'And...?' the commander prompted.

She took a long deep breath before she said, 'I have never cared for Antoninus, and I sent it back. I did not want to seem to be accepting gifts from him. Can you understand? It was a signal that I did not want him calling at the house when I was vulnerable and on my own.' She turned to face us, and there were tears upon her cheeks. 'But then when I heard that he was lying dead ... well, you can imagine what I thought. It would be a kind of dreadful justice, wouldn't it, if Antoninus died from eating his own poisoned food. The same food that had poisoned my husband earlier?'

'But Antoninus wasn't—' Redux had begun, but I interrupted him.

'Surely the garum was unopened, though? You would not have sent it back to him half-used? And how could anything your husband ate last night possibly have affected him so suddenly today?'

She looked startled for a moment, then she gave a nervous laugh. 'You are quite right, of course. It was stoppered, and it was obviously full. So Honorius could not have tasted it today – I wondered for a moment if he might have done. Well, there you are, I have confessed my foolish act – I thought that I should tell you at once, while I was here.' She raised her limpid eyes to me and smiled.

I was still wondering if this might be relevant. 'You are quite sure that it was Antoninus who brought it?' I enquired. 'It could not have been a gift from someone else?'

'I'm as certain as I can be, in the circumstance. The doorman confirms that he arrived with it. And I am sure, Libertus, that he would tell you the same thing, if you care to come and speak to him again. And now...' She was visibly shaking with what might have been relief. 'If there is no more that I can help you with, perhaps I might go home.' She tailed off and broke into little breathless sobs, until Pulchra bustled forward.

'There, there, madam. Do not distress yourself. This is not your doing. It will be all right.' She patted Livia's hand and murmured to her, as though she were a child.

The commander was clearly embarrassed by this emotional display. He was a military man, and not used to female ways. He gave an awkward cough. 'Madam citizen, your servant is quite right. You obviously haven't heard how Antoninus died?'

'But surely he was poisoned? I thought ... That is, I supposed ... After Honorius...' She made a helpless little gesture with her hands.

Redux had been bursting to say something all along, and now he could contain himself no longer. 'He wasn't poisoned. He was lying dead across his desk. Somebody had stuck a knife into his back.'

'Stabbed?' Her voice was almost shrill with shock. 'But who? How?' She paused and with an obvious effort to regain her self-control, turned to the commander. 'That's why you asked about the knife?'

He nodded. 'Though it is just possible the blade was poisoned, I believe. The tribune thought it was. Largely because the victim had clearly died at once.'

She got up abruptly from the stool at this. 'So, it might yet have been dipped in that amphora?' she began, pressing her hands against her heart again.

The commander looked at me. I shook my

head. 'I doubt that very much. The toxin would not be strong enough to kill him,' I explained. 'Not if it was diluted in the garum. Remember that it took your husband a little time to die – he stumbled and the servants thought at first that he was merely taken sick – and he would have swallowed quite a lot of poison in the wine. So it would be surprising if Antoninus died at once from the small amount of the same concoction that could be carried on a blade.'

'Ah!' She let out a little sigh and smiled tremulously at us. 'So it was not my fault at all? You are quite sure of that? So you won't be needing me?' This time she did drop the veil across her face again.

'I think it would be sensible to test the garum, though, if the commander could arrange that for us?' I said. 'I'm sure he could find a convicted criminal, who would be glad of a swift death – just in case there should be anything amiss.'

'Of course. There would be several candidates – specially if I offered a pardon should the man survive.' The commander seemed delighted that he had found a job to do. He turned to Livia, who was looking dubious. 'Don't worry about the fate of the criminal, my dear. He would have died in any case. And Libertus is quite right, we should do the test. Somebody poisoned your husband, after all.'

'Perhaps we should test the other food as well,' I said. I had been watching Redux all this while. He had lost his demeanour of effete, plump elegance and was twisting his fingers together like an impatient girl, as if he were uncertain whether to speak out. I decided for him. 'Though I think we can ignore the wine jug on the window shelf, since Redux has already tested that for us.'

He had turned scarlet. 'How did you know that?'

'I wasn't certain of it – until now – although I thought it possible. When the tribune came and was half-accusing you, you were ready to pour yourself a drink, though there were people watching and it was a very unusual thing to do. It all suggested that you turned to wine in moments of distress. When you found the corpse you were in the room alone. It must have been a shock. It seemed very likely that you would have had a drink – and when the tribune mentioned poison, you were quite alarmed. And you have just confirmed it.'

'You can see why my master is so good at solving mysteries!' I had forgotten Minimus who was standing behind us all this while. He and the pageboy must have heard all this. I turned to rebuke him, but the words died on my lips as the tribune reappeared with a clatter of hobnailed sandals on the stairs.

He stood at the doorway with my salver in

his hand, and the soldier I had entrusted with it at his heels.

'Your pardon for this intrusion, sir, I beg.' The tribune looked flustered, and embarrassed, too. 'But this soldier is wanted on parade and he refuses to part with this to anyone, until he has sight of the receipt. Says that he was half-promised a reward.'

'This is insubordination, tribune. I shall see you later on. I made it clear that we were not to be disturbed.' The commander sounded coldly angry, and the young man quailed. 'But I suppose, that since you've brought the fellow here...' The commander opened the compartment on his desk and took the tablet out. 'Is this what you require?'

I stepped forward to claim it, but it was the page who spoke. 'But, madam, surely that's your lost writing block?'

Nineteen

There was a moment's startled silence. Everyone looked from me to Livia, but she didn't say a word. She had pushed her veil back again, and was staring at the writing tablet with evident dismay. Redux, I noticed, was also eyeing it, with the same anxiety that

234

he'd evinced before. The commander waited, but no one moved or spoke.

The stillness seemed to hang heavy in the room. We could hear the barking of orders down below as the detachment in the courtyard began to march away and some hapless laggard being singled out, and put on extra duties and penal rations for a week. At this the soldier with the salver gave a nervous little cough, and I realized that he was anxious to be allowed to leave. No doubt he feared additional fatigues and a diet of thin porridge for being late himself.

I felt rather guilty. He was here at my behest. I broke the tension by speaking suddenly. 'Thank you, soldier, for bringing in the tray, and for taking charge of it for me,' I said. 'There will be a reward for you, when Marcus Septimus comes back from Rome – and these citizens are witnesses to my word on that.' I spoke with what I hoped was confidence, but secretly I prayed that Marcus would honour my contract when he heard. 'In the meantime you may leave the salver with the commander here. I'll ask him to keep it in the garrison, until my patron comes. It is much safer than my carrying it home with me tonight – miles in the dark on unfrequented roads.'

'And that document you wrote as a receipt? You'll erase my name from it?'

I gestured towards the writing tablet in the

commander's hand. 'There it is. You can countersign it now. These citizens will witness that you brought the salver here, and therefore you are entitled to a reward.'

The soldier took the tablet. He made a show of reading it, scrawled his initials on the wax again and gave it back. Then – with obvious relief – he put the salver on the table, saluted and withdrew. We could hear him clattering pell-mell down the stairs. The tribune, after a moment, sighed and followed him.

The commander turned to Livia and me. 'I'm happy to take charge of His Excellence's tray. But what am I to do about this writing block? There seems to be some question as to whose it is. Lady, your servant appears to think that it is yours.'

Livia had recovered her composure now. She gave a little laugh. 'It looks like it certainly. But I lost mine a long, long way from here. We were on the way to visit relatives, and it was stolen from the luggage wagon when we were in an inn. Pulchra will remember.'

Pulchra did. She nodded eagerly. 'Your husband was angry at your carelessness. He had them search the inn from floor to roof, and flogged the servants who should have been on guard, but it was never found.'

'You see?' Livia said sweetly. 'How could Antoninus have got hold of it? Besides, I'm not so sure that this is so much like it, after all. May I examine it?' She took it from the officer and undid the ties. 'What do you think Pulchra?'

The woman examined it, and then gave it back. 'Well, it is certainly very similar, but I don't think it's the same. For instance, I think this one may have been rewaxed and yours had certainly never been repaired.'

I nodded. It is not uncommon for a favourite tablet to have the wax removed and replaced with new, especially if the casing is a fine one – as this was. There is a limit to how many messages can be written and erased before the writing surface becomes too thin, and the stylus begins to scratch the wooden backing block or even cause damage to the case itself.

The pageboy refused to be deterred. 'But surely, mistress? This fretwork near the hinge...? It's so unusual, there can't be two of them.'

'Foreign handiwork, so Redux tells me,' I remarked. 'It may be that he can throw some further light upon its history. Let him have a closer look at it. I have the impression that he recognizes it.'

I thought to shame him, but he took the block and turned it reverently in his hands. 'Ivory, from the African provinces, by the look of it. Fine work, and as you say, un-usual. Hand carved by an artist – and quite a masterpiece. I have never seen another quite as intricate.'

'But you have seen this before?' I tried to press the point.

He gave me that poisonous look again. 'Or something very like it – as the lady said. My partner Zythos had one for a while. I cannot swear that it was this – I did not get so close a look at it – but it was similar. I suppose there may be others carved by the same man.'

Livia clapped her hands. 'Then that explains it. Don't you see? Zythos was the one who provided me with mine. No doubt he imported them all from the same source. Perhaps Antoninus bought one from him too. My husband meant to pay for ours, of course, but Zythos insisted on giving it to us – a pretty trinket for a pretty lady, he declared.'

'Then he was a fool! This is no trinket, it's a lovely thing. This would command the highest price in any marketplace.' Redux was speaking angrily, but Livia shook her head.

'I think he hoped to influence my husband to a deal. Something about a statue he was hoping to import.'

Redux relaxed at this quite visibly. 'Ah, perhaps you're right. Compared to Minerva, this tablet is a trinket, I suppose. But if he imported these, he did so privately. I have never dealt in anything like this – I only wish

I had.' He turned it over and opened it again. 'Though it seems that this has been much used. Your servant is correct. The wax has been replaced.'

'Well, that settles it!' Livia declared. 'If there had been any damage to my writing block, Honorius would have bought me a new one instantly. So it is certain that I have no claim to this.'

'Then I'll give it to the pavement-maker,' the commander said. 'It was sent to him – and Antoninus won't be needing it again.'

'By all means,' Livia murmured graciously.

'But...' Pulchra began. Her mistress silenced her.

'Even if it were mine – which it is clearly not – I would let Libertus have it,' she declared. 'I wouldn't want anything which Antoninus had defiled – and the pavement-maker has deserved a gift from us. He has spent his whole day trying to clear Pompeia's name – and see what his kindness has resulted in! Brought in for questioning about a death! I only hope my coming here to speak for him has helped. Speaking of which, commander...?' She dropped the veil again.

'I must let you go – of course!' The commander was playing his gallant role again. 'You have rituals to attend to and you will be missed. I apologize for having kept you here so long.' He turned to the page. 'You, lad, go out into the street and find a litter quickly for this lady citizen. Tell the bearers they are to take her home as fast as possible, and the commander of the garrison will pay.' And then, since the slave-boy was goggling in surprise: 'Well, boy, what are you waiting for?'

The pageboy still looked startled but he trotted off downstairs and we heard him speaking to the tribune at the door.

The old commander cocked an eye at me. 'And I suppose I shall have to let you go as well – and your companion in the fancy sleeves. Ah...!' He broke off as the pageboy reappeared again.

'I have found a litter, it was right outside. They are waiting for you, mistress, at the outer gate. Only...' He hesitated and I saw that his ears were turning pink. 'The bearers want to know if you will pay them now, or whether they should come back for the money afterwards.'

The Roman looked as if he might explode, but Livia put a gentle hand upon his arm. 'It is all right, commander. Do not concern yourself. I will see that the litter slaves are paid when I get home. But thank you for your kindness. Pulchra, follow me.' And she turned and went downstairs, before the soldier had the chance to offer her an arm.

'So we may go as well?' Redux and I exchanged glances of relief, but we were too hasty. The commander spoke again.

'I fear that we have not finished with you yet. I shall have my troops search Antoninus's house for useful evidence, and question the people in the neighbourhood. When they have done that, I'll speak to you again. Tomorrow, at the sixth hour, I'll expect you here. On pain of being sent for and arrested, otherwise.'

That was a surprise, and not a pleasant one. 'Arrested!' I exclaimed.

The commander turned to me. 'I've done my best for you. I am exceeding my authority in letting you go now. And don't think I won't imprison you, Libertus, because I will – I will be obliged to, since the tribune has accused you of a crime, and brought you before me according to the law. If there is no other suspect by the time that you come back, I will be forced to take you into custody. And make sure you appear on time, the pair of you, or I shall have to send my guards to come and bring you in – and they will be a good deal less gentle than the tribune was.'

I nodded glumly. 'You'll take the noonday trumpet as a sign?' I asked. The sixth hour was only approximate to me, but the army had good methods of assessing time. Halfway through the day was naturally noon, and trumpet was always sounded at that hour on the steps of the basilica each day, to mark the end of court proceedings. It was reasonably accurate if the day was fine. But if the sky

241

was overcast, as it had been today, the trumpeter had to make an estimate of when the sun had reached its height – and once the call had sounded it was officially too late. I would have to ensure that I allowed sufficient time for the trumpeter to get his calculations wrong. 'Let us hope that it is sunny, then.'

The commander grunted and went back to his desk. 'Remember. Tomorrow. Make sure you're not late.' And he busied himself with his affairs again, evidently expecting the pair of us to leave.

Redux was already on the topmost step, but I still lingered by the stool. The commander looked up sharply. 'Well?'

'The writing tablet?' I ventured. I hardly liked to ask, but he handed it to me without another word, and I followed Redux down into the yard, sending Minimus ahead to try to find a hiring-carriage that would take us home. We emerged from the stairway, blinking in the light.

The tribune was standing by the entrance looking grim. 'So, he has let you go?'

'Only till tomorrow,' Redux said, and made him smile.

'Tribune?' A voice came roaring from above, and the soldier was forced to race upstairs again.

But I was not smiling as I strode towards the gate. Matters had taken a sorry turn for me. If I could not offer a solution very soon, it seemed as if I would be brought to trial – and without even Marcus to speak up for me. I wondered if Junio could take over my role and try to make enquiries into this unhappy mess.

The courtyard was deserted now, the cohort had all gone and only the off-duty centurion in his den and the gatekeeper on duty were there to see us go. I could hear my sandals ringing on the cobbled yard – and I was aware of someone else's hurrying after me.

I turned to find Redux, already out of breath. 'So, clever pavement-maker, what do we do now? Have you got some other lead you wish to follow up?' He saw my startled look. 'Well, I'll have to help you, won't I? For my own sake now. You heard what the commander said about arresting us, if there was no other likely candidate.'

I gazed at him, hopelessly. 'And what do you suggest?'

He shook his head. 'You are supposed to be the expert, I believe. Though I can't say I'm delighted with your progress up to now. Apart from getting us arrested and having us brought here, it doesn't seem to me that you've done anything at all.'

I said sadly, 'I believe you're right. We now have two corpses, instead of only one – and I have no idea exactly how either of them died. Or what there is in common, between the two of them—'

He interrupted. 'But surely, there was poison in both cases, wasn't there? The tribune said he thought so.'

'I know what he said. But Redux – you are a man of some intelligence. You have demonstrated that to me a dozen times. And you saw Antoninus – how he was slumped at the desk. Did he look like a man who'd died of poisoning to you?'

He stopped and stared at me. 'I don't know what you mean?'

'Oh, the usual symptoms. Skin a funny colour, foam around the lips, looking as though he'd died in agony. Anything like that?'

'Great Mars!' Redux was suddenly alert. 'Of course there wasn't, now you mention it. He looked quite peaceful – or perhaps surprised – as though he'd died of fright. You think that's what happened?'

'Died of fright, but with a knife stuck in his back?' I said. 'That doesn't sound a likely circumstance to me. But something happened, and I don't know what.'

'There must be lots of people who would like to see him dead,' Redux mused. 'I was afraid, when I saw that writing block, that he'd had some hold on poor old Zythos at one time – but it seems that it wasn't necessarily the case. But you'll question other

244

people. Gracchus possibly? I've noticed him avoiding Antoninus once or twice. It makes me wonder if he might have had dealings with him, in the past.'

That might explain why Gracchus was in debt, I thought. I said aloud, 'You're right! I'd better talk to him. And probably to Maesta and her husband too, but that will be tomorrow – if I can manage it. For now, I'm going home. It's getting late. The sun will soon be setting and the guards will shut the gates. It may be the last time that I walk out of them. Besides, my wife will be anxious for my safety by this time. She must have expected me to come home long ago.'

Redux surprised me. 'And mine will be throwing a pretty tantrum too.' I had never heard any mention of a wife – indeed, I had the impression he was not the marrying kind. He grinned at me. 'I know what you're thinking – but I do have a wife. Isn't it the duty of every citizen? Marry and raise up new generations for the state. Zythos thought so – and my brother too. Though he has only a daughter to show for it, so far.'

'Miles was married before Honoria?'

He grinned. 'He was – but it's Honoria's daughter all the same. His first wife perished, giving him a son who was weak and died a few days afterwards. That's why Miles was so anxious about the latest pregnancy – insisting that Honoria always slept in her own bed and didn't come to Glevum to see her family. Ironic that it should be that which killed her in the end. Honoria was healthy – she'd have borne him heirs. But I thought you already knew all this?'

I shook my head. But of course, I should have done. Honorius had made a new will, hadn't he, disinheriting 'his eldest daughter and her heirs'. But his eldest daughter and her unborn baby were already dead – there was no call to write a new will over that. I should have realized that there had to be a living child.

'I am getting very old,' I said, and I went through the gate, though not without a strange look from the man on guard. People who have been arrested by a tribune and brought in, do not often walk so calmly out again. Near the archway that led into the town, I could see Redux's servant leaning on the wall, with a pair of stouter sandals in his hand. The last I saw of Redux, he was changing into them. I turned the other way.

The garrison was adjacent to the south gate of the town, and Minimus was waiting outside with the carriage and driver he had hired.

Twenty

It took a long time to get home, even so. We had to go the long way, on the military road – no carriage-driver would willingly take the older Celtic track, with its boggy hollows, corners and vertiginous descents – but the newer route was mostly quicker anyway, especially in the dusk. The road was busy, as it always was towards the end of day, with carts and wagons coming to make deliveries; no civilian horse-drawn transport was permitted on the streets, until the town gates were ready to be shut.

There were few things going in our direction, though, and we made good progress. There was no military traffic to force us off the road – we did not even catch up with the soldiers from the garrison. I wondered if they had gone another route but as Minimus pointed out: 'They are trained to march twenty or thirty miles a day carrying full equipment, so a two-hour route-march is simple exercise to them. I wouldn't be surprised if we met them coming back!'

Indeed, as we turned off the main road on

to the gravelled spur that led to Marcus's estate – and therefore to my roundhouse which was built on part of it – I thought I did hear the sound of approaching marching feet and the clanking of armour from somewhere up ahead. But there was no time to think of that. The sun was setting further in the west, and the shadows of the forest were distinctly lengthening. The chill wind of evening was rustling the leaves and the first owl was hooting as it searched for its prey. The driver slowed the horses to a walk. At any moment, I thought, he might refuse to take us any further in this light. That would be a serious predicament. It was dangerous to be walking on unfrequented roads, in the forest, un-armed and in the dark.

I rapped on the back of the planks behind his seat. He stopped and craned over to look in on me. 'You wanted something, citizen?'

'Not much further now. I'll give you a brand to light yourself back home.'

He muttered something about not having realized how far it would be, and how he would not have taken the fare if he had known, but he did urge the horses slowly on again. After a few minutes, which seemed an age, I saw the roundhouse coming into sight and I signalled to the driver that it was time to stop. He drew up at the gate to the en-closure.

Minimus jumped down at once and helped

me to the ground. As he was doing so his partner, Maximus, came running from the house.

'Oh, master, you are home at last. The mistress was concerned. She was beginning to think of sending out a search party for you.' He grinned at Minimus. 'How was the wedding? Was it a good feast?'

'I'll tell you in a moment. First I have to pay.'

The driver named a sum that made me pale. But I would have to pay it, and persuade him to come back. My freedom depended on my being early into town and making some breakthrough with the problems that I faced.

The driver saw my frown. 'A double journey, citizen, and a slow one in this light. I might have had a dozen customers by now.'

I turned to Minimus. 'But didn't you agree a price before we left?'

The slave boy shook his head, shamefacedly. 'I'm sorry, master, Marcus never did.' Of course, I had not thought. He was not accustomed to such bargaining.

I turned to the driver. 'I will pay what you ask. But only on condition that you come back here in the morning as soon as it is light, and take me back into the town again.'

The driver looked mutinous. 'Another double trip!' Then he brightened. 'I'll take it in advance.'

I was prepared for that trick. 'When you come tomorrow. I will pay you then – for both the journeys.' That should ensure that he came back for me, I thought. 'In the meantime, here is something on account. Maximus, go inside and find a sestertius for him. Minimus, you go and find a brand to light him home.' The two boys ran to do this, and I turned back to him. 'Tomorrow morning, as soon as it is light. I am going back to the garrison, so don't be late.'

I left the two boys to pay him and fix the torch on to the metal hook which was provided for that purpose on the carriage frame. I went into the roundhouse to my wife.

She was sitting spinning by the central fire. She smiled as I came in. 'Minimus says you've had a trying day.'

I was about to answer when she raised her hand. 'Tell me later on. Junio is coming and you can tell us then. You are tired and hungry. Take your toga off and sit down on that stool, the boys will fetch some water and wash your face and hands. There is vegetable stew in that pot on the fire, and I have baked those oatcakes that you like so much.'

I sat down gratefully and did as she had said, willing to delay bad news as long as possible, while Minimus tended to my every need. How much longer would I have the luxury of slaves and home-cooked food like this?

I glanced at Minimus. He had been given a great bowl of stew as well. I was not hungry somehow, but he wolfed his down, and – seeing the disappointment of my wife – I forced myself to eat. It was fragrant and delicious and I did not speak a word until there was not a morsel remaining on the plate. Just as I was mopping up the very last of it, my adopted son Junio came into the house.

I told the story then, trying not to dwell too much upon the threat to me.

Junio and Gwellia listened carefully, and did not interrupt – except to ask for every detail I could recollect. I was grateful for their help. I had encouraged Junio to do this many times, and he had an aptitude. He often saw things I had not seen myself, and Gwellia had a gift for spotting discrepancies from a female point of view. This time how-ever, they seemed mystified.

'Let's go back to basics,' Junio said. 'Who would stand to profit by Honorius's death? Pompeia does, I suppose. Not Helena Domna, she has lost her home, and will only have her own allowance to live on from now on.'

'And not Livia either,' Gwellia put in. 'She's worse off than before. If she wanted to be rid of him, she only needed to sue for a divorce. They are not so difficult to come by nowadays – any good lawyer could have got her one. She has been dutiful and Honorius is cruel – he has shown that by executing his own daughter in that way. She would have got her dowry back intact, and the freedom to do anything she liked. As it is, she gets a guardian and shares the estate with Pompeia and the child. She'll need the guardian's permission to do anything at all.'

'So it rather depends on who the guardian is,' I said. 'If it is Gracchus, he might have a motive, I suppose. And the doorman, too. He was hoping for his freedom, and Honorius might have been standing in his way. But how could they have murdered anyone? Or Miles, the son-in-law whose wife Honorius killed? He had a grievance, but he wasn't there.'

'Redux?' Gwellia put in. 'He had a private grudge concerning Zythos, it appears. But how could he have brought poison to the house? Which brings us back to Antoninus, possibly. Suppose that Livia is right – there really was poison in that garum and Honorius somehow tasted it today. Somebody realized that and killed the murderer. They might even have filled the amphora up again. That makes a kind of sense. It could even have been Livia herself – she seemed anxious that no one else should taste it afterwards.'

I made a doubtful face. 'But why should Honorius begin that garum today? It was a small amphora and they had many guests.'

'Well, he was tasting all the wedding wine,' she said, obviously unwilling to let the theory go.

'Of course he was,' I murmured, and then stopped with a frown. 'But, come to think of it, why was he doing that? It isn't usual for hosts to test the wine when it has come directly from the vintners only hours before. Did something happen to make him question it?'

'And why did he taste the wine himself, in any case?' Junio was sounding interested and excited now. 'Most people would have someone do it for them, wouldn't they?'

'As Helena Domna did, in fact!' I said triumphantly. 'Junio, you're right. Did he ask the servants to taste the wine at all? Do you know, Minimus?'

There was no answer. The slave boy was sitting on the upturned pail which served him as a stool, and his empty bowl was still balanced on his lap, but he had slumped forward, his ginger head leaning upon his arms.

For an awful moment I felt my blood run cold. 'Minimus!'

But my voice had roused him, and he slowly stirred. He opened one eye drowsily, then pulled himself upright, obviously horrified to realize where he was. 'I'm sorry master – I was fast asleep. There has been so much to see and do today. It won't occur again. What can I do to make amends to you?'

He clearly feared a beating, but Gwellia caught my glance. 'You can rinse these dirty bowls for me, then smooth the straw and spread the blanket out to make your master's bed. Then, I suggest that you should go next door into the servants' sleeping room and go to bed yourself. You'll be wanted first thing in the morning, so I understand. Your master has enough concerns without your carelessness.'

Junio smiled. 'And I must go back to Cilla. She'll be waiting up for me. She would have come to see you, father, but she's not been well. I've been away from her all day – working on that pavement you started yesterday. I haven't even had the time to go into Glevum and open up the shop.'

'Poor Cilla! What's the matter?' I was all concern. Junio's young wife had been a slave of ours, and had always been the picture of robust good health.

Gwellia nudged me sharply. 'Nothing serious. But he should get back to her. Maximus, you can take a brand and escort him up the path.' Junio's roundhouse enclosure was very close to ours.

My son turned at the doorway. 'Shall I come with you tomorrow, father, when you go into town? It seems to me that you could do with my support?'

'If you would like to and if Cilla's well

enough,' I said. It was as close to begging as dignity allowed. 'There are several things that you could do for me.'

And he was gone, with Maximus holding a torch to light his way. Minimus murmured a blessing and withdrew, leaving my gentle wife and I alone. The evening rituals of the household seemed precious suddenly.

I helped her with the fire, raked the ashes over the clay pot in one half of it, so that the bread would cook in the embers overnight, and banked the other half with slower-burning logs, not only to warm the round-house, but to ensure that we still had a means of cooking when the morning came. Then I lay down on the bed that Minimus had prepared and Gwellia drew the covers over me, settled down beside me and blew the tapers out. A moment later her soft breathing told me she was fast asleep.

I was grateful for the comfort of her sleeping form, but I could not rest. My mind was too full of the worries of the day and fears about the morrow. It was not just the murders – though, Jove knew, they were sufficient problems in themselves – but there were little questions which niggled at my brain. That writing tablet for example, and the way that Livia and Redux had both been shocked by it. Livia's astonishment was explicable enough, but could I really believe that Redux had merely been anxious for his friend? Antoninus had clearly possessed that writing block – he'd used the thing to send a note to me. Had Zythos bribed him with it, in exchange for silence over some misdeed? Was it about that statue, that it worried Redux so? I was sure the information was in that writing block, but for the life of me I could not work out what it was. And my future might depend on it.

In the end I got up quietly, so as not to wake my wife, and groped my way to where Maximus had folded up my clothes. I fumbled in the pouch and found the writing block. The ivory of the cover glimmered at me in the dark, and when I opened it I could just make out the paler colour of the wax. Of course, the new wax which had replaced the thin and damaged piece! Why had I not thought of that before?

I hurried over to the glow that was the hearth, and lit a taper from the burning wood, shielding it by placing it inside a wooden bowl, so that its light did not disturb the house. Then I placed the trivet on the hottest section of the fire, and carefully balanced the open writing tablet on the rim of it.

I was so excited by my new idea that I was not alert, until a voice behind me made me whirl around. 'Master!' Minimus was standing in the entrance, watching me. 'What are you doing?' He padded towards me, rubbing bleary eyes and I saw that he was tousle-headed and barefoot, with only his thin under-tunic on. 'Are you trying to destroy that lovely thing?'

I shook my head, and placed a finger on my lips. 'The cover is ivory, it will take no harm. And if I am careful, I will not scorch the wood. But see, the wax is already soften-ing and I will be able to lift it from the frame.' I took it carefully from the trivet as I spoke, burning my fingers a little with the heat. My method had been more effective than I hoped, and the wax was dripping of its own accord. I took up a knife and helped it on its way, then lifted the taper to look closely at the wooden backing frame. 'Just as I thought. There are scratches visible. But in this light, it is impossible to see.'

Minimus grinned impishly at me. He kept his voice low, just as I had done. 'If you rubbed it with black dust from the fire, it would get into the grooves and show the marks up more.'

He suited the action to the word and I saw that he was right. There were a lot of scratches, and at first it seemed a maze – fragments of numbers and disconnected words, each new message obscuring the one underneath. But when I risked a second taper and rubbed in more black dust, it was possible to convince myself that I could make out words.

' "A S tomorrow",' I read aloud, 'then something undecipherable, then the words "usual ajar".'

Was that what it said? I stared at it. It made no kind of sense. It sounded like an invitation to a robbery. The statue possibly? That sounded plausible. And could the AS stand for Antoninus, in that case? Antoninus Seulonius – wasn't that what Marcus had called him long ago?

'Well done, Minimus,' I murmured, and he preened.

He whispered back, 'It's something we used to do – Maximus and I – when we were small and wanted to pass messages between ourselves without the chief slave finding out. Just a piece of wood and a nail to scratch it with. Silly really, but we were not allowed to talk and we had to spend hours waiting to be called.' He looked anxiously at me. 'Have I atoned for dropping off to sleep?'

'I suppose so,' I said with a laugh. 'But now go back to bed or you'll be doing it again.' I reached out and rubbed his tousled hair. 'And I've enough troubles without that, Jove knows. You gave me quite a shock.'

He nodded ruefully and padded off. But it was true, I thought, as I blew the candles out and went back to lie down on my own bed again. For a dreadful moment, while he was slumped like that, I had seriously feared that he was dead. Perhaps it was because my mind was full of poisoning. Or he had reminded me of Antoninus at his desk. There had been something very similar. Almost as if he were...

'I wonder!' I murmured to myself, recalling something that Redux had remarked. Well, that would have to wait until tomorrow too. And feeling that at least I had a path to follow now, I closed my eyes at last.

I woke to find Gwellia shaking me and thrusting a glass of water into my hand.

'Wake up, husband. The carriage is here. Junio is waiting and it's time to go. I'll cut a piece of bread and cheese for you, and you can eat it on the way. Minimus will help you to put your toga on. I've given him the money for the carriage fare, but if you want any extra you'll have to get it from the shop, because until I sell some eggs and cloth, that's all the cash we have.' Her voice trembled – just a little. 'Send the boy home to let me know what happens, husband. And good luck!'

She kissed me as the boy deftly wrapped my toga round my form. Five minutes later, we were on our way.

Twenty-One

Redux was waiting for me at the city gates. He grinned at my evident surprise.

'You weren't expecting me? I said I would assist you, since it concerns me now.' He was wearing a different tunic today, I noticed – this one had red and gold embroidered hems and he had topped off his toga with a Grecian coat to match, though he had plain, comfortable sandals on his feet. He fell into step beside us, and looked at Junio.

'Junio, this is Redux,' I explained. 'Redux, meet my son. It's kind of you to offer to assist, of course, but he'll help me from now on.'

'I already have.' Redux was not to be deterred. 'I went to see Gracchus, when you left last night. I have my suspicions, as I think I said, that he was one of Antoninus's "special" customers. I thought it would be interesting to know what he got up to when his wedding was postponed.'

'And what did you find out?'

He made a little face. 'Proof that he could not have killed Antoninus yesterday. When

260

the wedding was cancelled he did not go home, except to take his wedding garments off, it appears. He went off with his friends and tried to drown his woes. He was in a tavern all the afternoon, betting on the dice – and there are half a dozen others who will swear to that.'

'And have you tracked these people down, to check?' It was Junio who asked.

Redux looked at him with a mixture of surprise and reluctant admiration on his face. 'I spoke to two of them. They both told me the same. And so did the tavern keeper when I found the place. And I don't think he's mistaken: Gracchus couldn't pay – lost too much on the game, so the fellow says – and there's a tally of what's owing scratched up on the wall. So Gracchus is accounted for.'

'All the same,' I said, 'I'd like to speak to him. If you are serious in your desire to help, you could go and find him now. Ask him to meet me at Honorius's house, in ... let me see' – I did a little calculation in my head, allowing time to get to the garrison by noon – 'in perhaps an hour if he has a water clock, or in any case before the sun is halfway overhead. I think he'll come, since he's employing me.' Redux looked affronted and I added with a smile. 'You can come with him, and repeat what you've just said. It might serve to alter Helena Domna's mind about his suitability as a match for Pompeia. I don't think she approves of drunkenness and dice.'

'In an hour then.' Redux nodded and set off down the street, skirting the rubbish on the pavement with fastidious care.

'So that is Redux,' Junio said. 'Intelligent, at least. And he must be wealthy, too. He must have spent a fortune on that red Grecian coat – though it's a fashion more suitable for women I'd have thought. You can understand what his friend Zythos might have seen in him. But Zythos isn't here, so I wonder who he is trying to impress. The commander possibly?'

I had a horrid suspicion that it might be me, but I suppressed the thought. 'You seemed to doubt his story about Gracchus though?'

Junio looked thoughtful and then shook his head. 'On the whole, I think it must be true. After all, a tavern is a public place, and if Gracchus spent time there, there will be witnesses. There's no point in either of them lying about that. Besides, from what you told me yesterday, Redux may know the tavern keeper fairly well himself. Didn't you say that he was fond of wine?'

'That's why I sent him to Gracchus's again. I want you to go and see Vinerius and his wife. Tell them the same thing – that they are wanted at Honorius's house, but let them think it's Livia who has summoned them. I doubt that Vinerius would deign to come, if it was only me. Oh, and ask Maesta to bring her cures with her – anything that she's provided to the womenfolk before.'

'Where do I find Vinerius's wine shop?' he enquired. I gave him directions and he hurried off.

'And me, master?' Minimus piped up. He had been very quiet up to now.

'You and I will go directly to the house. The back door for preference. I don't want to be caught up in streams of visitors, coming to pay homage to the corpse – and I suppose that they'll be lining up by now.'

They were, too. All the senior councillors that I'd seen yesterday, and a good few that I hadn't: magistrates and senior tradesmen from the town, even the clerks from the basilica, all of them waiting to pay traditional respects. They would be shown in, I knew, to spend a few moments with the corpse – a few would utter a token wail or two – and then they would be ushered out and given fruit and wine, while another visitor would come and take their place. Not many of the waiting crowd were bearing gifts, I saw, though that was not uncommon when a wealthy man had died. This time however, there was no one to 'impress' (as Junio might have put it) since there were only females remaining in the family – and there are no business or political favours to be had from them.

There were so many waiting that a queue had formed, and a street musician was walking up and down, trying to earn a few brass coins by entertaining them. His raucous singing was an affront to the dead, and very soon a slave came out to order him away. It was the lugubrious doorkeeper of the day before.

I pulled Minimus quickly out of sight. 'I don't want him to see us. We'll try the other way – in through the stables and the kitchen, if we can.'

It was not as easy as I had hoped that it would be. The stable hand was very loath to let me pass. 'I am responsible for guarding the back gate, and this is no place for strangers. Especially after what happened yesterday. It is more than my life is worth to let you through.'

I sighed. I should have thought to take my toga off – with just a tunic I might have been taken for a slave – but just as I thought that we'd be turned away, the steward from the house came bustling in.

'We need a bale of straw to strew outside the gate and muffle...' he began. Then he caught sight of us. 'Citizen! What are you doing here again? The queue for mourners is around the front.'

'And I don't want to join it, for the moment anyway. I'd hoped to speak to Pompeia, if she's awake again. I tried to come this way to avoid the crowds,' I said. He looked uncertain, so I tried flattery. 'This stable slave is rightly dubious, but I know that you are able to vouch for who I am.'

It worked. The steward smiled, and obviously decided to postpone his present task. 'Follow me then, citizen. And your servant too – unless he would rather go and wait upstairs?'

Minimus caught my eye and fiercely shook his head.

'I will take him with me. We shan't be very long,' I said, rewarding him for his useful trick with wax the night before. Though if he had been Junio, I thought, he would have seized the chance to go upstairs and hear the servants talk, but as it was he simply tailed along. The steward led us past the kitchen block, and through the back gate into the courtyard garden of the house.

He skirted past a massive stone Neptune with a trident, and stopped outside the room I'd been to yesterday. The bar was back across the door again. 'This has been turned into Pompeia's room,' he said. 'I think you'll find her in.' He tapped discreetly on the door, removed the bar and opened it a crack.

Pompeia was sitting on the bed. She was no longer in her wedding finery, but in a dark-coloured stola which quite suited her. When she saw the steward her face lit up at

once. 'Pentius...' she murmured, then realized we were there. The smile vanished instantly and she was plain again.

'Lady, this citizen would like a word with
you.' His manner was perfectly correct, but I
noticed that he had turned rather pink
around the ears. 'May I show him in? And do
you require a maid as chaperone, or will his
manservant suffice?'

'Oh, let him in alone. What difference does
it make? I couldn't be in more disgrace than
I already am.' He obeyed her, and shut the
door again. She turned to me. 'You know
they've locked me in? They wouldn't even let
me join in the lament without a pair of slaves
to keep an eye on me. On Helena Domna's
orders, naturally!' She did not look tragic or
emotionally distressed – she looked and
sounded simply murderous.

'That does sound unreasonable,' I said
placidly. 'Does she still believe that you
caused your father's death?'

She glowered. 'She claims that I would try
to run away.'

'And would you? Even if you could not
have taken all your things with you?' I
gestured to a little stack of wooden crates,
clearly packed ready for her new home
yesterday, but now brought back into this
house again. A pile of stolas had been half-
pulled out of one, presumably in search of
the mourning clothes she wore.

My question surprised her into a small smile. 'I suppose I might have done, since no other method works.' The smile faded. 'You know she's going to make me marry Gracchus after all? I wish I'd taken poison like...' she tailed off, confused.

'Like your father?' I was momentarily startled by the thought, but her bitter laugh convinced me that my guess was wrong. Suddenly I remembered what Maesta had confessed. 'Or like the convicted criminals that avoided worse, by drinking hemlock of their own accord?'

'Ah! The convicted criminals ... of course. That is what I meant.'

But it wasn't. I could read it in her face. I searched my mind, and suddenly things settled into place – like pieces of mosaic that make a pattern suddenly. 'It was your mother, wasn't it? She was so unhappy she committed suicide. How did she manage it?' But even as I asked, I knew what it must be. 'She took some of the poison that your father had – for those convicted criminals – and swallowed it herself?'

She didn't answer but she scarcely needed to. It was clear from the expression on her face that I was right.

'I should have realized that it was something of the kind. Maesta said that one of the victims hadn't died at once, but that the dose should have been strong enough to kill an ox. She had an explanation which I doubted at the time. But of course, the poor wretch didn't get the full amount. Your mother had abstracted some of it. Maesta actually told me that she'd died soon afterwards.'

'She did not mean to make him suffer,' Pompeia said. She had screwed her two hands tightly into fists and was staring down at them, as though she was physically holding on to her self-control. 'My mother never intended to be cruel.'

'Then tell me. Make me understand.' I sat down, without permission, on the stool that Maesta had used.

'I suppose I might as well, since you know anyway...' She let her hands relax and moved her gaze to me. 'It was clear that the doses were very strong indeed – because too little hemlock may not kill at once. They were to be distributed on successive days. My father came back and told us how the first two men had died, and how they had not even finished what had been poured for them. When my mother learned that, it gave her a way out. She had these phials of so-called love potions – she emptied one of them, and put the poison in, and topped the criminal's container up again – probably with the other philtre she had saved. It should have been enough to kill him anyway. She only drank a mouthful and she died within the hour. It was just that the last criminal must have been a giant.'

I stared at her. 'How do you know all this?'

'She left a letter, for Honoria and I. We found it in our clothes chest after she had gone, with the remainder of the poison phial. In case we needed to escape ourselves, she said. Of course we didn't realize how bad things had become. And naturally it was never mentioned at the funeral, or anywhere else as far as I'm aware – my father simply told us that she'd died.'

'But you think he knew that she had killed herself?'

'I'm not sure that he did. Certainly he never admitted it to us, and of course, he never found the phial. Died of a broken heart, the servants said. Only the steward knew the truth, and he could hardly tell, since he was the person who had let her out.'

'She must have been desperate.'

'I believe she was. It was the love potions that caused it – according to her note. She tried to put them in my father's food, and he accused her of attempted poisoning and trying to affect his mind with sorcery. She was not allowed to speak to us: he told us she was ill. He locked her in her room – this one, hence the bar across the door – had her beaten, and threatened to exile her for life. He was about to bring a case to court – and his word would always have carried against hers. But she bribed the steward and he let her out, one evening when the rest of us were busy with a feast. And then she found the poison – and you know the rest. Of course, she must have been unhappy for a long time earlier, or she would not have needed the love potions at all.' She looked at me at last. 'Can you see why I'm determined not to marry Gracchus, now?'

'Yet you didn't resort to drinking the remnants of the phial? To make your own escape, as your mother might have said?'

She gave a long, defeated sigh. 'Oh, but I did. I actually did. Honoria had left it with me when she went away, and the night before the wedding – when all else had failed – I screwed up my courage and drank the contents down. But either it was too diluted or time had weakened it. It had no effect. It made me a little queasy, but that was all it did.' She got up suddenly and paced around the room, picked up the stolas and began to thrust them roughly back into their box.

'It must have been distressing,' I said, with sympathy, 'to brace yourself to die, screw up your courage to take the fatal step, and then find that you are very much alive.'

She stuffed the stola violently away. 'With the added consolation of feeling slightly sick.' She turned to me. 'You know I even wondered if my father had found out, and had changed the contents of the bottle while it was in my care. But I can't see how he can have done. It was a secret between Honoria and I – we couldn't help our mother, so we never mentioned it. Besides, Honoria had already met Miles by that time. It was her dowry – and she loved him. What else was there to do?'

'You never sought redress. Not from your grandmother?'

'What could we say to her? My father was not actually guilty of a crime – not under the law he cared so much about. He would simply have turned his anger on to us – disinherited the pair of us, so Honoria said.'

'And you would have minded that?'

'Not the lack of luxury – I would not have cared – but how could we have made a living if he'd cast us out?'

I should have thought of that. Girls of her status were not brought up to work, and they had no skills that they could offer in the marketplace. They would have had to sell themselves as slaves – and, since Pompeia was so plain, she might not have found a buyer, even then. Perhaps that's one reason the mother took her life – in order to protect them from a fate like that. If she'd been exiled and disgraced, the father was entitled to disown the daughters too. 'So you stayed here and kept silent. And then your father brought another woman to the house? You must have hated her.'

Pompeia looked surprised. 'Oh, you can't

object to Livia, she didn't choose her fate. In any case, she's more like one of us. She was always kind to me – protected me from Helena Domna when she could – and she was really great friends with Honoria you know. Even when my sister wed and went away to live, she was always writing to ask Livia to come. Wanted her there when her first child was born – even called the girl Lavinia as a kind of compliment.' She sat down on the box.

'So Livia did go there? I had the impression Honorius went alone.'

'He did do, sometimes, but often she went too. I was never permitted to accompany them, of course – though I should have loved to see my sister's house. It was a fine one, so everybody says, with handsome frescos in the dining room, and a proper little walled courtyard at the back – even if it was right next door to an inn. Honoria's bedroom looked out on a tree – she used to lie in bed and watch the blossoms grow when she was expecting Lavinia, she said.'

But I was hardly listening. A startling possibility had just occurred to me – something which might hold the key to everything – but I did not want to alarm Pompeia by expressing it. 'But you have never been to visit her yourself?' I improvised. 'I suppose your grandmother would not approve of that? Too much expense for a girl of no account?'

She gave a rueful smile. 'My sister used to write me letters, though – and so did Livia when she was away. Miles would get them brought up by some passing wagon. Helena Domna disapproved of course, so we used to get the doorkeeper to keep a watch for them and smuggle them to me.' She clenched her fists again. 'But that's all over now. Honoria is dead. Is all this important, citizen? If it isn't, I think I've had enough of questioning.'

'You've been more help than you imagine,' I said truthfully. 'Thank you for daring to confide in me. I'll do my best to be worthy of your trust.'

'I've talked too much. You won't tell anyone?' She tugged my toga sleeve.

'I cannot promise that. But I won't tell anyone unnecessarily. Will that be good enough?'

'Then I hope Helena Domna doesn't have to know. She's my custodian and she hates me as it is – I'll be lucky if she even sends me any meals.' She turned her head away. 'What difference does it make? She'll make me marry Gracchus, and I might as well be dead.'

'She can't do anything before the will is read,' I pointed out. 'And then you'll have a guardian—'

She interrupted me. 'And that's likely to be Gracchus, or so Livia thinks.' She brighten-ed. 'But he mightn't need to marry me, in that case, I suppose – he would still have the money, which is all he wants. Though Helena Domna would be furious. And,' she added, sounding positively cheerful at the thought, 'I don't suppose he'd let me marry anybody else.'

Especially not a freed slave, I thought suddenly – remembering the way she'd said the steward's name and the warmth with which she'd smiled at him. It would have been entirely impossible, of course – a freeborn woman cannot marry her own slave, even if she decides to set him free. If she does so, she becomes a slave herself – and a man in slavery cannot marry anyone. Poor Pompeia – her case was desperate.

So all I said was: 'Your grandmother may have some questions to answer herself. And if I am to ask them, I had better go. I think I know now, what the questions are, but unless I get some answers I will be in jail by noon.'

'Then you are lucky, citizen. I am imprisoned now,' she murmured.

It was true, and I felt truly sorry for her as I went outside, and allowed my waiting slave to put the bar back across her door.

Twenty-Two

The bar was heavy and it took a moment for my slave to heave it into place. When he had finished, he gestured to the Neptune and made a wry grimace. 'Master, I'm glad you've come. I haven't dared sit down. I had the feeling it was watching me.'

It was a relief to laugh, but I knew what he meant. This was a house of secrecy and spies. The feeling was made all the more oppressive by the distant wail of the lament and the insistent plangent twanging of a lyre. I found that I was moved to whisper, as I said, 'Have you seen anyone since the steward left?'

He shook his head. 'He was going to tell the family that you were here, he said, but he has not been back. Oh, but here's Pulchra coming for us now.'

And indeed the stout maidservant was bustling towards us down the court, though her face did not look very welcoming. Her greeting, when she reached us, was not encouraging. 'The mistress isn't very happy that you've come. She says she did as much as possible for you yesterday. It isn't right, you know. Interrupting a family during mourning rites.'

'I am still working to clear Pompeia's name,' I said. I didn't mention that I also had to clear my own. 'And we now have two murders, not just one, to solve.'

She made an impatient little clucking noise. 'Well, Pompeia didn't murder Antoninus, did she, citizen? She was fast asleep and guarded the whole afternoon. She never left the house. Nor did Helena Domna either, come to that – and nor did my mistress – till you sent for her, by which time Antoninus was already dead. The whole of the household are witnesses to that. And you questioned them all yesterday about Honorius. So I don't know what you hope to gain by coming here like this.'

'Pulchra,' I said gently, 'you love Livia, I think?'

She glowered at me uncertainly. 'Well, of course I do. I've known her all her life. And who wouldn't love her – Juno bless her little heart? Even her pompous husband thought the world of her.'

'So you can't think of anyone who'd tried to poison her?'

The scowl vanished and she stared at me, surprised. 'Whatever do you mean? Who'd do a thing like that? And how could it happen, in a house like this?'

I nodded sagely. 'That is what I'm trying to find out. But it occurs to me, that it's remotely possible. Livia took some medicine in the mornings, didn't she? Against the morning sickness, I think Maesta said. And she opened a new phial of it, only yesterday. Did anyone handle it but Livia herself?'

'I don't think so, citizen.' She pulled her lips down at the corners in a sort of a grimace. 'I broke the seal and poured it out myself.' She looked at me, aghast. 'You think that Maesta might have substituted poison in the phial? And that Honorius took it by mistake?' She shook her head. 'I really don't see how. The master would never deign to take anything like that – and you could not have missed it. The stuff smelt horrible. Besides, I saw her drink it, and she was quite all right.'

'And the watered wine that she took afterwards, to take the taste away? I remember that you mentioned that she always needed some.'

She had turned white, as if the notion had shocked her to the core. 'She did think that there was something a little odd in that – but then she often did, when she'd been taking that revolting stuff. Made me have a taste of it, and Honorius too – though it tasted perfectly all right to me. But she insisted that Honorius should go and test the wine, in case there was something the matter with the batch. He laughed at her, but he did it all the same.'

So that was the solution to that riddle, I thought. 'And what happened to the jug that she'd been drinking from?'

She shrugged her shoulders. 'I don't really know. She sent me out to test the water in the well. The wedding guests were already beginning to arrive. Oh...!' She gave a little gasp. 'You think it was that wine that might have poisoned him – and not the stuff in the new amphorae after all?'

I nodded. This was a new theory and I was pleased with it. 'I wondered what it was that made him decide to test the wine – one doesn't generally do a thing like that. But Livia thought there was a problem – tasted something unusual, perhaps – and she persuaded him...'

She seemed pleased. 'Of course. He would taste every amphora in the house, if she'd requested it. But wouldn't he have died a little earlier, in that case?'

'A small dose, especially diluted with water in a jug, might have taken a little while to take effect – and that would still tie in with the events of yesterday.'

'So you think it was my mistress that the murderer was really aiming at? Dear Jupiter, I hadn't thought of that. You're very clever, citizen.' She frowned. 'But how can that be right? I tasted the mixture in that jug myself, and so did she – and we're as alive as you are, aren't we, citizen?'

She clearly had a point. I shook my head. 'There's something missing in my thinking, and I don't know what it is. But I do think it may have been related to Livia's medicine. You see now why it is important that I came?'

'Of course you had to, citizen. I can see that now. I'll go and tell my mistress what you have just said. Then I'm sure she'll come and speak to you herself.' She made to go but I put out a quick restraining hand.

'I don't want to frighten her. Just tell her that I think I'm on the right track, and keep on guard yourself. Oh, and tell her that I've brought that writing block. I think I have established whose it really is, and that Antoninus had no right to it. So I can hardly keep it, when he sent it to me. She ought to have it, if anybody does.'

Pulchra's plump face beamed with happiness. 'There now! Aren't you generous? What a nice idea. I thought she was overhasty giving it to you. Even if it isn't hers, it's so like the one she lost she ought to have been pleased to have it – that's what I would say!'

'But the initials on it show that it was sent to Anton...' Minimus began, but I gave him a fierce look and silenced him. He went and stood by Neptune in something of a sulk, but I had other plans.

'Go and tell the doorkeeper I'd like a word with him,' I said. 'About Antoninus and his dealings with the house. Ask the steward to send him a relief.'

Minimus nodded and trotted unwillingly away. I took advantage of a private conversation with the maid. 'Just before you go and bring your mistress here, there's one other question I'd like to put to you. Pompeia tells me that her sister liked your mistress very much. Would you agree with that? There was never any jealousy between the two of them?'

Pulchra looked at me in mock reproach. 'Not a bit of it, citizen. Why, they were as close as' – she looked around, as if she was seeking inspiration in the colonnade – 'as that fellow Remus and his twin. You only had to see them together to know that.'

'You went with Livia to visit her step-daughter, I suppose? I can't imagine she'd have taken any maid but you.'

Pulchra grinned proudly. 'You're right there, citizen. She wouldn't go without me, not on a trip like that. She took me every time, and I was glad to serve – despite that awful journey, which always jolted me till my poor old teeth were rattling my head. It's a long way, in a carriage – especially in the rain, when it's harder for the heavy luggage cart to keep up behind. We couldn't do what the master sometimes did, and go ahead by horse.'

'And on that final visit, was that what he did?'

She shook her head. 'The mistress was hoping she was you-know-what' – she patted her own ample stomach to show me what she meant – 'so he decided that he would travel in the carriage too. I'm lucky he didn't make me follow in the luggage cart – that would have been a trial.' She gave another grin. 'But it was worth it when we got there.'

'In what way worth it?'

'They made a proper fuss. Honoria always did when Livia came to stay. Turned out of her own beds, more than once, and made Miles do so too, so that the master and mistress could have the nicest sleeping rooms. Even I was given a private cubicle. They put on banquets and entertainment every night, and always gave the mistress an expensive gift.' She gave me that hostile glowering look again. 'And see how the master repaid them for all this!'

'You did not like Honorius very much?'

'I did not, citizen. I'll say it, now he's dead. Livia was too good for him, and that's the fact of it. And as for his mother – oh, but here she comes. I'll go and get the mistress, excuse me, citizen.'

I could not blame her for avoiding Helena Domna's company today. The older woman's stony countenance was a match for any statue in the colonnade. She was still draped from head to toe in black, though today devoid of any jewellery. She was attended only by the page and she was not so much leaning on her stick as carrying it as a sort of potential baton in her hand. Remembering her prowess with the wedding fan, I promised myself that I would keep a wary eye on it.

The stick, however, could not have been more stinging than her words. 'Pavement-maker! The steward informed me that you had come back. Presuming on your vaunted patronage again? Well, I hope you have something of importance to impart. Did you imagine that you'd be welcome here?'

I took a swift decision. Attack, I concluded, was my best defence. 'Not as welcome as Antoninus, I suppose.'

There was a silence. Then: 'What do you mean by that?'

'Only that he was a fairly frequent visitor. And at such unsocial hours, I understand. The other night for instance.'

The grim face hardened further. 'And what of that? It was my son Honorius that he came to see.'

'And now they both are dead. Is that coincidence?'

There was a sudden spark of colour in the sallow cheeks. 'I heard that Antoninus had collapsed and died. It's most unfortunate.'

'And just before I was due to visit him,' I said, softly. 'Was that a coincidence as well? Or was there somebody who knew that I was going to call on him – and that he had something he was going to tell me when I arrived? Something that they'd rather I didn't hear?'

She turned away, the fingers gripping more tightly round the stick. 'I don't know what you mean.'

'Oh, I think you do.' I was insistent now. 'You knew that I'd been asked to call there, didn't you? Not immediately – as one might have thought – but later on. Now why would Antoninus stipulate a thing like that? So there was time to pay him off, if a sufficient bribe was to be offered him? And who – apart from you – knew what was in that note?'

'I don't have to answer this,' she said. 'Besides, it is pure conjecture. You have no proof at all. In any case, the note was sent to you – why should he suppose that I should even learn of it?' But she had waved the page away, so he was out of earshot, I observed.

'Because he sent a writing tablet that he knew would catch your eye – indeed, the eye of almost anyone living in the house – because it looked like one that Livia had lost.'

She stamped an impatient foot at me. 'But, fool, how could he know that I would see it – as I said before?'

'He made sure that it was delivered to me here. I would obviously receive it in the company of you or Livia. I've heard that Antoninus had a little trick of taunting people with the evidence he had – and I think that writing tablet was a case in point. He let this household know he had it, and that was itself a threat.'

She looked at me stonily. 'It was no threat to me. I simply knew that Livia had lost one like it, at one time – through her own stupidity. Carelessly left it where a thief could get at it, though it was a rare and valuable thing. She never did appreciate the fine things in this house...' She broke off as hurrying footsteps echoed in the court and Minimus came hastening back to us, nodding to signal that his mission was complete.

I gestured to him to remain where he was, beside the figure of Minerva in the court. I turned to Helena Domna. 'Fine things? Like that statue where my servant's standing now?' I said.

That silenced her. For a moment, anyway. She slashed at the pathway in frustration with her cane, and when she spoke again her passion frightened me. 'Get out of my house – you tradesman – before I throw you out. Mourners or no mourners, I will have it done. What right have you to come here and insult me in this way?' Her voice was rising to an impressive pitch. 'Get out, do you hear me? Seize him, page, and thrown him out of doors.'

Given that page was no more than eight years old, and that even Minimus could have felled him with a single blow, it was not a realistic prospect. The poor lad gazed at me, then galloped off towards the atrium as fast as he could go, shouting as he did so, 'Mistress! Steward! Come!' It echoed round the courtyard, and even the tuneless wail of the lament, which had been issuing from the atrium all this while, momentarily faltered before it rose again.

Livia burst into the courtyard, from the little passage to the front part of the house. She was accompanied by Pulchra and the steward too. 'What is this disturbance? Libertus, is it you? And mother-in-law, whatever is the meaning of this irreverence? You, of all people, to disturb your son's lament!'

Helena Domna had recovered a little of her lost patrician poise. She glared at me with baleful hatred in her eyes. 'This upstart pavement-maker is accusing me of personal involvement in this sordid affair concerning Antoninus. He insulted me. I simply ordered that he be removed, but all that useless little page could do was shout for help. But now that you have come you can throw him out yourself. You should have had him locked up yesterday, when I suggested it. I will not be insulted in my own home like this.'

Perhaps it was that last remark that saved the day for me. Livia bridled. 'But, Helena Domna, I am mistress here. If Libertus has accusations, then we should hear him out. But not here in the courtyard. Let us go inside. In the *triclinium* would be the best, I think, where there are seats enough for all of us and the steward can bring us some refreshments while we talk.'

And with quiet dignity, she turned and led the way.

Twenty-Three

The feasting room had been returned to something like its normal state by now. All the additional seating had been whisked away, leaving only the main table and the three enormous dining couches round three sides of it. I wondered what had happened to the other furniture – no doubt it would be required for the funeral feast: Honorius's household would be careful to observe the traditional three days between a man's death and his cremation pyre. I smiled. Given what I had to tell the family, I was unlikely to be invited to the feast.

Livia took the top couch, rather self-consciously, and indicated that I should sit down on her right-hand side, which left Helena Domna in the inferior seat. We were sitting, not reclining, obviously – since there was no question of a proper meal – but we were grouped around the table on three couches all the same.

The steward had already gone to fetch the 'refreshments' that were spoken of, but Livia signalled that the page and Minimus should leave. 'This is clearly private business – not for servants' ears.' And the two of them reluctantly withdrew to wait outside. Pulchra however, made no move to go.

'I'll go, mistress, if you insist, of course,' she said, but I held up my hand.

'I think there are matters which you could help us with, if your mistress will permit it?'

Livia nodded. 'Very well.' The maidservant looked pleased and took up a position behind her owner's chair.

'Now then, citizen Libertus,' the young widow began, but she was interrupted by the steward bursting in.

'I'm sorry to disturb you once again, madam, but there are three citizens out here. They have forced their way in past the mourning queue and say that Libertus is expecting them. The usual doorkeeper has been relieved' – he shot a look at me – 'and his deputy could not deal with them. They were making a disturbance, and he's had to let them in.'

I ignored the implied rebuke. 'Three citizens?' I murmured. 'I'd been expecting five. Do you know who they are?'

'Gracchus, and Redux and another younger man. I don't know him, citizen, but he claims to be your son.' The steward managed to convey polite affront.

I frowned. Where were Vinerius and Maesta in that case? I was about to ask the question when Helena Domna spoke. 'Oh, show them in, by all means. Let the whole of Glevum come. This house is no longer private property, it seems. This ... pavement-maker,' she said with real venom, 'appears to treat it as his own inviting anyone he likes.'

Livia looked rather doubtfully at me. 'Is this connected with the accusations that you spoke of, citizen?'

'I hope these gentleman will be able to help confirm the truth.'

'Then we'll have them in by all means. In any case – your son apart – they are not strangers here.' The steward had bowed himself away and she turned to me again. 'So you shall have your way. But I hope, citizen, that this is justified. Otherwise I shall be compelled to send out for the guard and have them throw you into prison for impugning our good name.' She said it gently, but it was a threat – and a real one, as I was aware. *Injuria* was a criminal offence, and the punishments for it were surprisingly severe.

I nodded wryly. 'I am in danger of arrest in any case. I am due to report to the garrison at noon – and if I have not found a full solution by then to both the deaths, then the commander is threatening to imprison me. There has been a formal charge against me by that tribune that you saw.'

'You see!' The grandmother was on her feet again. 'The man's a criminal. How can you believe a single word he says?'

'Perhaps, Helena Domna, I should be the judge of that – with the help of these three citizens, who are at the door.' She rose to meet them, very graciously, and after greetings and introductions had been made, she indicated that they should find a seat. Helena Domna was compelled to shuffle up a bit and allow Gracchus a corner of the couch that she was on, while Redux and Junio sat down on either side of me.

'What happened to the vintner and his wife?' I asked my son.

He shook his head. 'They're both under arrest.'

There was a sudden hush. Everyone was looking at him now.

'There were some documents discovered in Antoninus's apartment,' he explained, 'which proved that Vinerius had been watering his wine, so that for every ten amphora of

289

Rhenish wine he bought, he somehow managed to sell eleven on.'

'Vinerius?' Helena Domna muttered furiously. 'And after all that wine we bought from him! I'll see him flogged. I'll go and see him tried and get our money back. He will be tried, I suppose?'

Junio nodded. 'It seems that the garrison commander sent to bring him in and Maesta was discovered in the act of making hemlock draughts – so she was taken into custody as well, on suspicion of abetting a conspiracy to kill.'

'And Citizen Libertus has some views on that,' Livia resumed. 'He has some accusations that he wants to make. They concern Helena Domna, I believe?'

I saw the three newcomers exchange a baffled glance. 'That is correct,' I said. 'Her dealings with Antoninus, in particular. He was a blackmailer of course – as I think other people around this table know – hence his sudden rise from nowhere and his undoubted wealth.' Gracchus and Redux were both staring at their feet, and looking rather embarrassed by these words, I saw – and Livia had allowed her jaw to drop and was staring at Helena Domna with disbelief.

'Antoninus was blackmailing my mother-in-law?' She sounded more incredulous than shocked.

Helena Domna set her wrinkled face. 'So

this man alleges. He has no proper proof at all.' If I had hoped that she might break down and confess, then I was wrong – the old woman was clearly made of sterner stuff.

I returned to the attack. 'Then what was your gold necklace doing in his flat? I noticed it when he was lying dead. It was looped around the water clock. I saw it at the time, and simply thought that it was decoration round the base – a beautiful and intricate festoon of gold and jet. I should have realized earlier what I was looking at. It was not until this morning, when I saw you in the court, and realized that you were not wearing it today, that I put two and two together.'

'And made five,' she snapped.

I forced myself to smile. 'Then demonstrate your innocence. Send for your necklace, and you prove me wrong.'

Angry red colour washed up her cheeks and neck. 'I have mislaid it temporarily...'

I shook my head. 'I think you sent it to Antoninus yesterday when you affected to be sending out to the musicians' guild. You used the doorman as your messenger. I thought I glimpsed the fellow in the street outside the flat, but I did not pay much attention to him at the time. Shall we ask him? I have sent for him.'

She glared at me again. 'Do so, if you want to. I know what he'll say.'

'Do you, Helena Domna? Are you sure of

that? We'll offer to pay him good money for the truth, and you might be surprised.'

Patrician matrons do not often spit, but Helena Domna came very close to it. 'Well, if you mean you'll bribe him, of course it's different. In that case he might say anything at all.'

'And what might he say about that statue in the court?'

The old face crumpled slightly. 'What do you know of that?'

'Only that it came illicitly from Rome, and that Honorius was probably aware of it,' I said.

'So that cursed Antoninus did tell you, after all?' She had lost her calm. She was white and shaking and her eyes were bright with tears. 'And after I...' She stopped, and glared at me, aware that she had already said too much.

'And after you had sent him your gold necklace as a bribe? Just as the citizen suggested?' Redux said, before I had the time to make the point myself. 'And I can confirm what Libertus said about the clock – I noticed the gold chain around the base myself. Fine gold – it must have been worth a tidy sum.'

Livia was shaking a bewildered head at me. 'What's this about a statue?'

'That Minerva in the courtyard – it's a stolen one. Probably from the palace of the

Emperor himself,' I said. 'Zythos arranged it when he was alive, and Redux shipped it and delivered it to you. It was disguised beneath a plaster cast, I hear.'

'The Emperor?' She was horrified. 'I had no idea.' She shook her head again. 'It came when I was out, and when I got home it was already in the court and looked exactly as it does today. Honorius was always buying statues for the house, and I thought no more about it – except to wonder how much it had cost. He will have used my dowry money to pay for it, of course.'

'I suspect it cost him even more than he had bargained for. Antoninus had discovered the details of the sale – he had been blackmailing Zythos all along, and now he was demanding money from Honorius as well. That's why he came the other night – as I think Helena Domna can confirm.'

All eyes turned to the mother-in-law at my words, but she said nothing.

I was forced to speak again. 'You told me, Livia, that she came along and prevented you from listening to the men yourself. But I think she stopped and eavesdropped, on her own account. And what she heard appalled her. She discovered that Honorius – her son – was guilty of dealing in illegal goods, and more than that – Imperial property. She spoke to Antoninus at the wedding yesterday – I saw them whispering together in the hall. She must have been unwise enough to tell him what she knew, and he, of course, demanded bribes to keep the secret safe.'

Helena Domna had started to her feet.

'We can ask the doorkeeper if he took that necklace there or not,' I said.

She looked at me bitterly, and sat down again. All the fury had ebbed out of her, and she almost seemed physically smaller all at once. 'Antoninus didn't keep his word,' she muttered. 'I wanted to protect our reputation, that is all – and now, I suppose, the whole colonia will know. You were quite right, citizen. I knew when that note arrived for you – in that writing case that looked so much like Livia's – that it was intended as a veiled hint to me. He'd already told me he would be in touch.'

'So you made a point of reading what he wrote?'

She nodded. 'I knew that he would tell you everything, if I did not find some way of paying him. And – as you say – he set a later time, so I could find the money and get it to him first. I do have a little, but it was not to hand and all I could think of was to send him gold. That necklace is a fine one, the jet is good as well – Zythos imported it from somewhere in the East. And even when I sent him that, the wretch betrayed me and told you anyway.'

'Antoninus would never have done that,' I said. 'If he once told the secret, he had lost his power. He would have gone on making his demands for years – if he thought you could be made to pay. He didn't tell me anything. He didn't have the chance – by the time I got there he was already dead.'

She stared at me. 'So how did you learn about the stolen statue then?'

Redux answered for me. 'I told him, lady – and, I think that you should know that I told the commander of the garrison as well.' She half-rose as if to hit him, and he raised his hand. 'I was being suspected of murder at the time, and I might have been tortured if I did not tell the truth. I did not steal the statue, and I do not know who did – but Antoninus knew that I had been involved in shipping it, and he was extorting money out of me as well. I don't know exactly what evidence he had – I looked through the papers, but I couldn't find a thing. No mention of Honorius or Zythos anywhere. That should be some comfort to you, madam, anyway. I rather think that somebody had burned the documents.'

Helena Domna brightened. 'So there will be no proof?' She shook her head. 'Burned them, do you say? Let's ask the doorkeeper...'

'So, it was the doorkeeper you sent?' Junio's satisfaction was on my account I

knew, because my deduction had been proved correct.

She didn't answer.

'Rather a bad choice, Helena Domna,' I
remarked. 'I think that he was passing information on. You used him as a messenger, as
your son had done. Perhaps you even heard
him mentioned when you were listening in.
It was clear to me already that he knew the
place, and had carried things to Antoninus
several times before – that's how the blackmailer knew so much about this house.'

'So that's what you meant about the statue,
citizen?' Helena Domna had turned very
pale. 'He told Antoninus? And I sent him
there...' She paused to take in the enormity
of this. 'I'll have him flogged for this. Flogged to within inches of his wretched life.
Pulchra, send the slave to fetch him. I shall
have him flayed!' She sat down heavily on
the couch again. 'How could he betray me?
The doorman is our slave. He owes us
loyalty. We own him, after all.'

'So you got the doorkeeper to murder
Antoninus?' Redux said, as Pulchra came
back into the room again. He was addressing
Helena Domna with a smile, which almost
suggested that he felt some sympathy. 'How
did you do it? Put poison in the wine? Or
even in that pot of garum that you sent back
to him? But I suppose the doorkeeper was
anxious to make sure, and thrust a knife into

his back as well.'

Gracchus was listening avidly to this, though he had made no contribution up till now. 'All the same – as a patrician lady – you deserve respect for making the attempt to save the family's name. Though it seems you may have killed your son for nothing, after all. You tried to save his honour, but the truth has all come out. Nonetheless, I'm sure the court will understand, and not exact the highest punishment.'

Nobody answered, and he turned to me. 'Well, it seems you have succeeded in your efforts, citizen. I salute you and agree to pay you what I owe. Pompeia is not guilty, and she can be my bride. An honour killing is not the kind of thing that would prevent one seeking alliance with a family. Honorius had already done the same thing with his eldest daughter, after all.' He looked around the table, as if seeing confirmation of his words.

But Helena Domna was on her feet again. She was very nearly trembling with rage. 'I did not instruct the doorkeeper to murder anyone. I did not touch the garum. It was returned intact – Livia herself is witness to the fact. She was the one who sent it back to him. And as for colluding in the murder of my son, of course I did nothing of the kind.'

'But you admit the other allegations?' Redux said.

She threw a furious look in my direction,

then: 'Oh, very well. The pavement-maker's right. I did send a necklace to pay Antoninus off, because I'd overheard the conversation in this house that night, about the statue and its illicit past. I never had the chance to tell Honorius what I knew – I was going to wait until the wedding guests were gone and try to persuade him that he should send it back, and maybe even apply to Commodus for reward – but he died before I had the chance. All I could think of was the honour of his name – and the fear that Antoninus would publicize the crime and maybe seize the statue on his own account. I knew he'd want the money that he was asking for.' She banged the table with her stick and glared around the room. 'But I have never stooped to murder, and I've never planned to kill. The doorkeeper will tell you, when we bring him in. When he left, Antoninus was very much alive – tucking into a meal of bread and cheese and sending demands for further jewellery.'

Twenty-Four

A little hush greeted this impassioned outpouring.

Gracchus turned to me. 'So what do you think, pavement-maker? Have you earned your fee? You have managed to get Helena Domna to confess to paying bribes and being in possession of illegal goods – in front of four Roman citizens, too, which is sufficient evidence for a court of law – so there's no escaping blame. So why is she denying the remainder of her crimes? Any magistrate would honour her for her protection of her son, and sentence her to exile at the very most. I would be prepared to pay the cost of a good advocate myself – Pompeia's dowry would allow for that.'

'I'm not interested in an advocate!' Helena Domna sat down heavily. 'I tell you, I am not guilty of the deaths. In fact, I would pay almost any sum myself, to see the person brought to justice who poisoned my poor son. But we seem no nearer to knowing who that was – though I have been humiliated for my lesser sins.'

'On the contrary, madam!' Junio jumped up. 'I know that expression on my father's face – I think he knows who did it, or he thinks he does.'

He broke off as the steward came in with the tray. 'I'm sorry, citizens. I know you were asking for the doorkeeper, but he cannot be found. I've got every slave that can be spared searching the house for him.' He set down a plate of nuts and dates, and put a drinking cup in front of each of us. 'I will bring him, with the wine, as soon as possible.'

I waited until the steward had disappeared before I spoke again. 'I believe the door-keeper will tell us the same thing, when he comes. Helena Domna behaved unwisely, but she did not conspire to kill. I think we must look elsewhere for our murderer.'

'So Antoninus's murder was not connected with the statue, after all?' Redux contrived to look relieved at this.

'Indirectly, I think it may have been. It was what brought Antoninus Seulonius here the other night, and that's what caused his death. But Helena Domna and her door-keeper were not the only ones who feared what Antoninus could reveal. Zythos, for example, was a victim too.'

'Zythos, dear man, is unfortunately dead.' Redux's plump face was pink and crump-ling. 'I think we can keep his reputation out of this.'

'Of course he arranged that Minerva should be stolen, shipped and sold.' Gracchus was attempting to be judicious now. 'But he could hardly be responsible for what has happened since. Certainly not for either of the deaths.'

'And yet, you know, I rather think he was involved,' I said, as gently as I could. 'Not only these deaths, but Honoria's as well.' I turned to Livia. 'And doubtless, madam, you would agree with me – if you can be prevailed upon to admit the truth.'

Livia had risen to her feet. She was as pale as marble, though her eyes were bright. 'Citizen Libertus, you have made your point. Helena Domna has admitted to every charge you raised. I cannot imagine what you hope to gain by blaming a dead man for my husband's death – far less the death of a man I hardly knew. Let Gracchus pay you, as he promised, and we will say no more – lest Zythos's spirit be offended and return to haunt us all.'

'As he already haunts you, madam?' I enquired. 'The "fair-haired beauty" to whom he wrote his poem? Oh, don't look startled – Redux told me that he had seen the verses though he did not suspect they were composed for you. No doubt he could also identify the lock of hair that you are wearing in that locket ring. I should have noticed at the time that you referred to it as "the dead

301

man's hair", not "my husband's", as one might expect.'

I looked at Redux and he swallowed hard then said, 'I only knew that Zythos had lost his heart – and that it was not to me.'

'It was you, lady – I am quite sure of it,' I said. 'It was you that he was hoping to encounter on that night, when he was discovered in Honoria's room – the bedroom that she usually gave you, when you came to stay.'

Helena Domna looked triumphant now. 'So it was you, you hussy! Let me see that ring.' But Livia simply went on gazing in a kind of trance, as if she were trying to read the mural on the wall.

'It must have been convenient for a lovers' tryst,' I said. 'The house was next door to an inn, and Honoria's bedroom looked out on a tree. Zythos was young and vigorous – it was not hard to climb – once he had let himself into the grounds. And you left the shutters open, by arrangement too, so that he could come and find you in the room.'

Livia let out a tiny sound, but went on staring blankly at the wall.

'Only, on that fatal night,' I went on mercilessly, 'it all went wrong. Honoria had announced that she was with child again, and this time she did not offer you her room. So when Zythos entered for a night of love, it wasn't you he found. What happened, Livia?

She cried out, I suppose? Why else would your husband have burst into her room? She screamed her innocence, but he killed them both. The deaths must have been on your conscience ever since.'

Pulchra stepped forward from behind the couch and put a hand upon her mistress's arm. 'What nonsense, mistress. Take no notice of the man. Of course you would never have done anything like that.'

'But Pulchra, you were in a private cubicle in the servants' quarters of the house,' I said. 'You told me so yourself. How can you be certain what she did or didn't do?'

Pulchra turned crimson and stepped back again. 'I know my mistress, that's all I can say. Anyway, it's only guesswork. Where's your evidence?'

'Antoninus had it, but I have it here.' I reached into my pouch and took out the writing tablet in its pretty case. 'This is your writing tablet, madam, I believe. There was a message scrawled upon it, in such haste that the stylus went right through and scratched the wooden frame. The marks had been covered with a layer of fresh wax, but when that was melted it showed up again.'

I held it out to Livia but she looked away. 'I have told you, I don't believe that is my writing block at all. Pulchra will tell you, the one I had was lost.'

'On the way to visit relatives, you said.

What relatives were these? You had no family of your own, I think. It was your step-daughter and her husband you were going to see. "A.S." Can you see it, madam? You wrote that, I think. A.S. Not Antoninus Seulonius as I thought at first, but Aqua Sulis – where you hoped to be. And that makes sense of the other scratches, too. "To-morrow. Usual ... ajar." It was a message to Zythos, wasn't it? You could not give it to a messenger openly, as you might otherwise have done, because Honorius was riding in the coach with you. So you had to send it in secret and pretend the block was lost.'

Redux was looking with fascination at the block. 'And I saw Zythos with it – but he wouldn't let me look at what was scratched on it. He laughed at me and hid it in the folds of his toga. It was the last time I ever set eyes on him in fact.' He had been sound-ing mournful, but he sat up suddenly. 'But how did Antoninus lay his hands on it?'

Livia let out a little moan again. 'That doorkeeper again. It must have been. When Zythos sent me a reply on it.'

Junio nodded, quite excited now. 'And then Antoninus saw the scratches and work-ed out what they meant – and he has been blackmailing Livia ever since.' He stopped. 'But why should she suddenly kill him in that case? And why kill her husband? That makes no sense at all.' He sat back to permit the steward to come in, pick up the drinking cups and fill them from the wine crater that he'd brought in with him.

'It's because she's carrying that wretched Greek man's child!' It was Helena Domna, with a sudden energy. 'He was always round here – courting Pompeia they said – and therefore invited as a dinner guest. Yet looking back it was clearly Livia that he'd come to see. I don't know why I didn't spot it at the time. But if that is his child that she is carrying, then it is just as well that Honorius is dead. He would have killed her for dishonouring the family otherwise.'

'Precisely so, Helena Domna,' I said carefully. 'Or if he didn't kill her, he'd have divorced her and sent her away. And that would have left her penniless, of course. Her dowry would be forfeit if he proved unfaithfulness. She couldn't even hope to inherit when he died – Honorius had already shown that he had no sentiment, and would disinherit anyone who strayed – and their descendants, too. Neither Livia nor the child could have hoped for anything.'

'What makes you assume that this is not my husband's child?' Livia was shaking with emotion as she spoke. 'That is mere conjecture on your part, and it is libellous. It was said in front of several Roman citizens as well. When the funeral is over, and the will is read, I shall sue you for *injuria*, pavement-maker – see if I do not. And I did not kill my husband, if that's what you imply.'

'But you had the means to do so, didn't you?' I said. 'You knew Honoria's mother had left a poison phial behind. And on the morning of the wedding it would not have been hard to slip the contents into the watered wine that you yourself had sipped – to take away the taste of Maesta's morning sickness cure – and persuade Honorius to take a drink of it. And if it tasted a bit peculiar – which it might have done – it was no great step for you to urge him to test the wedding wine. After which, of course, attention was wholly drawn to that wine. Fortunate that the diluted dosage took a little time to work.'

'It's all lies and conjecture. I deny it all.' Livia looked round wildly, but there was no escape. She was effectively imprisoned in her place. The central table was in front of her, and the two couches that we others sat on barred the route on either side. She sank back despondently on to her couch again, and added in a bitter and reproachful tone, 'Citizen Libertus, I am surprised at you. I did my best to help you when you were in trouble yesterday, but you repay me by alleging that I killed Honorius. And what about Antoninus? Are you going to claim that I murdered him as well?' She seized the drinking cup and drank it at a gulp.

'You certainly had a motive for wishing he was dead. And you felt yourself in sudden danger the other day, of course, when Antoninus came to see your husband late at night. By your own admission you listened at the door – but you told me that it was very difficult to hear. I think you heard the name of Zythos mentioned several times. You didn't know about the stolen statue of Minerva, then, and you thought that Antoninus had betrayed your love affair. Pulchra, didn't she come and tell you something of the kind?'

Pulchra had turned pink about the ears. 'Well, I can't deny it, citizen. She was so upset, poor lamb, she hardly closed her eyes and slept a wink all night. If I'd had Maesta's sleeping potion then, I would have given it to her.'

'Instead of to Antoninus, as you actually did?'

The whole room had turned silent and was looking at me now.

Pulchra glanced about her. 'I don't know what you mean.'

'Of course you do. It was a clever plan. You didn't have the poison, you'd already used that up. You gave it to Honorius that morning, didn't you? I don't know whether Livia knew what you had done, but you got that poison from Pompeia's room – not hard to do when you are packing up her things – and

307

put it into that jug of watered wine, after your mistress had sipped it and pronounced it odd, of course. It did occur to me to think of this before, but you assured me then that you'd tasted it yourself. But of course you hadn't – I had just your word for that.'

There was a sudden scuffle from behind the chair as Pulchra tried to make a run for it. Redux and Gracchus jumped up as one man, seized her bodily and pinned her to the wall.

'So you admit it?' Helena Domna cried. 'Wretched woman. I'll have you flayed for this.'

'Pulchra?' Livia's voice was almost a childish tearful cry. 'Why did you do it? I told you it was mad.' She turned to me. 'It's my fault, citizen. I was the one who told her about the poison phial. I heard about it from Honoria – and of course I told the maid, as I told her nearly everything. Have mercy, citizen. She used it, not from malice, but to save me from disgrace, and poverty and divorce, or – worse – from sharing Honoria's awful fate. I always said that Pulchra would protect me with her life.'

'And so I would have done,' the servant said, then broke off with a gasp as Redux took her arm and twisted it behind her.

'So you can tell us about what you did to Antoninus too.' For an effete and overweight young man he sounded threatening.

Pulchra said nothing. He yanked the arm again.

'You went there, Pulchra,' I said sympathetically. 'Livia virtually told me that you did. She said that she'd arranged to have the garum taken back – and who would she have sent on any message except you? And you had the clever notion of the sleeping draught. I thought of it last evening when I saw my slave asleep – in just the same attitude that Antoninus was. What did you do? Slip it into his drink of wine?'

Gracchus did something with his knee and Pulchra yelped again.

'Oh, don't hurt Pulchra!' Livia exclaimed. 'It was my doing as much as it was hers. I agreed that she should use the phial. It wasn't meant to kill him – just put him to sleep, so he couldn't talk to anyone and let my secret out. I thought he was intending to do that, naturally, when I heard that he'd asked you to call round later on, especially when Helena Domna told me what the note was written on.' She gave a bitter laugh. 'Ironic. I thought Antoninus was making a hidden threat to me – and for different reasons, she thought just the same.'

'Well then, Pulchra,' Gracchus snarled at her. 'You heard what Livia said. She was as much responsible as you. Will you make a full confession, or shall we start on her?'

Livia looked defeated, but Pulchra raised

her head. 'It was my doing, citizens. Mine and only mine. It's true that my mistress knew about the sleeping draught, but making someone fall asleep is not against the law. I managed to slip it into his water jug – I offered to fill it at the fountain for him while he dined – and after a little while it seemed to take effect. He wandered to the study, sat down and seemed to doze. But I wasn't certain how long the dose would last, so when he had been nodding for a little while, I took his dining knife and stuck it in his ribs. He didn't shout or struggle, just gave a little groan and even then I wasn't absolutely certain he was dead. He didn't seem to bleed much, but I didn't dare to stay. I tipped away the water, emptied out the jug and stole back down the stairs into the street again.' She looked at me, and there was almost the faintest glimmer of a smile. 'It must have been after the doorkeeper had been. I noticed the decoration on the clock as well.'

But I was struggling with a notion of my own. 'His knife,' I muttered. 'Of course it was his own. I should have noticed that there wasn't one on the table with the food. Who eats bread and cheese without a knife?'

'And Honorius?' Gracchus used his knee to good effect again. 'Did your mistress collude with you in that?'

'I told her to ask him to taste the wedding wine. That's all – I swear by all the gods. She had her sickness medicine before she came downstairs, and said – as usual – that it tasted foul and she wanted something to take the taste away. So I went and got it and took it up to her. She had a little and then she went downstairs. I had the poison ready, and I put it in the jug. Then I took it to Honorius. Of course, I carried it, like I always did – he was busy greeting the wedding guests by then – and Honorius drank it like a lamb. He actually told me that it tasted fine, and I had to persuade him to go and try the new amphorae as he'd promised to. I didn't tell the mistress what I'd done till after he was dead.'

Helena Domna gave a disbelieving sniff. 'You ask me to believe this? That my son took a cup of drink from you, and drank it without question because you asked him to?'

I raised an eyebrow at her. 'Just as you have just partaken of watered wine and dates. The steward brought them, and you accepted it.'

She reddened and put her drinking cup down hastily. 'Steward! Leave the room! And fetch that doorkeeper – we've already waited far too long for him.' I realized that she'd hardly noticed that the steward had been there – and must have been listening to much of what had passed. Such is the peculiar position of a slave.

A moment later, though, the man had reappeared. 'Madam?' His face was ashen.

'They have found the doorkeeper. He was in the servants' quarters. He had hanged himself.'

Helena Domna gave a bitter laugh. 'Then he's escaped my vengeance. How dared he act like this. Betraying our household, when he was our slave?'

'Exactly, madam,' I said. 'That is what you see. A slave, a mere possession, not a man at all. No matter that he may have been on duty half the day, you sent him out on extra errands when he is relieved, with no thought of how he was to eat or when he was to rest. He was simply a tool for you to use. And your son was just the same – promising freedom which he never gave. Did it not occur to you, the fellow might have dreams? He was saving for his slave price, were you aware of that? And no doubt Antoninus paid him handsomely, at first. Even the pageboy noticed how much cash he had.'

'At first!' Junio had seen the force of my remark. 'But it would only be at first. Once Antoninus had persuaded him to betray the household's trust – of course he would threaten to tell Honorius, who would have meted out dreadful punishment or death. So Antoninus had another victim – it was a slightly different kind of blackmail, that's all – and the doorkeeper would have been forced to carry on.'

I glanced at Livia but she was staring

blankly at the wall. 'So many deaths,' she murmured, 'and it is all—'

She was interrupted by a commotion at the door, and the arrival of the little page. 'Citizen Libertus. There's a troop of soldiers here. They're coming to arrest you – they say that you are late. And, Citizen Redux, they're asking for you too.'

'Tell them we have a culprit, and she has confessed – in front of Roman witnesses, so it will stand in law. They can take her to the garrison commander under guard. We will come with them – as we are bound to do by law – and tell the story there. Gracchus – you were offering an advocate, I think?'

Gracchus looked furtive. 'Not for just a slave. And this was hardly an honour killing, after all.'

'It was dishonour killing!' Helena Domna cried. 'That woman Livia has betrayed my son. I shall disown her publicly before the magistrates. We shall see then whose house this really is.'

'And I shall make it known that you were giving bribes, and knew about the stolen statue in the court,' Livia retorted, with a flash of her old self. 'You've admitted it, in front of witnesses. By the way, I hope you've got enough to pay the fine. Honorius hasn't left you anything.'

'Pompeia's marriage portion is provided, all the same,' Gracchus said, looking a little thoughtful. 'Though I suppose I shall have to start again, and apply for approval from the guardian.'

'But surely you are to be the guardian yourself?' I said, surprised.

He looked at me. 'I don't know where you got that idea from, citizen. Honorius did approach me to do it, at one time, but in the end he nominated Antoninus in that role. I ought to know. I was witness to the will.' He frowned. 'I suppose it will fall now to the residuary legatee.'

Which meant Marcus, I thought wryly to myself.

Gracchus was still fretting. 'I hope it works out smoothly, I need that dowry sum. I don't know where I shall find the money to pay you otherwise. In the meantime, I'll come and speak for you. Ah, here are the soldiers, come to make arrests.' He followed Livia and the steward out into the hall, while Pulchra, Redux and myself were unceremoniously seized by burly hands.

'How could you do it, Pulchra? To your master too?' Helena Domna had remained in the room, and was watching as we were firmly bound with ropes, and roughly linked together by a loop around our waists.

The old slave woman gave a weary sigh. 'I couldn't have him kill her as he'd killed Honoria. What had her crime been, when all is said and done? Just loving somebody a bit too much – that's all.'

And Livia was not the only one to be guilty of that, I thought – as we were marched in an ignominious line out of the house and past the mourning queue.

Epilogue

It was a relief to be walking up the forest road and back into my own comfortable little roundhouse once again, with Minimus trudging slowly at my heels. Gwellia was waiting for me at the outer gate, a bucket of rose-madder petals in her hand, ready to be used for something in the dyeing house.

'Husband,' she greeted me, 'you have come at last. Junio has been here an hour or two at least. You persuaded the garrison commander to let you go, at last?'

I nodded. It had been a long and trying afternoon. 'Pulchra's confession convinced him straightaway that Redux and I had no charge to answer now – but the tribune was much more difficult to appease. I believe he still thinks we had some part in it.'

Gwellia laughed softly. 'And what about that vintner and his wife?' she asked. 'They are still in custody?' We had reached the entrance to the house itself by now, and as we went inside the good smell of cooking floated from the fire.

I grinned. 'He is. On charges of watering the wine. I was able to speak for Maesta – and they set her free. She told me yesterday that her husband wanted her to make a lethal potion that they both could take, if there had proved to be a problem with the wedding wine. That explained the brew that she had made. Of course it was her potion that killed Honorius, but the court accepted it was no fault of hers. But she has been forbidden to make lethal draughts again – and the authorities have confiscated those already found.' I sat down on my favourite stool and took my sandals off.

'And what will happen to them now?' Gwellia was ladling soup on to a dish, and Maximus was pouring warm water in a bowl, ready to kneel down and wash my feet in it.

I leaned back and abandoned myself to domestic luxury. 'I hope the commander will let Pulchra swallow it. Poor woman, her fate will be dreadful otherwise. And her mistress is not likely to be much better off. Helena Domna has exacted her revenge and raised a question with the council about the father of the child. It will be up to the guardian to decide its fate – and hers.'

'And that will be Marcus?' Gwellia took a taste and added a few grains of precious salt from the little pile that was drying by the hearth.

I nodded. 'He is the residuary legatee. If he declares the child a bastard he'll inherit everything. I've got the garrison commander to write to him in Rome, telling him about it, and explaining everything. I've also suggested that he sets the steward free.' I took the dish and spoon from her, and allowed the fragrant liquid to warm me inwardly.

'So he can marry Pompeia?' she grinned. 'Junio was telling me you had a plan for that.'

'If Marcus manumits him, things are different. Pentius will be a freeman and she can marry him. She may not get a dowry, that's a decision for the guardian – but when he comes back I'll do my best for her.'

She picked up a ladle and refilled my dish. 'While Helena Domna escapes with just a fine. She sounds a horrid woman, it doesn't seem quite fair.'

I laughed. 'Not everyone has your advantages – or mine. And few people can make a soup as good as this.'

'I didn't do it, husband. Cilla made the soup.'

'Of course she was trained in a Roman kitchen once,' I said, disappointed that my attempt at flattery had failed. 'How is she, by the way?'

My wife grinned down at me. 'She has been sick again. The third time in a week. And always in the mornings. Do you know what I think?'

I nodded, moved by her evident delight. We had not managed to have children of our own – thanks to the years of separation in our youth – and though we had adopted Junio, of course, a grandchild would put the final touches on our happiness.

I adopted a carefully professional tone of voice. 'Vulvaria – stinking arrach – that is what she needs. It's a well-known cure for morning sickness. It smells and tastes disgusting, but it does the trick.' I grinned at Gwellia's evident surprise. 'And,' I added, thinking of Maesta and her herbs, 'I think I know exactly where we can get some from.'